CROSS

DISCARD

HADEON DROP

CALEY CROSS

AND THE

HADEON DROP

THE CALEY CROSS SERIES, BOOK ONE

JEFF ROSEN

Published by SparkPress, a BookSparks imprint,
A division of SparkPoint Studio, LLC
Phoenix, Arizona, USA, 85007
www.gosparkpress.com

Published 2020
Printed in the United States of America
ISBN: 978-1-68463-053-0 (pbk)
ISBN: 978-1-68463-054-7 (e-bk)
Library of Congress Control Number: 2020906194

Edited by Sarah Riley
Book design by Stacey Aaronson

To Natalie and Emma, my inspiration.

CHAPTER ONE

Dead (+ Zombie Frogs)

In three and a half hours, Caley Cross would be dead. Which wasn't even the worst thing to happen to her that morning. The zombie frogs took that prize. Some days, it's better to stay in bed. But like most things, Caley didn't exactly have a choice, because when she woke up there was a large greasy rat on her pillow.

"Good morning."

Said the rat. Or did it? If it did, it was pointless. A rat in your bed automatically made it a bad morning. Especially one that *talked*.

Caley screamed. The scream spooked the rat, and it shot off wherever rats go. Caley closed her eyes and tried to breathe normally again. A shard of the dream she'd been having came back. She was swinging in a hammock outside a cottage on the edge of some northern sea. The screen door swung open, and her mother was standing there with smiling green eyes, her red hair caught in the wind. She held her arms out, and Caley went reaching for that perfect embrace. Then the sky split apart and a black rain fell, vaporizing everything it touched. The cottage, her mother . . . it all melted away. And the hooded man was coming for her.

It was always the same dream. And always the same nightmare that followed . . . her *actual* life.

Caley would have to hurry if she didn't want to be late for school, each move executed with military precision. She tidied her room, which was really a basement cold storage crammed with shelves of prehistoric pickle jars and headless mannequins. The mannequins belonged to the Gunch, who was a seamstress before she caught the "rheumatoids." Now she ran the Gunch Home for Wayward Waifs, a foster care facility where Caley lived.

Deciding what to wear was easy. Caley dressed in whatever rags the Gunch threw away. The last time she asked for clothes the Gunch had said, "New clothes? What on earth would a thirteen-year-old girl want with new clothes?"

Caley hurried upstairs to the bathroom. There was already a line of little orphans, and despite the fact that she'd be late doing her chores she let a few in front of her. Caley was by far the oldest, and, she reasoned, the others all had smaller bladders. By the time she got in the shower, it was ice-cold because the Gunch turned the hot water off at exactly 6:15 each morning. ("Who needs heat when the sun is coming up?")

Caley studied herself in the mirror. Her bright red curls—which normally looked like a nest of flaming snakes—were even screwier than usual. There was no shampoo left, so she coated her hair with baby powder so she could at least drag a brush through it. As a result, her hair looked (and smelled) like baby barf. Her freckles seemed to have spontaneously multiplied overnight, making her pale white skin appear poxified. She considered her eyes, green and large, to be her best feature, but today all she saw was the intense combination of red, white, and green and decided she looked like a Saint Patrick's Day parade float.

Definitely a hat day.

Caley set out food for the orphans crowded around the kitchen table. There was just toast this morning. Everything else had run out, and the Gunch only shopped on Saturday, when the grocery store gave a seniors' discount.

"Is there jam?" an orphan asked.

The Gunch was poking behind the fridge with a broom, presumably for the rat. She screwed up her buzzard face at the little kid as if deciding if he was roadkill worth devouring. Her forehead vein began to bulge like it did whenever she was angry.

"I'm *soooo* sorry, Your Lordship, but our private yacht from Marmaladeland was rerouted to acquire fresh salt from the Dead Sea!"

The poor little kid started to sniffle, and Caley slipped her own toast to him as the Gunch turned her attention back to the rat hunt. The broom was suddenly snatched right out of her hands by a giant dead ivy vine that snaked out from under the fridge. The Gunch wheeled around to Caley with a vinegary look.

"There was a *rat*. I told you not to bring food to your room, and now vermin have infested my house!"

"Maybe I should eat up here with everyone else," Caley said mildly, then braced for the rabid response.

"Yes, by all means, eat *here*," the Gunch began reasonably enough, turning to the table. "Hmm . . . eleven orphans . . . ten chairs. I'll just run out and purchase a new chair, perhaps a *throne* for Your Highness. And then we can all drink jam and gargle with caviar like they do in Buckingham Palace!"

Her vein was swelling like a python swallowing a rabbit. The Gunch turned to a long list addressed to Caley, taped to the fridge:

NO EATING IN KITCHEN!

NO EATING IN ROOM!

To which the Gunch now added:

NO EATING IN HOUSE!!!

The Gunch snatched the butter dish from an orphan, plunked it on a high shelf no one else could reach, and stormed out of the kitchen.

"Caley Cross! Caley Cross!"

Albert dropped a piece of toast on Caley's plate. Albert the parrot belonged to the Gunch and was in even worse shape than Caley because the Gunch fed him moldy seed she made Caley steal from the neighbor's bird feeder. He looked like an old feather duster.

Caley crammed the toast in her mouth and began mopping the floors, thinking about her dream. It was weird, because she'd never met her mother. Knew nothing about her. Didn't even have a picture. But the Gunch knew. She always promised she'd tell her where to find her one day if she worked hard enough and didn't cause trouble. Never would say why she left her there in the first place.

The Gunch was primping in her hallway mirror, so Caley mopped around her. With her face-lifted face stretched like an overblown balloon, teetering bleached blond beehive, and fox collar wrapped around her neck (she always wore heaps of jewelry and furs and loud-patterned jumpsuits), she looked like one of those killer clowns.

Mahjong!

The Gunch's mahjong group would be arriving any minute

for their game. That's why she was getting all clowned up. Caley shooed the orphans to their rooms where they spent their days mending clothes for the Gunch's seamstress business. One of her mahjong players worked for the government, and the Gunch was paranoid she would tell the cops she was running an illegal sweatshop on the side.

The Gunch gasped. A cricket had wriggled out of her fox fur and sprang onto her lipstick, which she squished into her lips before she could stop herself. The squished cricket dropped to the floor, jerked a bit, came back to life, and hopped away. The Gunch turned to Caley, her cricket-smeared lips quivering.

"I'm *warning* you, girl, no more of your shenanigans or you're back on the street where I found you. Do you think anyone else would take you?"

The Gunch marched into her room and returned a moment later with a thick file labeled "CALEY CROSS ADOPTION." She dumped it out on the hallway table. It was an impressive pile of papers.

Caley had to admit she had a lousy record in the outside world. Every time the Gunch tried to get her adopted out of her group home, something went wrong. The line for "REASON FOR RETURN OF ADOPTEE" on the form varied from "UNSUITABLE" to "WITCH" or was sometimes just left blank with the word "HELP!!" scrawled across it in blood.

The Gunch always said, "Caley Cross, you are *my* cross to bear. But I try and see the positive in everyone."

Caley supposed the "positive" she saw was the part about having a personal slave who was forced to listen to her rant about robots coming to take her job. Anyway, there she was, living with the Gunch, probably the world's oldest orphan. At least she got to go to school, unlike the others, because, as much as the Gunch loved free labor, she *hated* Caley and would do anything to get her out of the house.

The bus!

Out the front door, Caley could see her school bus making its way up the hill. She crammed her hair in a hat.

"What about my feet?" The Gunch kicked off a snakeskin stiletto. She always wore super swanky shoes that seemed way too small for her fat sweaty feet, which seemed way too large for her little weasel-like body. "I had to chase a rat this morning. And me with the rheumatoids."

"Sorry, Ms. Gunch. I'll massage them when I get home."

The Gunch fixed Caley with a speechless stare like she'd just informed her she would have to amputate. Albert flew out the door. The Gunch went hobbling after him on one shoe. She always caught Albert because, like Caley, he was too weak from hunger to move fast. Seeing her chance, Caley made a break for the bus. It began to rain, great sheets that made an instant mud puddle just in time for the bus to drench her as it screeched to a stop. As she bent to wipe off her soaked sweater, her hat blew away.

Could her day get any worse?

Yup. (Loads)

CALEY scanned for an empty seat on the bus. Each time she spied one, the kid sitting beside it said it was saved or just sprawled across it with a stupid smirk. Caley hadn't made any friends at school, and things weren't looking promising. Bouncing from foster home to foster home with a new school each time wasn't great for making lasting connections. Wearing the Gunch's hand-me-downs didn't help either (today: a moth-eaten leopard-pattern jumpsuit two sizes too big and flaking ostrich pumps two sizes too small). Her clothes along with her electric eel hairdo made her look like someone who'd been unearthed from a time capsule. So Caley kept to herself as much as she could and tried to be invisible, which made the kids decide she was stuck-up, so they were mean and paid way too much attention to her. Life was funny.

(But not "ha-ha" funny.)

Caley sat beside Daphne Doyle, a frog-faced girl from her class who was too busy taking selfies to notice her. The bus stopped for another kid whose mom kissed her and handed her a lunch bag. Caley wondered what that must be like, having someone who would miss you.

Or lunch for that matter.

A thin shriek was followed by another. Caley sometimes heard bugs scream when they hit the windshield. No one else ever seemed to. It had been happening her whole life, the awful cries of animals killed in awful ways. She put it down to her starvation diet. She had read books about people lost in the wilderness who hallucinated when they didn't eat enough. It didn't get any wilder than the Gunch's.

Caley stared out the window. The run-down town in a run-down part of the coast had been declared a disaster zone a while back because of a chemical spill. The bus was passing the poison ponds. The ponds were because of a tire-burning plant that filled the air with stinking gunk that stuck to your clothes and skin. Dead fish were washed up on the banks, their gaping mouths making a pathetic gasping sound. It made Caley angry when she saw what happened to poor, helpless creatures. Maybe if everyone heard them scream like she did they'd stop.

Probably not. People were the worst. Caley clamped her ears and didn't unclamp them until they were safely past.

"Who said you could sit beside me?"

Daphne Doyle glared at her.

"I don't need your permission—" Caley began.

"You do if you *stink*," Daphne cut her off. "She *stinks*," Daphne repeated to several of her girlfriends, who turned to Caley.

Caley noticed they all seemed to have identical sideswept bangs today. They must have coordinated their look on social media or something. Caley didn't have a phone, or a computer, or *anything*, and was always out of the loop fashion-wise (and every *other*-wise).

The bus stopped outside the school. Daphne Doyle and her sideswept-bangs gang shoved past Caley like she was a particularly obnoxious speed bump.

Just let me get through this day, Caley said to herself, tugging on her amulet. She had no idea where it had come from, but she'd worn it as long as she could remember. It was just an old hunk of amber-colored stone hanging from a chain around her neck. It didn't look worth anything or the Gunch would have stolen it. Caley considered it her good-luck charm (though if it ever had any luck, it had worn off). Sometimes she tried making a wish on it. The wish usually went something like, "Please, if anyone out there is listening, change my life. Let me be anyone, anywhere, other than me. And straighter hair."

Caley noticed a dead cricket wriggling out of a hole in her sweater and swiped it onto the sidewalk with a sigh.

.

IN science class, the teacher placed a tray with a pickled frog on each desk.

"Today we will be dissecting frogs to analyze their anatomy."

Why do we need to take frogs apart? Caley shuddered to herself. *Everyone already knows what's inside them.*

A kid puked at the sight of his frog, and the teacher herded him off to the nurse's office after warning the class they had thirty minutes to remove the frogs' organs.

Caley regarded her frog warily. At least it wasn't screaming.

Daphne Doyle snapped selfies with her frog while her sideswept-bangs gang laughed as if she had just done the funniest thing any of them could think of (which was probably true because thinking wasn't exactly their go-to). The frog looked a bit like Daphne or vice versa, and for a happy moment, Caley imagined dissecting Daphne.

That she would have no trouble doing.

Caley felt something cold and slimy before realizing Daphne had dumped a frog down her back. Caley began squirming around, trying to get the frog out, and as she did, her janky jumpsuit began to fall apart. Everyone laughed and pointed, and Daphne took a picture. It would probably get loads of "likes" or whatever.

Caley's amulet started tingling against her chest. Her hands were red-hot and burning, like one of those tires in the factory. It was happening again, but she couldn't stop it. She never could. One second Caley was holding the dead frog; the next it jumped onto Daphne Doyle. Everyone began to scream as frogs—some already partially dissected—began leaping off their trays, their bursting bellies spurting frog guts over everyone. Daphne jumped out a window in a fog of frog parts.

Good thing the classroom is on the first floor, thought Caley. *Or not.*

Caley just stood there. The burning was gone, but she felt shriveled, like a dead match, and could barely move.

She noticed a crow on the monkey bars in the playground staring straight at her. It opened and closed its mouth as if it was saying something and then flew off unsteadily. One of its wings looked like it was made of metal.

Then Caley died.

WHEN she opened her eyes, Caley lay in a stretcher in the nurse's office. Paramedics fiddled with their emergency equipment with vexed expressions. The principal and a police officer had a hushed conversation, occasionally eyeing Caley. Just how serious an offense *were* zombie frogs, she wondered. Would she be expelled? Jailed?

It would be an upgrade from living at the Gunch's.

Caley sat up. Her skin felt stung all over like she'd fallen into a hornet nest, and her body felt weak and floppy as if her bones had been boiled.

The principal turned to her. "According to the paramedics . . . your heart stopped."

"Her vitals were flat," a paramedic said, tapping a monitor perplexedly. He shrugged and turned to Caley with an uneasy grin. "Probably an equipment glitch. She seems fine."

"Nevertheless, we're sending you home for rest," the nurse told Caley.

"Home? Rest?" Caley repeated. Those were two words she'd never used together in a sentence before.

"Can your mother pick you up?" the nurse went on.

"Mother . . ."

"Or . . . caregiver?"

"If by 'caregiver' you mean 'the person who keeps you in a dungeon and only lets you out to steal birdseed . . .'"

The principal and the officer had another hushed exchange.

THE police officer drove Caley home. She wasn't sure how they could pin this frog thing on her, but if they did it probably meant detention or even a week's suspension, which meant no dinner for a week because the Gunch was furious any time she was home from school early, "using up the electricity."

"Can you let me off somewhere else?'" Caley asked woozily.

"Norway . . ."

"I'd like to have a look inside," the officer said as they pulled up to the dilapidated orphanage.

Inside, the mahjong game was raging. When the Gunch saw the officer, she tried to hide a pile of money behind some tea sandwiches and scurried out, slamming the door behind her.

"What's she done *now*?"

Her python vein was already bulging.

"She attacked a classmate with a frog," the officer read from a notebook. "A . . . *dead* frog. Several . . . dead frogs," he added, looking mystified. "We are investigating the matter. After that, she appears to have . . . died. The paramedic's equipment was probably faulty."

"She *always* does that." The Gunch glowered at Caley. "And she *always* comes back."

The officer began to write something, then scratched it out. He looked up at the Gunch.

"She claims she's being kept in a dungeon. I thought it

would be good if I spoke to her . . ." he regarded the Gunch skeptically, "grandmother?"

The Gunch made a face like she was being accused of murder. "She's an *orphan*," she said, glaring at Caley like it was *her* fault.

"And you are . . . ?"

"Edwina Gunch."

By now, the orphans were peering out their doors to see what all the commotion was about.

"*I* don't ask for extra jam," one called in a quavering voice.

The officer regarded the children, who were all holding clothing they were mending, then looked at the sewing machines and ironing boards in their rooms.

"The little darlings love to sew," the Gunch said innocently. "Keeps their minds off them being orphans. Bless their sorry souls."

You could see the officer slowly piecing things together in his head; then he turned his full attention to the Gunch.

"Ma'am, are these children *working* for you?"

The Gunch was frothing herself into one of her classic frenzies. She couldn't help it.

"Not hard enough, Your Lordship! Do you know what it *costs* to keep children? They . . . *eat!* This isn't Versailles! I don't have a hundred chefs waiting around to whip up suckling pigs! I'm on disability owing to the rheumatoids. And they . . . *grow*," she raved on, "so they need *clothes*. So they have to sew old clothes together. And me with the rheumatoids!"

"Yes, you mentioned that."

Caley could see the officer had written, "Disability . . . Mental?" in his notepad. He told the Gunch to expect a visit from Child Services.

"We'll discuss the frogs another time," he added to Caley.

As the officer left, the Gunch stood in the hallway until her vein stopped throbbing. Her face was as mean and nasty as Caley could ever remember (and that was really saying something). Then she began hitting her with a snakeskin stiletto.

"LAZY . . . ! LYING . . . ! LITTLE . . . ! WITCH!"

Each word brought another stiletto swat. The Gunch bent over the umbrella stand to catch her breath, then spoke in a quiet, reasonable tone that made her seem even more demented.

"I *warned* you, girl. It's too bad because I was thinking it was time to tell you about your mother. But I can't see her—or *anyone*—wanting *you*. No, Caley Cross, you're *my* cross to bear. *Forever!*"

CHAPTER TWO

Follow the Mole

Caley lay in bed that night listening to the Gunch's TV blaring upstairs. The Gunch was addicted to medical dramas. Caley always paid special attention to the various ailments she heard, sifting for clues to her condition (other than "witch"). Following the latest zombie attack, her body felt as if it had exploded from the inside out, which could mean appendicitis. Or gastroenteritis. Thrombosis? It was definitely *something* bad, and she jotted down a few possibilities in her notebook.

Caley put down her pen. Edwina! Who knew the Gunch had a first name? It made her seem almost human (which, for some reason, was even more disturbing). Then she remembered the crow with the metal wing. She was sure it had said something to her . . .

"Found you."

The walls creaked. The old house often made sounds. Another loud creak from the wall right behind her made Caley jump to her feet. A pair of beady little eyes were peering at her from under the bed. She grabbed a pillow to throw at whatever was in there.

"Please don't scream," came a squeaky voice.

A pair of whiskers poked out from the bed, and a little pink nose sniffed the air testingly.

Caley lowered the pillow, and a rat crawled cautiously out. It looked like the same one from that morning, though rats often look the same. (Then again, how many *talk*?) And since she wasn't screaming at it, she noticed that instead of ratty claws, *this* rat seemed to have tiny humanlike hands and was wearing a little plaid vest.

"I have a message from Master Pim," announced the rat.

"*Who?*"

The rat wasn't listening. He stared around at the room and gave a low, unimpressed whistle.

"I must say, this is a fine place for a princess to live."

"I'm not a princess, but the Gunch *did* mention she was getting me a throne."

"Wouldn't count on it," said the rat. "The human who runs this dump is too cheap to even put cheese in the traps."

The rat dragged a trap out from under the bed. It was baited with an old cricket-bitten sock.

"So *that's* where my other good sock went," said Caley. "Anyway, you were saying. A message?"

The rat removed a small scroll from his vest pocket and cleared his throat in an official-sounding manner.

"'Follow the mole.'"

"That's a weird message. Even from a *rat*."

The rat moved his finger along the scroll, reading to himself. "That's . . . all it says." He put the scroll back in his pocket and glanced around nervously. "If I may offer a word of advice, Your Highness, be warned. Foul things are afoot." He lowered his voice. "It's rumored Olpheist—"

Caley heard a distant sound. It wasn't the sort of dead-animal scream she usually heard—this was deeper and dead-lier—like some prehistoric beast. She looked out the window. Nothing.

"Did you hear—?" She turned back to the rat, but he was gone.

Caley crossed out "thrombosis" in her notebook and entered a new diagnosis: "brain tumor."

AFTER that, things got worse in Caley's life (if it was even possible). Child Services shut down the Gunch Home for Wayward Waifs and took away the waifs. They could not find anyone to adopt Caley because of the file on her (*see *witch*), so they reluctantly allowed the Gunch to become her legal guardian.

Having lost her orphan sweatshop (not to mention her marbles), the Gunch decided to repurpose her collection of furs, purses, and shoes into "high-fashion contemporary accessories." These included assorted atrocities such as snakeskin sundresses, fox-fur flip-flops, and ostrich onesies. She was convinced she could unload the grotesque things over the "interknit," as she called it. On top of her usual endless chores, Caley had to sew them together. She sometimes heard the animals shriek as she stitched.

Back at school, Daphne Doyle and her sideswept-bangs gang were too nervous to be nasty right to Caley's face (*see *zombie frogs*), but they *did* post a photo of her with the dead frogs and with devil horns photoshopped on Caley's head; the post went viral.

When she got home one afternoon, the mahjong game was in full tilt. The players (a bunch of killer clowns like the Gunch) were drinking champagne, gorging on chocolate truffles and French cheese, and complaining about their families. Caley noticed they were wearing the fur and lizard mash-ups she had been sewing, and they seemed pleased to be on the cutting edge of "contemporary fashion." It was like a zoo had exploded over a senior citizen's home.

Caley got into the server's uniform the Gunch had designed for her. It was meant to "class things up" at mahjong, where the Gunch was now charging for everything from seat-cushion rentals to snacks. The costume was sewn together from scrap ends of fur and lizard skin. She looked like road-kill.

The killer clowns were now complaining about the heat, but the Gunch wasn't about to turn on a fan. She ordered Caley to haul the tables and chairs to the front lawn: "Plenty of free air out there!"

The sun slammed down, and Caley's roadkill costume was soon soaked in sweat and weighed a ton. She almost passed out from the heat and hunger but somehow managed to get everything set up. She organized the chocolate truffles into a pyramid, the way the Gunch liked, then glanced around. Everyone was still inside. She grabbed a truffle.

"Caley Cross! Caley Cross!"

Albert the parrot was jabbing his beak warningly against the window. Caley saw the Gunch heading out of the house and shoved the truffle into her mouth before she saw her, but she made the fatal error of biting down on it and then beginning to chew. She couldn't stop herself. It was soooo good. The Gunch saw a truffle missing from the pyramid and wheeled around to Caley like a hawk spotting a rabbit.

"I didn't mean to take it!" Caley swallowed and swerved from the lunging Gunch, who yanked off one of her rattlesnake sneakers. "I may have spasmodic dysphonia: involuntary muscle spasms."

The Gunch began smacking her with her sneaker.

"WORTHLESS . . . ! EVIL . . . ! THIEF . . . !"

"Or juvenile diabetes! Jaundice! Jet lag! Jock itch!" Caley howled as she was hit.

Her amulet began vibrating so powerfully her whole body was practically buzzing and her hands were on fire. The rattlesnake sneaker in the Gunch's hand began wriggling, came to life, and bit the Gunch on her face.

Then Caley died. (Again)

When she came back to life, her body felt hornet-stung and bone-boiled, as usual. She sat up unsteadily and saw the killer clowns running around the yard, howling. Their high-fashion contemporary accessories had also come to life, and various cobra capris, polar bear pedal pushers, and wolverine windbreakers were attacking them. The Gunch was collapsed in a chair. Her face had swollen to the size of a basketball, and a beaver beret was making a lodge in her beehive hairdo. She turned to Caley with a deranged look on her face, halfway between a smile and a scream.

"*You* did this, didn't you?"

A killer clown ran past, screeching, with a chinchilla ball cap clamped on her neck.

"I did my best, Caley Cross, but there's no hope." The Gunch shook her head. "Time for you to go."

"Please, tell me how to find my mother," pleaded Caley. "I promise you'll never see me again."

The Gunch let loose a hysterical cackle. "Your *mother*? Don't bother looking for *her*! She never left you here in the first place. You want to know who dropped you on my doorstep? A *demon*. Saw it with my own eyes. A winged *demon*. And you know what that makes *you*, don't you?"

Albert flew out the open doorway and left a sizeable deposit on the Gunch's head as he made his break for freedom.

"Go!" repeated the Gunch.

Which seemed like a perfectly reasonable idea. *What is there to stay for* now? Caley wondered. The real question was, go *where*? As usual, she didn't exactly have a choice because at that moment there was a howl, like the one she heard in her room, but closer, followed by more howls. In the distance, Caley made out what looked like a pack of huge silvery wolves bearing down on her. Which made zero sense because there were no wolves in that part of the world. She tried to sort out her thoughts. She had probably died after the zombie attack, as usual, and was still passed out on the lawn.

Or . . . she really *was* dead this time.

"Princess Caley, I presume?"

A mole popped out of a hole in the lawn, whisked some dirt off himself, and snapped a smart salute to a fire hydrant. He wore a crisp khaki military jumpsuit and a beret and carried a backpack.

"Are you talking to me?" called Caley.

The mole blinked blindly at the hydrant, then spun around to her.

"Ah, there you are. Splendid. Major Fogg, at your service."

"A lot of people have been calling me 'princess' lately," said Caley. "Well, a lot of *rodents*. No offense."

"None taken. I'm a marsupial, technically, but why split hairs?"

The mole had a curiously humanlike face: squinty eyes,

jowly jaws, and a pug nose. He reminded Caley of Winston Churchill.

The sound of snarls made Caley turn back to the wolves. They were charging across the neighbor's lawn, their glowing yellow eyes riveted on her. Instead of fur they had needle-like spikes as well as steel jaws and claws.

"Right-e-o. Remain calm. I have the situation under control." The major rummaged in his backpack and pulled out an odd-looking camera with a big fish eyeball–like lens. "Everyone say cheese!" he called to the killer clowns trying to flee from the zombie accessories. "You all look very chic, by the way. Is that the look for fall? Afraid I don't follow fashion."

The eyeball-lens made an enormously bright flash that momentarily blinded everyone. The wolves stared around vacantly, stunned. The zombie accessories all went back to their normal (hideous) appearance without the additional (hideous+) zombie effect. The killer clowns sat back down and began playing mahjong again as if nothing unbelievable had just happened.

The major removed what looked like a spindly, sticky bug from his camera and waved it cheerily at Caley.

"Little invention of mine. Memory stick–insect. They won't be needing *these* memories."

"You erased their minds?"

"Only holds the last ten minutes." The major shoved the insect and camera back in his backpack. "Can't have civilians seeing that sort of thing," he added, pointing at the still-stunned wolves. "Bad for morale. Now, if you wouldn't mind terribly, could I ask you to follow me? I'm afraid the effects will wear off shortly."

The major scurried behind the house and hopped into a black open-topped horse carriage waiting in the woods that bordered the backyard. Caley noticed the horse had a woebe-gone humanlike face. She had seen horse-faced people but never a person-faced *horse*.

"Do come along, Your Highness," called the major. "I'm afraid we're in a bit of bother. Or a bit bigger than a bit . . ."

The wolves started to stir as if coming out of a deep freeze. Caley somehow managed to move her body into the carriage, the major gave a smart flick of the reins, and they were off at a brisk pace through the woods.

"Teatime! Mind steering for a spell?"

The major handed Caley the reins and pulled out a steaming tea service and scones from the trunk. The carriage hit a root and tilted crazily, nearly throwing them over the side.

"Watch where you're steering," groaned the horse-human. "I have bursitis."

"Inflammation of the synovial fluid?" Caley nodded knowledgeably. "Painful. Sorry, I've never steered a . . . whatever you are . . ."

"That's Cecil." The major nodded toward the horse-human. "Splendid of him to volunteer for this mission. Been out to pasture. But we've all got to do our part. Just head toward the end of *that* . . ." He pointed at a rainbow appearing through the trees.

"Seriously?" said Caley. "You want me to follow a *rainbow*?"

The metal wolves shook off the last of their deep freeze and continued tearing toward them.

"Maybe we should take a car or something!" suggested Caley, eyeing the rapidly closing wolves.

"Cars are not practical where we're going." The major shook his head. "And they offer little protection against . . ." he looked back at the wolves, "*those*. Fortunately, we're well equipped." He pushed a button, and a panel popped open with an assortment of knobs and levers. "This carriage has a variety of built-in defenses." The major squinted at a yellow knob. "*This* should do the trick . . ."

He yanked the knob and a bunch of piñatas shot from the carriage.

"No, that's for a bazkûl. Terrified of piñatas for some reason. One of my cleverer inventions. But perhaps not what we need here . . ."

He yanked another knob and a cannon appeared from the side of the carriage and fired bubbles everywhere.

"No real use for that. I just love bubbles."

"Who doesn't?" shouted Caley, surprised to find her voice was several octaves higher than normal.

At least all the bubbles seemed to confuse the wolves because they began running around in circles, trying to spot the carriage again. The major grabbed a manual and started to frantically leaf through it.

"Mechanical wolves . . . Mechanical wolves . . . This is written in some foreign language!"

"You're holding it upside down!"

"Sorry! Blind as a bat. Or a marsupial, technically. Pull up here."

The rainbow seemed to stop at an enormous old tree. Caley yanked the reins, and the major hopped out and knocked on the trunk. A tiny man with a large woodpecker beak and plume-like hair poked his head out of a knothole and stared down at them suspiciously.

"State your business," said the woodpecker-man.

"Major Gilly G. Fogg, escorting Princess Caley on orders of Master Pim."

He held out a scroll with a gold wax seal and showed it to

the woodpecker-man with obvious pride that he was on such an important mission. The woodpecker-man began to peck furiously at the tree.

The major turned to Caley with a slight shrug. "Must have heard a grub or something."

The woodpecker-man turned back to the major, swallowing a large ant.

"Ah . . . *ant*," corrected the major.

The woodpecker-man, cross-eyed from the pecking, regarded the major as if he'd never seen him before.

"State your business."

"Major Gilly G. Fogg, escorting Princess Caley, etc.," the major repeated patiently. "Look, the thing is, old chap . . . uh . . . bird, it would be awfully decent if you opened the gate at this particular point. We have a bit of a wolf-type situation."

The bubbles were popping and the wolves had spotted them again. They instantly changed direction and began to charge, their steel claws grinding up the ground. The woodpecker-man pecked at the tree some more, then turned back to the major. This time a caterpillar dangled from his beak.

"State your business."

Major Fogg sighed at Caley. "Woodpeckers have a difficult time staying focused. No doubt due to all the pecking. Still, marvelous birds. Love the plumage." He turned back to the woodpecker-man. "Sorry to be repetitive, but now would be an exceptionally good time for you to open the gate."

The wolves were so close Caley could hear their steel teeth snapping.

"OPEN THE GATE OR WE'RE GONNA DIE!" she shouted.

"Why didn't you say so in the first place?" huffed the woodpecker-man, and he disappeared into the knothole.

The major hopped back into the carriage and grabbed the reins.

"Giddyap, Cecil!"

The carriage went hurtling toward the tree. They were going to crash right into it. The wolves sprang at Caley on their pistonlike legs. Just as they were about to collide into the tree, the knothole shot out a blinding burst of rainbow light and the carriage disappeared into it.

"Please keep your arms inside the vehicle at all times," called the major. "Do not panic if you find yourself scattered around the universe a bit. Or a bit bigger than a bit . . ."

Caley felt like her body was being pulled apart. Not unpleasantly, just like a really good yoga stretch . . . in every possible direction. Then she felt folded up like origami into an infinitely small speck. Then all the lights went out.

"State your business," the woodpecker-man said somewhere, faintly.

CHAPTER THREE

Erinath

When the lights came back on, the mole with Winston Churchill's face was steering the carriage.

Still dead, Caley told herself.

She blinked. Then she blinked harder, stunned by what she saw. They were rolling past a village—but not like any village Caley had ever seen. The mushroom-shaped houses seemed to have grown right out of the ground. They were covered in pieces of polished glass and shells washed up from some strange shore in mosaic patterns: waves, fields of flowers, tiger stripes, giraffe spots, peacock feathers. The roofs were topped in shaggy moss trimmed like hairdos in wild styles: beehives, bird crests, buffalo horns. Each house had a round door and eyelike windows that were beginning to blink shut in the slowly setting sun, giving them the appearance of heads of giant sleepy creatures about to doze off. The cobbled streets teemed with people wearing clothes made of what looked like leaves and bark and vines, adorned with minerals and crystals like they'd grown around their wearers.

"Scone?" The major offered Caley the plate. "They're quite tasty."

Caley hoovered them all down without even breathing. She had forgotten in all the excitement (*see *zombie frogs, steel* *wolves*, etc.) that she hadn't eaten all day (not counting that truffle).

The major regarded the vanished tray of scones wistfully and patted his belly.

"Right-e-o. Really should watch my weight anyway. By the way, good job opening the gate." The major regarded Caley admiringly. "How did you manage that?"

Caley shrugged. "I just told the woodpecker . . . uh . . . person."

"Fearless, talking to a gatekeeper like that. You remind me a lot of your mother."

"My mother?" Caley felt her heart skip a beat.

"Looked a lot like you. Same green eyes. Red hair too. Not quite as curly . . ."

"She wasn't . . . a demon?"

"Gracious, nooooo." The major shook his head emphatically. "Where would you get an idea like that?"

"Is she . . . here?"

The major shook his head again. "Queen Catherine disappeared years ago." He lowered his voice. "Of course, everyone suspects . . . Olpheist."

"Olpheist?"

"Think of your worst nightmare, and have that nightmare think of its worst nightmare, and that might begin to sum him up. Nearly destroyed our world once. Imprisoned in the Black Gate. But he escaped somehow. Perhaps that is why you were sent to live with the old buzzard. No one would think of looking for you there."

"With . . . the Gunch?"

"No, the bird with the unfortunate plumage. Wasn't *he* looking after you?"

Caley could see how someone would think Albert was looking after her. At least he fed her toast now and then.

"At any rate, you're where you belong now." The major nodded. "Erinath."

"Erinath?"

"You *do* know where we are?"

"The afterlife?"

"It is a world. Located somewhere between the green and blue parts of a rainbow at a transcendent bijection of the space-time continuum. 'Wormhole,' I believe your people call it. Although I think it is more accurately a *woodpecker*-hole. Science was never my forte in school. More of a sports athlete myself. Quite the hundred-meter dasher . . ."

The major did a deep-knee bend, flinging his arms vigorously. Caley heard a loud pop, and he groaned and sat back down quickly, rubbing his knee.

"Bit of a gammy leg from the war, I'm afraid."

"Try having *four* of them," Cecil said with a snort.

The major steered the carriage down a wide cobbled road leading to a castle perched on steep cliffs in the distance. Its leaded glass windows twinkled in the late afternoon sun.

"Is that where we're going?" asked Caley.

"Where else would a princess of Erinath live?"

Guards waved the carriage through the gates of a formidable wooden wall being built around the perimeter of the castle. They passed gardens filled with the craziest looking flowers. Some resembled little old ladies in skirts and bonnets that curtsied as they passed. Others were shaped like ballerinas in petal tutus who pirouetted in place. Flutelike reeds played soft music, as if the wind was singing. Everything gave off fantastic scents: vanilla, blueberry, marmalade, pistachio ice cream, and even, Caley thought, a whiff of armpit. There were hedges and bushes carved in the shape of various animals that seemed alive. Caley was certain she saw a group of shrub-monkeys picking stray leaves off each other. She leaned over the carriage door, craning back for a look.

"Admiring our gardens, I see," said the major. "A thousand years old. Best to keep your head inside the carriage."

As if in reply, a hippo made of holly charged them. The major pulled another knob on his panel, and a huge toilet plunger shot out and sent the hippo tumbling back into the garden in a scatter of leaves, looking aggravated.

"Another of my little inventions," the major informed her. "Useful for a variety of bushy beasts. And, of course, blocked toilets."

Despite the eye-popping gardens, Caley's gaze was drawn to the castle coming into full view at the end of the road. It was surrounded by the gardens and a deep wood beyond. Like the houses in the village, it appeared to have grown out of the ground. Its towering walls were made of massive tree roots that seemed ancient and petrified, like stone. The windows were studded with balconies with wrought iron railings in winglike shapes that reminded her of bats clinging to the sides of a cave. Endless sloping towers and turrets with eye-shaped windows were covered in wooden shingles and looked like giant fossilized fish.

Caley had the feeling it wasn't a castle so much as some sort of colossal tree creature.

The carriage pulled up to a grand staircase. A row of trumpet-shaped flowers in pots blew a fanfare. A crowd of important-looking people—wearing the same plant-clothes as the villagers but fancier—all peered expectantly at Caley. Everyone bowed or curtsied as she stepped from the carriage. A swarm of what looked like electrified bees buzzed up and began flashing little lights at Caley's face.

"No photographs!" a stern voice called.

The bees zipped off as a tiny woman trailed by several maids marched up to Caley. She had a beaky nose, dramatically arched eyebrows, a permanently disapproving mouth and wore a feathery black dress that went from her chin to the ground. She bowed sharply to Caley. It reminded her of a crow pecking at a worm.

"Welcome to Castle Erinath, Your Highness." The woman spoke in a high, chirpy voice that made her seem even more birdlike. "I am Duchess Odeli, Mistress of the Royal Household."

Caley was dismayed to see a zombie cricket peeking out from her ridiculous roadkill costume. It must have come from the Gunch's. She hoped no one would notice, but it jumped on her shoulder and began chirping loudly.

"Common gryllidae," said the duchess, snatching up the ex-cricket and handing it to a maid. "Please see our extra guest gets a leaf to munch on. It does not look particularly well nourished. This way, Your Highness." The duchess fairly floated up the wide stairs leading into the castle, then turned to see Caley wasn't following her.

"Oh, you mean *me*," said Caley, setting off after the duchess, with the maids giggling behind.

Caley gazed in awe at the entrance hall, hundreds of feet high, with walls made of the same giant petrified roots as the outside. Dozens of hollow trunk-like pillars held up the roof with branches overhead forming arches. Bulging here and there on the pillars like knotholes, openings covered in stained glass with leaf and vine patterns flooded the wooded-looking hall with rainbows. Curving staircases spiraled off in all directions, like steps on a titanic tree house. Carved statues of kings and queens and fearsome animals appeared to be growing right out of the roots. As Caley passed under an archway, a wooden cherub waved at her and a queen turned to it ever-so-slowly with a disapproving look.

The duchess shot on ahead. She had a way of coasting along, her floor-length feathery getup fluttering over her unseen feet, her arms gently flapping, which made it seem like she was hovering slightly above the ground. She made no sound at all as she moved, like a gliding gull.

"Sorry we're late." The major raced on his little legs to keep up. "Bit of a dust-up en route. Or a bit bigger than a bit . . ."

"I expect the Council will want to hear all about it," said the duchess. "I believe they are arriving for a meeting."

"It takes more than a few wolf-type situations to throw Major Fogg off the trail . . ." The major blinked blindly around. The duchess had rounded a corner with everyone, and he had kept going in a straight line. "Right-e-o, carry on," he said, saluting a cherub.

Caley followed the duchess into a great hall with vaulted ceilings covered in coats of arms. A startled stag leaped from one coat of arms to another. A huddle of people, many with odd animal features like Major Fogg, hurried past, talking heatedly. Caley thought she heard her name and "Olpheist." Everyone stopped when they noticed her and bowed.

A tall, gaunt man with a graying goatee wearing a black military uniform, long leather gloves, and a cape trimmed in wolf fur stared at Caley with unblinking black eyes. Unlike the others, he did not bow, and something about the way he was

looking at her made her stomach feel funny, like she was trying to digest something rotten.

Caley hustled after the duchess. She had the impression
the wolf-man was still staring at her, but when she glanced
back, he was heading off with the others.

The duchess led Caley through endless twisting hallways
lit by torches holding what appeared to be glowing stones.
They finally stopped in front of a door with a royal crest carved
into it with the initial C. They seemed to be in a tower of the
castle, though it was impossible for Caley to tell because the
tree house stairs sometimes went up, sometimes down, sometimes, it seemed, in no direction at all. She hoped she wouldn't
have to find her way to the bathroom in the night.

"These are your quarters, Your Highness."

The duchess flung open the door. The grand room was
filled with beautiful furniture, all in powder blue. Carved
flowers decorated the root-covered walls, and as Caley passed,
buds opened. Flute-shaped blossoms played soothing music
like you might hear on an elevator. The floor was carpeted in
moss and fireflies flitted from it, lighting their way.

"This is . . . my room?" asked Caley.

"This is the outer receiving room," said the duchess, opening another set of doors to another, even grander room, this
one decorated in pale yellow. "And this is the *inner* receiving
room."

The duchess kept opening doors, with Caley and the
maids trailing after her. One room was trimmed in royal blue,
another in ruby red, and yet another was all warm white. The
duchess announced each room as they swept through.

"The outer formal sitting room. The inner informal sitting
room. The outer bedchamber. The inner bedchamber."

This last room, decorated in deep forest green, had a four-poster bed hung with thick velvet curtains. More of the glowing stones warmed a small fireplace. On a tapestry, a deer drank from a pool in a forest. The deer startled at the site of everyone and ran into the woven trees. Caley noticed a table laid with silver trays of fruit and pastries and chocolates. Her stomach rumbled loudly.

"They are for you, Your Highness," offered the duchess. "If you are hungry."

"Even when I'm dead, apparently," Caley muttered, and she began gobbling as much food as she could before she got reincarnated somewhere. She did a quick head count of the maids lined up behind the duchess. At least ten. Tons of room for everyone. Way less crowed than the Gunch's. Trouble was, there was only one bed.

"Should I sleep on a couch? Or the floor? Or the bathtub when nobody's using it . . ."

"These rooms are for you alone, Your Highness. You and your friend."

The duchess took a wooden cage from a maid and put it on a table. The cricket was inside, munching happily on a leaf.

"If these are not adequate, I'm sure I can arrange more suitable accommodations."

"No, they're . . . suitable," Caley said quickly.

"These were your mother's rooms." The duchess turned to a portrait over the fireplace, her lips tightening into a frown.

Caley stared at the image of the young woman with red hair, green eyes like hers, and a penetrating, almost fierce expression. A shiver ran down her spine.

It looked exactly like the person she always saw in her dreams.

"Do you know what happened to her?" Caley asked without taking her eyes off the portrait. "Major Fogg said someone named Olpheist—"

"A hot bath, then rest, I've found, does wonders to help one settle in," the duchess cut her off sternly. "Do not wander about at night. The castle is . . . It's best to stay in your rooms."

The duchess curtsied and shooed the maids out ahead of her, closing the doors behind them.

Caley fell into the bed, too exhausted to have a bath or even take her clothes off. The carved flowers on the walls closed, and the sculpted starlings in the rafters settled into their nests for the night in a small flurry of splinters. The eyelid window blinked shut. Caley watched the deer reappear on the tapestry and lie down by the pool. Her eyes drifted to the portrait over the fireplace, and then she fell instantly asleep.

CHAPTER FOUR

The Oracle

I t was the dream again: the windswept cottage ... the sky split apart ... the black rain ... her mother melting from her fingers ... and the hooded man. This time, he lowered his hood.

The face staring back at Caley was her own.

Caley bolted upright, her heart pounding. She squinted around the darkened room. It was still night and she was still ... *wherever* she was. The room suddenly began to shake. Caley stumbled from the bedroom, flinging open the door. To her surprise, the outer bedchamber was gone and in its place was one of the root-riddled hallways. Flickering torches cast shadows across it that made her think of claws. She turned back to her bedroom, but it was gone, too, replaced by another hallway. She began wrenching open doors, but they all led to more hallways that started to writhe like she was inside the belly of a giant snake. She went tumbling from one hallway to another until she landed in a passageway barely big enough to stand up in.

The shaking stopped at last. It was pitch-black except for a small circle of light from a knothole in the wall. Caley heard voices and peered through the hole.

Inside a dimly lit grotto-like chamber, a group was seated on flat rocks, hovering in midair around the edges of a stone pond. Caley recognized a few of the people from the great hall. Everyone was shouting at once. A man in a gold-and-black-striped robe with a white beard and round, furry ears that made him look vaguely like a tiger called above the din.

"The Council will come to order. Order!"

A toad-faced man in a maroon tunic turned to him.

"Chancellor Abbetine, we have a report from Major Fogg that the daughter of Queen Catherine has been found on a place called 'Earth.'"

"Never heard of it," said a woman with praying mantis arms.

"It's in *Grenthorne's Galaxy Guide*," said the toad-man. "Terrible reviews. The tenants have really trashed the place. Really more for the backpacker type—"

"How did the child come to be here?"

Everyone turned to someone Caley hadn't noticed in the shadows. It was the wolf-man.

"Sent for," replied Chancellor Abbetine, "by Master Pim." He held up the scroll Caley had seen Major Fogg show the woodpecker.

"Who has let our enemy in the gate," the wolf-man said. He had a way of speaking that was low and menacing, like distant thunder.

"General Roon, what are you getting at?" Abbetine stared at the wolf-man.

"Interesting the child should possess the same power as Olpheist," Roon continued smoothly. "The power to raise the dead."

"It's true," the talking toad said uneasily. "My cousin has it on good authority she made several frogs come back to life. Just for fun."

"And there was an incident involving crickets . . ." added the praying mantis woman.

"Olpheist can take many forms . . . hidden in the darkness," said Roon. "Some, perhaps, among us now."

His inky eyes snapped toward Caley. She yanked her head from the knothole. Had he seen her? Her heart beat so hard, she was sure everyone could hear it, but when she looked again, a man in a military uniform with an armored rhino horn for a nose stared accusingly at Roon.

"Aside from a few foul beasts on the loose, the only darkness I see is *you*, General Roon. You defile this Council wearing the fur of an animal around your neck."

"Perhaps it should have put up more of a fight, Commander Pike," Roon replied with a thin smile. "Perhaps it is time we were *all* prepared to fight."

Everyone began shouting again.

"The alliance has kept the peace for a thousand years!" Abbetine held up his hands in an appeasing gesture. "There is no need for rash action."

"Olpheist's power is beyond your feeble comprehension," Roon said. "Non-persons threaten this kingdom once again. As the Sword to the Crown, I intend to protect it. By *any* means necessary."

Everyone's attention shifted uneasily to the man standing in rigid attention behind Roon. Well, not exactly a *man*, thought Caley. He was the size of a refrigerator, with metallic-looking hands the size of rakes, long, greasy hair, one dead eye, and a mouthful of burnt-bean teeth. His skin—which resembled lizard scales dipped in iron—had so many scars, it looked like he'd been fed through a wood chipper.

"*You* are the threat!" Commander Pike's little rhino eyes

were practically bugging out of his head at Roon. "And the term 'non-person' is a grievous insult! As is the construction of your so-called 'Freedom Wall.'"

"But, *if* . . ." the frog-faced man began haltingly, "Olpheist *has* returned, we cannot hope to defeat him ourselves. We need to summon the Watchers."

"The *Watchers*." Roon sneered. "A dangerous cult clinging to a dead religion. They were all destroyed long ago."

"Not quite *all*."

A tiny man with a long foxlike nose, gray whiskers, and fir-tipped ears in baggy gardener's overalls, muddy gumboots, and a pointy straw hat seemed to have appeared out of thin air. He bent over a wooden staff and had the most astonishingly bright orange eyes, like little suns. The talking toad was so startled he toppled into the pond, then floated around on his back, pretending he did it on purpose.

"Master Pim," Chancellor Abbetine started with a frown, "you are late."

"Late is something you can only be when you have not arrived, and I am clearly here," said the fox-man, hopping with surprising agility onto a floating rock. "I do apologize, however. I was hoping a special flower I have been growing would bloom tonight, what with the full moon." He pointed his staff at the ceiling that disappeared to reveal the starry sky. "Alas, it failed to do so. Or I failed to observe it doing so, because you see, the phantom flower is, sadly, largely invisible."

"We are all fascinated by your gardening hobby," said Abbetine, without sounding a bit fascinated, "but right now it seems some of us feel the End of Days is near."

"Olpheist!" said the talking toad.

"And nuts." Pim nodded. "We must not forget the nuts."

"Nuts?" repeated Abbetine.

"The squirrels' nuts. Quite concerning." Pim stared around as if everyone knew what he was talking about, which no one seemed to. "There is only one thing to do. We must consult the Oracle."

Everyone slowly nodded in agreement, except, Caley noted, Roon, who suddenly looked uneasy.

Pim tossed a pebble from a pocket of his overalls into the pond. The water began to boil. Steaming water formed the shape of a woman with three eyes and a crown made of wriggling serpents. She was terrifying, but Caley forced herself to watch. The Oracle began swaying violently, then went still. She seemed to be in a trance, her eyes staring around wildly at nothing that could be seen. Then she spoke in a language Caley had never heard before, a hissing sound like sparks hitting ice. When she was finished, she dissolved again into the pond, and Pim translated.

"From the morning and the night,
Born the Shadow and the Light . . .
Born as one, as one must die,
As one must die or dead return . . .
Worlds turn or worlds burn."

No one spoke for a moment.

"So . . . it's kind of a good news/bad news prophesy?" asked the talking toad.

"But what is the meaning?" demanded Abbetine.

"The 'Shadow' refers to the Shadow Raiser—Olpheist," Pim replied, "the 'Light' to the one known as the Last Watcher—the one destined to defeat him or help him destroy us all."

"A bit vague," Pike snorted. "Which is it?"

"Olpheist has escaped the Black Gate," answered Pim. "That much is known. But he is weakened. Perhaps he seeks something that may return him to power."

"And who is this so-called 'Last Watcher'?" asked Abbetine.

Pim let out a slow breath. "That . . . is unclear."

"Who is willing to risk our destruction on the word of a crazy old gardener who grows imaginary flowers?" Roon stared around the chamber with a challenging look. "I am at work on the ultimate weapon that will ensure our victory."

"Only a Watcher could have opened the Black Gate and freed Olpheist," Pim said evenly. "And only powerful magic can defeat him once and for all."

"There is no magic in this world," Roon spat, his gloved hand slowly curling into a fist, "only the will to crush one's enemies."

"Then we are truly doomed," Pim said quietly.

The chamber erupted in argument again.

"Who are you?"

Caley could hear Pim's voice in her head, but he wasn't speaking. He turned toward her. She couldn't seem to look away, and she met the penetrating gaze of his orange eyes for a split second before she managed to wrench herself from the knothole, amazed to find herself back in her bedroom, as if she'd never left.

She collapsed into bed, too tired and too scared to even think about what had just happened, and this time she slept without a single dream until dawn.

CHAPTER FIVE

Know Your Baest

Caley was woken by the sound of someone in her room. She sat up, half-expecting to see a talking rat, or a mole with Winston Churchill's face, but instead she found a maid carrying in a tea tray. Caley rubbed her eyes in the bright sunlight streaming through the opening eyelid window. The air from the gardens smelled of oranges and warm biscuits. The carved flowers on the walls opened, and the wooden finches in the branches of the ceiling rafters began to sing, like little alarm clocks. On the tapestry, animals—deer, rabbits, partridges—appeared from the woven forest and drank from the pond.

"Good morning, Your Highness."

Caley looked around before realizing the maid was talking to *her*.

"Can you call me Caley? I never know who people are talking to when they say 'Your Highness.'"

"Yes, Your . . . uh . . . Caley," stammered the maid.

"Who are *you*?"

"Neive Olander, ma'am."

Neive set the tea tray down and curtsied. She had a pretty, heart-shaped face, a dimpled chin, strikingly large chestnut-colored oval eyes, and spiky hair in the most amazing shade of gray, even though she seemed about Caley's age.

"Would you like to take a bath?" asked Neive.

Caley shook her head to try and snap herself out of it. "Sorry, I'm stressed out. I've been running some scenarios. I'm either in a coma, or I *could* be dead."

"You're not dead," Neive said solemnly. "I knew you were coming. The squirrels told me."

"Riiiiiiight . . ." Caley nodded slowly. *Transient ischemic attack? Paranoid schizophrenia with a side of psychosis?* She began naming maladies to herself from the Gunch's medical dramas. *Metanoia? Neurasthenia?*

So many diseases, so little time.

Neive drew a bath. The water looked real enough, so Caley decided to just roll with it. She was used to taking cold, quick showers, and the water was so warm she almost couldn't bear to end it. Eventually, her skin started to prune, so she climbed out and wrapped herself in a towel.

"Would you like me to comb your hair?" asked Neive.

"Not unless you have a rake." Caley frowned.

"I wish *I* had curls," said Neive. "Mine just sticks straight up. I have to use barrettes to keep it down, or it looks like I've been electrocuted."

Neive fetched a small wooden box with the "Cross" crest on it and held it open to Caley. Inside was a row of what looked like rose blossoms floating in water.

Caley regarded them, clueless.

"You'll want the school uniform." Neive pointed at a green-and-white blossom.

Caley kept staring. What was she supposed to do with it?

"Hold it out in front of you and blow," Neive instructed.

When Caley's breath hit the blossom, it dissolved into sparkles and the sparkles spread over her, instantly forming a school uniform: a green skirt and blazer with a crest for "Erinath Academy" on the front pocket, a crisp white shirt, and green tights. It was fibrous and slightly fuzzy, like cotton mixed with leaves and bark. It was also a bit big but quickly shrunk to fit her perfectly, like an octopus on a rock.

"This . . . is . . . crazy." Caley grinned.

"It's a clothes-rose. Don't they have them where you're from?" Neive held up Caley's roadkill costume with a look of mild horror. "Can I throw this out? I don't think you want to wear animals around here."

"No one should wear that *anywhere*," said Caley.

Neive dumped the getup in the mouth of what looked like a giant toad made of tin. The mouth closed, and there was a kind of grinding, gulping sound, like a garbage truck makes when you feed it a bin.

"Trash toad," Neive explained, seeing Caley's surprised expression.

There was a sharp rap on the door, and almost before they could turn, Duchess Odeli stood there in her black bird outfit, like a storm cloud had dropped from the ceiling. She bowed quickly to Caley.

"Good morning, Your Highness. If you would accompany me . . ."

The duchess set off out of Caley's room in that soundless, float-fluttery way she had. Caley bolted after her. She didn't want to get left behind in those hazardous hallways.

"Bye, Neive," Caley called, waving.

"Bye, Caley."

The duchess's head swiveled around, regarding Neive with a mortified look.

"I mean . . . Your Highness!" Neive curtsied, red-faced.

"Your class schedule." The duchess handed Caley a sheet of paper with the Erinath Academy crest above it. "Breakfast at seven forty-five. Classes begin promptly at eight thirty and conclude at three fifteen, at which time you have a period of unscheduled personal recreation. I suggest you use it to engage in miscellaneous social interactions with your subjects. Dinner is at six thirty, followed by homework and lights out at nine forty-five. The weekend schedule will be posted outside the dining hall on Fridays. Don't be late for anything. And don't be *early*. Especially for Professor Wormington's class."

Caley saw that Professor Wormington's class (Wednesdays at 2:15) was Black Holes and How to Avoid Them.

She followed the duchess though an arched doorway into a dining hall. Long, polished wooden tables that looked like they'd grown from the floor were lined elbow-to-elbow with students in school uniforms, all talking excitedly. Everyone stood and bowed when Caley walked in, staring at her and whispering. She wasn't sure what she was supposed to do, so she bowed back to a flamingo-faced student who kept bowing back to her, not wanting Caley to be the last to bow. They both stood there, bowing back and forth to each other like a pair of dunking birds until the duchess told everyone to sit, took Caley firmly by the arm, and led her to a table at the front of the hall. There were about a dozen or so girls around Caley's age in school uniforms and tiaras. The duchess gestured to a throne-like chair at the head of the table and float-fluttered off again.

Caley stared, slack-jawed. She had never seen so much food in her whole life. She had also never seen so much *cutlery*. She had three forks, at least as many spoons, and a row of knives. She wondered if other people were supposed to eat there after she did. She was trying to choose a fork when the girl nearest her fixed her with a warmthless smile and held out a hand to shake.

"Princess Ithica Blight."

Caley shook the girl's hand. It was like a dead fish.

"Hi. I'm Caley."

"Charmed, I'm sure," Ithica replied blandly, as if practicing lines for a boring play. She had a turned-up nose, sunless skin, iceberg-blue eyes, laser-straight blond hair, and a mouthful of gold braces that appeared to be on too tight because her face looked like she was permanently about to puke. She gestured lazily around at the tiara-topped girls who were all regarding Caley with unfocused faces, like a lot of girls Caley knew on Earth who were pretty but dull and knew they were supposed to be interested in things but couldn't quite figure out why.

"May I present Princess Fawna Fardsarrage, Princess Allison Von Vunderling, Princess Wilhelmina Poting-Sackson, Princess Addleton Semadult, and, of course, the Pingintee cousins, Pansy and Petunia of the Penninghast-Pingintees."

Ithica said all this without pausing for anyone to say anything, like she was used to talking a lot and no one interrupting. Caley couldn't remember a single silly name, so she just waved at everyone and said, "What's up?"

"We're all so frightfully pleased you could join us," said Princess Addled Semi-Adult (something like that?).

Nobody looked *pleased*, Caley thought. She realized with a shock that along with tiaras and braces, they all had sideswept bangs. It seemed all the popular kids had them (even in Rainbow Land or wherever).

"They're going to bring your throne." Ithica gestured sulkily to the throne Caley sat on, covered in gilded gold, so bright it nearly blinded her.

"That's Princess Ithica's," said one of the Pig-in-a-Trees (was *that* their name?).

"She *used* to be the highest-ranking royal. Before *you*," added the other Pig-in-a-Tree.

The two girls were pink-skinned and looked a bit like boars, with pushed-in noses and round little eyes that darted around hungrily, as if they were missing out on something. Ithica shot them a look, and they went back to staring at Caley's plate. Caley glanced around the hall and realized no one was eating and they were all watching her. Someone placed her napkin on her lap. It was Neive.

"Start eating. Second fork on your left," Neive whispered, and she hurried off again.

Caley hadn't had such a delicious breakfast in a long time (forever, to be exact), and she wolfed down the food—even faster than a wolf-faced boy at the next table. The tiara-topped girls stared at her with alarm, but she didn't care.

"I heard earthlings eat animals," said Ithica. "Is it true?"

"I ate toast and birdseed mostly."

"We don't eat them," said Ithica. "On account of the boggers."

"Boggers?"

"You know . . . non-persons. I'm sure you've noticed them, with their beastly features." Her eyes slid to the wolf-boy, and she lowered her voice. "It's disgusting the way some people let animals take them over. Do you have boggers?"

"We *do* have animals. Not as many as we used to. Other than pets and the ones we eat . . ."

Ithica and her friends exchanged impressed looks.

"How droll," said Ithica.

"*Droll* means you don't drool a lot," Pansy Pingintee informed Caley.

"Which you shouldn't do," Petunia Pingintee added glumly, wiping drool from her big pink chin.

"Don't mind Lumpy and Dumpy," Ithica said, scowling at the Pingintees, "they're ignoramuses."

"Meaning ingenious," explained Pansy.

"Inbred," corrected Petunia.

"Tell me absolutely *everything* there is to know about you," Ithica told Caley, and then she began talking again before Caley could get a word out. "I can help you get accepted around here in no time. I know everyone and any *thing* worth knowing. Hairdressers, for example." She pointed at Caley's hair. "I imagine you want to get . . . *that* . . . dealt with as soon as possible."

Caley started to help herself to more food when Neive appeared again and grabbed her plate.

"*I* better."

"Better what?" said Ithica.

"Better get the food," answered Neive.

"Better get the food, *Princess Caley*." Ithica poked Neive with her fork. "Or did you forget your manners?"

"It's OK," Caley told Ithica, "no one needs to call me that."

"Oh, but they *do*. Servants need to know their proper place, or we're no better than boggers." Ithica poked Neive again. "Isn't that right, *you*?"

The Pingintees made a mean snigger-snorting sound.

"Neive. Her name's Neive." Caley really didn't like Ithica Blight.

Ithica fixed her with a nasty look that Caley decided suited her better.

"You're probably not used to all this, owing to your up-bringing, but you'll find it's best here to keep everyone where they belong. It's no good upsetting the natural order."

"No good," echoed the hulking Pingintees, staring down at Caley menacingly.

"I'm full," announced Caley (two more words she had never used together in a sentence).

She got up and left the dining hall. This new life was beginning to feel awfully similar to her *old* life (at least so far as mean girls and assorted adults who thought she was a demon were concerned).

CALEY'S schedule said her first class was supposed to take place in room 11B in the academy courtyard, but she couldn't find the courtyard, let alone the academy, only endless root-riddled hallways that seemed to lead to even more hallways. A boy about her age hurried past in a school uniform hauling a bulging backpack and munching on an apple.

"Are you lost?" he asked, turning to her. "Everyone always gets lost. The castle moves."

As if on cue, the hallway gave a shudder, like it had the hiccups. A cherub fell from the ceiling and landed heavily beside them, rubbing its wooden backside, which had completely split in two.

"It's going to kill someone one day, you mark my words." The boy shook his head. "It's all made of wood, you know. Imagine a giant tree house bouncing around like a mad monkey. Total carnage. I'm Kipley Gorsebrooke. Everyone calls me Kip."

"I'm Caley."

"Caley *Cross*? No *way!*" Kip kept shaking her hand and stared at her like he had just spotted a unicorn. "Scarcely So!"

"Pardon?"

Kip took his hand back. "It's an anagram. The letters of your name rearranged. I'm a wiz at puzzles and riddles and things."

"Scarcely So," repeated Caley. It made sense. She usually felt scarcely *anything* (other than starving and slave-driven).

"Everyone's talking about you," Kip continued excitedly. "First earthling in Erinath. Follow me. I never get lost."

The two set off together, with Kip sniffing the air now and then as they went. He had thick yellow hair that stuck out at every angle, a long nose, and large hands and feet, as if they'd grown faster than the rest of him. His school uniform was completely rumpled, like he'd gotten dressed in a washer/dryer. He reminded Caley of a big wrinkly puppy. He tossed his apple core in a trash toad, then pulled a muffin from his backpack, which Caley saw was crammed with food.

"Breakfast started late, and I didn't get to finish," Kip explained.

"I think that was my fault."

Kip stopped in front of what looked like a broom closet and opened it. He pushed aside a jumble of buckets and mops to reveal a large courtyard surrounded by ivy-covered buildings made of giant roots. Students were hurrying to class. An entire school campus somehow managed to fit inside a broom closet, but nothing surprised Caley lately.

"What's your first class?" asked Kip.

Caley studied the schedule the duchess had given her.

"Something called Interspecies Social Skills."

"Mine too. It's good luck you arrived at the start of the

school year. You haven't missed anything except orientation. And that was mostly the first-years trying to find the academy."

"The castle moves." Caley nodded.

"Princess Caley."

Caley turned to the familiar nasally voice and saw Ithica Blight heading her way. The Pingintee cousins stomped alongside her like bloated bodyguards. Ithica bowed to Caley. It looked like it took a lot of effort.

"Would you like me to accompany you to class?"

"Thanks, Kip's taking me."

"Kipley Gorsebrooke." Kip held out his hand to Ithica, who sized him up sourly.

"Gorsebrooke. I read about your family in *Peeve's Peerage*. Stripped of your pathetic little title, weren't they? And wasn't your father kicked out of teaching here for being revolting?"

"*Revolutionary*," corrected Kip, retrieving his unshaken hand.

The Pingintees snigger-snorted, which they seemed to do whenever Ithica said something mean, which meant they were almost constantly snigger-snorting at something with a sound like rooting pigs.

Ithica turned to Caley as if Kip weren't there anymore. "You might take care who you associate with. This is first year. It sets the tone for your entire future. One slip and you could find yourself permanently backsliding, like the Gorsebrookes."

She made the world's tiniest bow and Caley began to bow back, but Ithica quickly turned and headed off again with the Pingintees in tow.

"A Bit Glitchhi," Kip pronounced, scowling after Ithica.

"Good anagram," said Caley.

"*You're* not supposed to bow." Kip led Caley into one of

the buildings. "You're the highest-ranking royal. *I'm* officially the lowest. They took Dad's title away, which wasn't much of one anyway, just some baron from someplace no one's ever heard of. My mom was your mom's lady-in-waiting. She got me in into the academy. Kids from all over Erinath want to come. It's where they train future leaders, though Dad says we should be overthrowing the system. But I'm here for one thing, of course: the Equidium." He stopped and turned to Caley solemnly. "I'm going to win it. And restore the Gorsebrooke honor."

Caley had no idea what an Equidium was, but Kip seemed so earnest, she nodded enthusiastically.

"You have to stay focused." Kip set off again with Caley. You can't get . . ." Kip was staring at her amulet.

"Distracted?" suggested Caley.

"I like your amulet," said Kip.

Caley realized her amulet was outside her blouse and tucked it back in, her face flushed.

"I like your bracelet."

Kip wore a studded bracelet that looked a bit like a small dog collar.

"It's against dress code," said Kip, "but Gorsebrookes are born rebels."

A teacher hurried past, and Kip nervously tugged his shirtsleeve over his bracelet. Kip flung open a classroom door. Inside, a swirling black disc shot out a blinding beam of light. All kinds of things were streaming into it: desks, books, blackboards, students, and a surprised-looking chicken with its neck stretched the length of a telephone line. Kip slammed the door shut.

"Wrong room!"

"Professor Wormington's class?"

"Black Holes and How to Avoid Them." Kip gulped, hurrying to the next door. "I don't know why they tell you to be on time for it. Even if you are, you're definitely going to be late in *some* universe or wherever."

Kip opened the door, and the class stood and bowed to Caley. A small owl-like man in a professor's gown led her to her seat.

"Class, please welcome Princess Caley," said the owl-professor.

"Welcome, Princess Caley," the class dutifully echoed.

A student raised her hand, which looked a bit like a hoof. "Is it true earthlings wear clothes made of animals?"

The class regarded Caley with alarm.

"There will be time to explore the interspecies relationships of Earth in the future," replied the owl-professor, "but let us continue our discussion on the horned lizard. If it thinks you are an enemy, it will shoot blood from its eyes. Who can tell me the best way to approach a horned lizard?"

"Who?" asked a student.

"Who?" the owl-professor hooted back.

"Who?" asked a student.

"Who?" hooted the owl-professor.

The students and the owl-professor continued to "who" back and forth until the professor fell fast asleep.

The class snuck out of the room and spilled into the courtyard, settling into benches under a tree with oddly glowing leaves.

"Useful interspecies social skill." Kip winked at Caley. "The best way to get free period with an owl is to say 'who' until it falls asleep."

A gangly boy sitting next to them with a serious case of green-tinged bedhead, like a badly trimmed hedge, suddenly slumped over.

"Is he OK?" asked Caley, alarmed.

"That's Lucas Mancini," said Kip. "He's a narcoleptic. This is Taran and Tessa O'Toole," he added, introducing Caley to a pair of identical twins.

"I'm Tessa," one of the twins corrected Kip.

"I'm Taran," said the other twin.

"And that's Lidia Vowell." He nodded toward a tall, serious-looking girl whose head was beginning to sprout elk horns. "She's first-year Head Girl, so watch your step."

"I'm not a girl," said Lidia. "I identify as species fluid."

Everyone plucked the glowing leaves from the tree and stared at them, absorbed.

"You're famous." Kip showed Caley a leaf.

To Caley's amazement, the leaf was like a small tablet computer. It displayed something called "Trixi Tells," featuring a woman with a mouthful of neon-white teeth and dramatically slicked-back black helmet hair. It reminded her of the gossip magazines she stole from the neighbor's trash for the Gunch.

The headline read:

PRINCESS FOUND ABANDONED
ON ALIEN WORLD!!

It featured a photo of Caley when she first arrived in Erinath in her roadkill costume. Then the leaves all went black, and a crest appeared from something called the Office of the Sword with a report.

NON-PERSON ALERT!

REPORT SUSPICIOUS ACTIVITY TO THE MINISTRY.

IF YOU'RE NOT US, YOU'RE THEM!

According to the report, a wolf had attacked someone in the village.

"I don't believe it," said the wolflike boy Caley had seen in the dining hall. "Wolves don't attack for no reason."

"I don't trust *anything* the government says," said Kip, crumpling a leaf. "Bunch of lying weasels."

"That's speciest," protested Lidia Vowell. "Weasels do not fabricate the truth more than other animals. Weasels use ingenious concealment methods, such as burrowing, to avoid predators, which has given them an undeserved reputation as being sneaky."

"Students!"

The class turned, startled, to face Duchess Odeli, who had appeared behind them, silent as a snowflake.

"If you have a free period, please absorb yourselves in quiet study. And someone wake Mr. Mancini."

The duchess float-fluttered off, the feather-like mulch on her dress flapping soundlessly.

Kip made a rude gesture at her behind her back.

"Detention, Mr. Gorsebrooke," called the duchess without turning.

"The old crow sees everything," Kip grumbled.

THE rest of the day was filled with classes, and Caley was relieved to discover she shared them with Kip (the classrooms seemed to shift around, like the castle). Kip barely looked where he was going, just sniffed like a dog on a scent, but he always seemed to find the correct room (aside from the false start with Mr. Wormington's).

The classes themselves were a whole other matter. Even Kip seemed to have a hard time getting his bearings. In science, which was never Caley's favorite subject (*see *zombie frogs*), the teacher was the toad-faced man she'd seen in the Council Chamber. She was initially relieved because she felt confident she wouldn't have to dissect any frogs in *this* class. But instead of learning about amphibians or atoms, the students were each given what looked like a floating marble. Everyone began setting up heat lamps around their marbles and watering them with eyedroppers. Caley was about to pick hers up to get a closer look when the teacher croaked with alarm and slapped her hand away from it. The marbles turned out to be tiny new planets, and Caley had almost rendered the recently hatched life-forms on hers prematurely extinct. She noticed photographs of past planet projects on a wall. One looked suspiciously like Earth. It was graded a D– (which made sense if anything did).

Animals and Botanicals took place deep beneath the castle, judging by how many stairs Caley had to descend, though you never really knew where you were going to end up when you opened a door. The damp, dark laboratory was bursting with bubbling beakers and furiously sparking equipment. There were herbs, potions, plants, bottles, and beakers of bizarre dead creatures stacked to the ceiling on uneven, teetering shelves—or possibly not dead, because Caley saw what looked a giant black amoeba with red horns crammed in a jar turn toward her with burning pinwheel eyes.

"Don't make eye contact!" cried Kip, herding Caley away from the thing to an empty seat.

"What was that?" asked Caley.

"Slugdevil. It hypnotizes you and sucks your brains out. Then the nasty stuff starts."

Caley sniffed the air. Something smelled seriously rotten.

A creature that looked like a tree stump with branches for arms and legs in a white lab coat skittered in. He picked distractedly at his bark-beard that grew down well past his knees —or knots—or *whatever* he had. The beard glowed faintly blue and writhed around on his face as if it had a life of its own.

"Good morning, class," said the stump.

"Good morning, Doctor Lemenecky," said the class.

The rotten smell seemed to be coming from Doctor Lemenecky, and Caley couldn't decide if he was an animal or a botanical himself.

"Where did we leave off?" Lemenecky hopped up on a chair behind his desk.

"We called the tree surgeon to free you from your beard," replied one of the O'Toole twins.

"Won't be necessary today. Theoretically . . ." said Lemenecky, still picking at his beard.

"We were giving our presentations," said the other O'Toole.

"Ah, yes." Lemenecky nodded. "Your assignment was to combine animals with botanicals using Fuze-Brew to create something unique. Ithica Blight, I believe you're next."

Ithica strode to the front of the class holding up a jar of what looked like fireflies stuck to glittery little flower buds.

"For my project," Ithica began in her dead-drone, "I combined fireflies with fireworks flowers using Fuze-Brew, then soaked them in Milk of Magnetium. I call it 'Tiara Magnififlee.'"

She removed her tiara and emptied the jar over it. The firefly goop was immediately magnetized to it. It looked kind of gross.

"It lights up your tiara. Activated by the heat of your head," explained Ithica, putting her tiara back on.

Nothing happened for a moment, and Ithica's eyes drifted anxiously up to her tiara.

"That proves it," Kip said with a smirk. "Her blood doesn't reach up there."

The flies affixed to Ithica's tiara began sparking, buzzing around, and sending up tiny fireworks. The Pingintees applauded rapturously—as if Ithica had just discovered the secret of fire—then the flies began exploding and smoking, like tiny popping light bulbs. Ithica flung her tiara off, mortified. It rolled across the room and toppled over, and one last firefly blew up.

The Pingintees applauded again haltingly, but a scalding look from Ithica froze their fat hands in mid-clap.

Doctor Lemenecky cleared his throat again. "While the concept was . . . illuminating . . . initially . . . the objective of combining animals and botanicals was undermined by the unfortunate demise of one of its principal components. I grade it a C."

Ithica shoved her tiara back on her slightly charred hair and returned to her seat, refusing to look at anyone.

Lemenecky called Lucas Mancini's name. He called it again, louder. Lucas was fast asleep.

Kip prodded Lucas and he lurched to his feet, pulling a tattered wad of notes from his pocket that he proceeded to drop all over the floor. He got his notes together and began to read in a halting voice.

"As many of you know, the castle is becoming increasingly unstable. After careful observation, I have concluded that it is rotting. For my project, I used termites . . ." He fumbled in his pockets and pulled out a vial of termites. "And bound them to planet-based silica with Fuze-Brew. As many of you know . . ." Lucas lost his place.

"We know this is *boring*," someone heckled.

A few kids snickered, but Lemenecky wasn't paying attention. He battled his beard, which was tossing pencils from his lab coat pocket.

"Silica is one of the ingredients in cement," Lucas soldiered on, "and if the termites find anything rotten, they will eat it and excrete a cement-like substance. This will turn all the rotten parts of the castle as hard as rock, hopefully making it stable again."

"Genius!" Kip nodded admiringly.

"Now for the demonstration . . ."

Lucas began to empty the insects onto one of the wall roots. To everyone's surprise, they skittered from the root to Doctor Lemenecky—who was on his knees—or knots—trying to pick up his pencils. The termites swarmed Lemenecky's beard, and he began to race around the lab, his little stick-arms swiping wildly at the termites while his beard thrashed about, knocking over beakers, Bunsen burners, bottles of bat wings— everything in its path. He almost knocked over the slugdevil, which teetered alarmingly on the shelf as everyone screamed and covered their eyes.

"Mr. Mancini! Do something!" shouted Lemenecky.

Lucas was fast asleep again.

"Out! Everyone out!" cried Lemenecky. "I'll deal with this. Technically . . . And someone call the tree surgeon!"

Kip woke Lucas as everyone ran out the door and up the stairs leading from the lab.

"Doctor Lemenecky should be locked up along with all the other boggers," declared Ithica Blight. "He's a disgrace to the academy."

"For once, I almost agree with her," Kip told Caley.

THE last class was something called Know Your Baest. Kip opened the door for Caley, and as soon as she entered, she figured the castle had moved because she was in some sort of jungle. She turned back, but Kip was nowhere to be seen. The door was gone, and in its place was a large, moss-covered rock. She looked behind the rock and out pounced a huge gold cobra. Caley stumbled backward, helpless, as the cobra slowly rose up in front of her, spreading its hood and baring fangs, which for some reason had braces. From out of the jungle leapt a dog in a studded collar, snapping and snarling at the cobra. The cobra slithered under a thorny bush. The dog backed off and, to Caley's absolute astonishment, turned into Kip. A moment later, the cobra slithered out again and transformed into Ithica Blight.

"Suppose you think that's funny, do you?" Kip glared at Ithica.

Ithica pretended to throw a stick, and Kip went bounding off after it.

"No, *that's* funny," Ithica smirked. "Stupid mutt."

Kip turned back to Ithica, red-faced, his hair bristling. "I'm a bloodhound. Ninety-eight percent." He wheeled around to a pair of snorting boars gorging greedily on the bush. "Quit it, you two!"

The boars transformed into the Pingintee cousins. A pair of Siamese cats appeared from the jungle and transformed into the identical O'Toole twins. An elk transformed into Lidia Vowell, and she shook the bush with her antlers.

"Lucas! Wake up!"

The bush turned into Lucas Mancini, fast asleep. He woke up groggily, staring perplexed at his chewed-up pants (courtesy of the Pingintees).

"Looks like Lucas needs some pruning," said Ithica.

"That means he's constipated," grinned Pansy Pingintee.

"Contaminated," said Petunia.

Kip glowered at Ithica and the Pingintees. "I'm warning you, leave Lucas alone."

"Can't he look after himself?" asked Ithica. "Oh, I forgot, shrubs have no spines."

"That's speciest," said Lidia. "Plants may not have vertebrae, but they have highly sophisticated structures. They transport nutrients through xylem and phloem and have roots for taking up water and minerals."

Ithica eyed Lidia's elk horns. "The rest of us are *human* again, by the way. Or are you rutting?"

The Pingintees snigger-snorted and pretended to know what "rutting" meant.

"Some of us prefer to remain boggers, it seems," Ithica went on with a disgusted tone.

"Some of us, like *you*, were never human to begin with," Kip countered.

"What's going on here?"

Everyone turned to a portly bald man in an elaborate robe and cap in a peacock-feather pattern striding toward them.

"Oh, Master Aramund," said Ithica, affecting an innocent

tone, "we were getting to know our baests. But it seems Princess Caley doesn't *have* a baest. I forgot; she's an earthling."

"Back to your studies," ordered Aramund. "Concentrate on experiencing the environment through your baest's senses."

The class headed back into the jungle, transforming into animals again (or plants, in Lucas's case).

Aramund took Caley's arm and began to lead her through the jungle, talking quietly to her as if reciting a bedtime story. Caley had the feeling *this* story didn't have a happy ending.

"There are many hidden paths in the baest realm. Some quite dangerous . . . even deadly for the uninitiated. When it is time to receive your baest, you must come to me and I shall guide you. There is the way out." He gestured to a tall group of ferns. "Take care, Your Highness. This can be a wild kingdom."

Caley watched Aramund melt back into the jungle. She walked through the ferns and found herself once again in the academy.

WHEN the final bell rang, the only thing Caley was sure of was that she knew less at the end of the day than she did at the beginning.

She was also pretty sure she was failing grade eight in two entirely different worlds.

CHAPTER SIX

The Cat's-Eye Crystal

aley hoped Kip could help her find her way back to her
rooms again after class, but he had the duchess's detention,
so she waited for him in the courtyard. She didn't want to open
the wrong door and end up floating in eternity with a
stretched-out chicken. She spotted Neive dragging a sack of
laundry across the lawn and went to help her.

"You shouldn't." Neive shook her head. "Someone got me
in trouble with the duchess. They said I was insolent. Now I
have laundry on top of my other chores."

"Ithica Blight. I bet it was her."

Caley didn't think it was possible to dislike someone so
completely and so quickly, but Ithica made it easy. She saw the
duchess float-fluttering her way soundlessly across the courtyard.

"I'm the highest-ranking royal, right?" Caley asked, turning
to Neive.

Neive gave her a nervous nod.

"Duchess Odeli," Caley called in a clear voice, "I require
Neive . . . er . . . that servant there—to tidy up my rooms immediately. They are most unsuitably . . . *untidy*."

The duchess's eyes narrowed a notch; then she flattened

her feathery dress and bowed sharply, shooting Neive a suspicious look as she fluffed off again.

"Did you see her face? I thought she would burst a blood vessel." Neive grinned as she escorted Caley back to her rooms. "I bet no one's ever ordered the duchess to do anything before."

"It reminded me a bit of the Gunch," said Caley. "Except her face *always* looked like that."

"The person who took care of you? The duchess told me about her."

"If by 'took care' you mean 'once used my arm as a pin cushion when she couldn't find hers.'" A curious thought came to Caley. "How does the duchess know about the Gunch?"

"Duchess Odeli knows all," Neive said dramatically.

"Kip says she's part hawk. I bet that's her baest."

"No one knows."

"So, Kip is a dog. And poor Lucas . . ."

"The story I heard was that Lucas went to get his baest and he fell asleep under a tree, and when he woke up he was a shrub. He can turn into any kind of plant. Pretty amazing, really."

"Ithica's a snake. Perfect. The O'Toole twins are Siamese cats, also perfect. I think I keep calling them by the wrong names."

"You can usually tell them apart because Taran always wears her hair in a ponytail. Or is that Tessa . . . ?"

"Is that why some people here look like animals?"

"The more you identify with your baest, the more you can begin to look like it. Some people practically turn into theirs."

It kind of made sense. Caley always saw pets who looked like their owners—this was just the other way around.

"So, this baest thing," started Caley, "I think they're kind of like spirit animals on Earth. But how does it work? How do you get one?"

"The Wandering Woods."

"The Wandering Woods?'"

"It's where you form the Unbreakable Bond with your baest."

"Sounds painful."

"It's more scary than painful," said Neive. "You're not allowed in the Wandering Woods unless you're seeking your baest, and not without Master Aramund's permission. Once you go in, you can never leave, unless you form the bond. You wander in there forever."

"I wonder what my baest would be."

"It depends on your personality. It's the animal part of your nature. And once you get your baest, you start to take on its power," explained Neive.

"Like Kip always sniffing things out." Caley nodded. "Baests are awesome. I can't wait to get one."

"Some people don't like them. They think it makes you less human. They call people who look like their baests 'boggers.' There was a war long ago where baests turned on people or something. There's supposedly all these baest attacks now, and everyone's afraid. There's even people talking about getting rid of baests altogether, but I don't know how they could do that."

"I'd much rather be an animal," Caley said with a frown, "considering most of the humans I've met. What's yours?"

"My what?"

"Your baest."

Neive quickly got the wooden box with the little floating rose blossoms and opened it for Caley.

"You better get dressed for dinner. It's Friday, so you can wear weekend clothes."

It didn't seem like Neive wanted to say anything more about baests. Caley picked a green rose (her favorite color). She blew on it, and the blossom twinkled and the light washed over her. Her school uniform faded and fell to dust and was replaced by an emerald tunic made of soft, woven leaves interlaced with tiny yellow buds that bloomed, held magically in the fabric like flies caught in a web.

Neive frowned. "It's a bit out of fashion."

"It's beautiful." Caley admired herself in a mirror (which was officially the first time she had ever done *that*). "I never want to take it off." She picked up the row of blossoms in the box. "Where did you get these?"

"They belonged to Queen Catherine."

"No one seems to know what happened to her." Caley turned to the portrait of her mother over the fireplace. "Or they won't tell *me*."

Neive stared at her thoughtfully a moment. "I need to show you something." She pulled the bed skirt away, revealing a hidden drawer, and retrieved a small black velvet bag from it. "This must have belonged to your mother too. I found it when I was getting the room ready for your arrival."

She emptied the contents of the bag into her hand. Inside was a crystal about the size of an egg with a dark crescent in the middle.

"It's a cat's-eye crystal," explained Neive. "You see things with it."

"Like what?"

"Things that are happening in other places. Even in the past. Maybe it can help you see your mother."

Caley felt her pulse quicken. "Let's try it."

Neive rubbed the crystal. Nothing happened.

"I've never actually used one before. I'm not sure how it works. Maybe it's broken—"

There was a loud knock on the door.

"The duchess!" Neive hid the crystal behind her back, but before she could open the door, Kip barged in and bumped into her. The crystal went flying, and Neive almost fell over.

"Hey," Kip said, waving to Caley. "Couldn't find you after class. Just wanted to make sure you were OK."

"I'm OK," Caley assured him.

"I'm fine too," said Neive as she straightened her uniform. "And please just walk right in. *Whoever* you are."

"That's Kip," said Caley. "Kip, this is Neive."

Kip cocked his head curiously at Neive, his hair bristling. Neive stared back at Kip, her nose twitching suspiciously. Kip snapped out of it, spotting the cat's-eye crystal.

"Is that a cat's-eye? I've only ever *heard* about them. Incredibly rare. Mind if I try?"

"I think it's broken," Caley explained.

Kip scooped the crystal up. "Probably just needs to be activated. 'A cat's-eye is blind until you take one of its lives.'"

"Take one of its lives?" Neive asked.

"It's a riddle. I have a nose for mysteries. Pretty much able to solve anything."

"Humble too," said Neive.

Kip hurled the crystal at the wall as hard as he could, and it shattered into a million pieces.

"You broke it!" Neive glared at Kip.

"Look!" implored Caley.

The shattered pieces of the crystal were floating across the floor and magically forming back together. In a moment, the cat's-eye was as good as new.

"Just as I thought." Kip nodded, looking relieved. "You only get one look for each of its nine lives." He handed Caley the crystal. "Hold it tightly and think about something you want to see."

Caley held the crystal. Again, nothing happened.

"I forgot," said Kip. "You have to have something from the person or place you want to see."

"I don't have anything from anywhere," said Caley.

They heard a chirp, and everyone turned to the cricket in the wooden cage.

"There *is* that. It came from where I used to live."

"Give it a try," urged Kip, handing her the cage.

Caley held the cage in one hand and the cat's-eye in the other. The crystal began to glow. She stared into in, and to her amazement she saw the Gunch's house. The Gunch was having a yard sale of all the hideous animal creations she had made Caley sew. There was a sign that read "PET-CESSORIES," promising the latest in high-fashion contemporary accessories that doubled as household pets. The Gunch carried on a one-sided conversation with some anaconda cargo pants that lay there, immobile. She began to shake them and scream, "Say something! *Do* something! I know you can hear me!"

Neighbors looked on nervously as a wagon pulled up from the local hospital and men in white suits began chasing around after the Gunch, who was clutching a salamander sun hat and howling, "It's alive! IT'S ALIIIIIIVE!"

Caley grinned faintly to herself. "I guess there *are* happy endings . . ."

The scene in the crystal shifted to her basement cold storage/dungeon.

"What's that place?" Kip asked, looking slightly horrified.

"My bedroom."

"Looks like a haunted house."

"I wish." Caley sighed. "Would've loved to live in a nice place like that."

"There's someone in there." Neive pointed at a shadow floating across the floor. The image was blurry, like they were looking at it through too-thick glasses.

"Try turning the cat's-eye," suggested Kip. "Maybe we can see a different angle."

Caley repositioned the crystal. They saw a hooded silhouette overturning everything in the room, hunting for something. Caley recognized him right away. He began to turn toward her. She gasped and dropped the cat's-eye. The image vanished.

"Who was that?" asked Kip. "Did he live with you?"

Caley shook her head. She felt cold despite the warm afternoon.

Neive and Kip stared at her questioningly.

"When I first got here, I overheard this meeting," Caley began slowly. "They were talking about him. I've seen before. In my dreams. I think it's him."

"Who?" said Neive.

"Olpheist."

Neive and Kip exchanged a look.

"He's supposed to be in some sort of prison you can never escape from," said Kip.

"Are you sure it's him?" Neive asked.

Caley nodded. "Pretty sure. And I think he's looking for me."

"But . . . why?" said Kip.

Caley had no answer for that.

CHAPTER SEVEN

Neive's Secret

I n the days that followed, Caley tried to find answers to the questions blowing up in her brain like little lead balloons, making her feel like she would sink under the weight of endless mysteries. Why was she in Erinath? What had happened to her mother? And what did Olpheist want with her? Most of the time, it was hard enough just finding her *class* (and sometimes the entire academy). Whole parts of the castle would be there one minute and gone the next. The dining hall was mostly reliable, except for lunch one day when it was replaced by a section of the royal gardens (apparently restricted) where naked shrub-nymphs frolicked in a fountain. The duchess immediately herded the students away, declaring the castle needed "a good time-out." The castle also shuddered and shook, seemingly more with each passing day, and various parts of it were always threatening to fall apart. A squad had been dispatched to deal with the situation, led by Colonel Chip Chesterton. Caley decided they must all have had beavers for baests because although she caught glimpses of them fixing the castle, mostly they gnawed on the wooden beams they were supposed to be using to repair it.

"Seems like a serious conflict of interest," Kip observed. "Beavers repairing a *wooden* castle."

Classes continued to be about as predictable as the castle floor plan. In Things and Nothings, the teacher (an ordinary-looking man with a large mustache) informed the students that the observable universe depended on how it was observed. To demonstrate, he put on a pair of "imagine-glasses," which looked like a pair of eyeglasses made for a giant housefly or something because each glass had about a million facets. The glasses seemed to have a life of their own and kept blinking and staring around at everything. The teacher looked at the class through the glasses, and everyone appeared as variations of the O'Toole twins. There were O'Tooles with two legs and O'Tooles with hundreds of legs, like centipedes. Some O'Tooles seemed to be made of slime; others were just mustaches in school uniforms. At that point, one of the actual O'Tooles got fed up with the whole thing and untied her ponytail. This was apparently the only way the universe (not to mention the class) could tell them apart because the universe seemed to get confused and everyone turned into the person they were looking at. This was even worse than it sounded because it turns out the one thing teenagers hate even more than being turned into slime is being turned into *each other*. Eventually, the teacher managed to restore order and everyone got back to being themselves—except the O'-Tooles now had faint moustaches.

"We're meant to be learning that anything can become anything else, I guess," Kip told Caley on their way to their next class, "but I'd just as soon not know. Being thirteen is hard enough. Got my first pimple yesterday. Plenty more of *those* to look forward to, I expect."

After class, Caley and Neive always hung out in the common room. The airy, window-lined room was full of comfortable old couches and tables centered around an enormous fireplace full of glowing stones. Neive explained they were bazkûl-breath gems (a bazkûl was apparently some kind of extinct monster, like a dragon). They also powered everything in Erinath. Kids usually sat in front of spiders' webs suspended between what looked like a tennis racket on a stand. This was known as "the Web"—kind of like the Internet on Earth, except . . . spiders. You touched the web, said whatever you wanted to search, and little electrified-looking spiders instantly spun out the information.

"We need to set you up on Bee-Me," Neive told Caley one day as they settled into a couch.

"Be what?"

Neive smiled. "Hey, Bee!"

A glowing bee streaked in front of them.

"Show Bee-Me," Neive told the bee, and it projected a social media site in the air in front of them, like a floating smartphone screen.

"Wow!" said Caley. "Where do these come from?"

"Machines and creatures can be combined in Erinath. If the creatures are OK with it. I think trash toads are kind of upset about what happened . . ."

Neive swiped her finger across the screen, and various profiles scrolled past with people's interests and hobbies, goals for the year, achievements, family background, and their baests. Caley noticed Ithica Blight's profile. Her photo made her tiara look a lot bigger, her braces were gone altogether, and her eyes were much bluer and shinier—not the typical dead-shark sheen.

Neive frowned. "She probably used the Perfect Princess filter."

Ithica's goal for the school year was to continue being "#1 ROYAL!!" Her interests were "SHOPPING, STYLE, AND PARTIES," and she disliked "FURRY THINGS." Caley noticed that all the *i*'s were dotted with ridiculous little tiaras. There was a photo of Ithica standing next to a handsome dark-haired boy named Ferren Quik. It said they were "in a relationship," and the picture was surrounded by more tiaras and hearts.

"Can we look at someone else's profile?" Caley asked (that was more than enough Ithica Blight for one day). "How about yours?"

Neive brought her page up, and Caley read it.

"'Interests: Being in nature. Climbing trees.'" Caley scanned the mostly blank page. "There's nothing about your family, or your baest, or *anything*."

"I've been so busy I haven't gotten around to it," Neive said, sounding a bit defensive.

"What are you guys doing?"

Kip loomed behind them, chomping noisily on a carrot.

"Bee-Me." He nodded. "Check mine out. Hey, Bee, show Kipley Gorsebrooke."

Neive's profile was replaced by Kip's.

"Please just totally interrupt us," Neive told Kip.

Kip's profile picture showed him proudly holding the Equidium Cup. Caley remembered him saying something about the Equidium—whatever *that* was. The cup looked like it had been pasted into the picture. Underneath it read, "FUTURE EQUIDIUM CHAMPION!"

Neive stifled a smirk.

"What?" Kip said testily.

"Equidium Champion?"

"It says '*future*.'"

Kip stared at Neive, his head cocked, his hair bristling. Neive stared back at Kip, her nose twitching.

"We were going to work on my profile," Caley said, hoping to calm everyone down.

"I'll help you." Kip plunked himself down on the couch beside Caley. "Hey, Bee: New profile. Princess Caley Cross." A blank profile page opened on the bee-screen with Caley's name on it. "Take photo."

The bee flashed and the next thing Caley knew, her blinded-looking picture appeared under her profile, with Kip hovering on the edge of the frame.

"Looks good," Kip said with a nod. "What about your interests and hobbies?"

Caley thought a moment. She never had any time for interests or hobbies with the Gunch. Did zombie-raising count? Probably not, so she just shrugged.

"We can leave that empty for now." Kip scanned the profile page. "Oh, here's one," he said blandly. "'Relationship status.' What's yours? Do you only date Earth people, or do you also date people from other worlds—"

"It's none of your business," Neive cut in.

"It's part of the profile," said Kip, his face getting flushed. "Just trying to help."

"She didn't ask you to help."

"She didn't *not* ask."

"I'm right here." Caley stared back and forth at two like she was watching a Ping-Pong match.

Loud snoring was followed by groans.

"Lucas!"

Everyone turned to Lidia Vowell, who was sitting nearby with a few kids, and Lucas Mancini, who was fast asleep.

"He heard you arguing," Lidia explained to Neive and Kip. "Conflict puts him to sleep."

"He was right in the middle of a tapestry," said one of the O'Toole twins, gesturing to a large tapestry on the wall in front of them.

Most rooms had a tapestry with nature scenes like the one in Caley's bedroom. It turned out the images could also show you any story you thought up. The little worm-like fibers that made up the fabric wove out the scene, except the tapestries made the stories much more exciting, adding characters and plot twists. It was like being the director of your own movie. Lucas usually got to control the tapestry in the common room because he had a knack for creating epic adventures. Right now, the tapestry was frozen on the image of a prince (who looked a bit like Lucas but without the greenish hedge-hair) who was battling a bazkûl. The bazkûl had trapped a princess (who, Caley noticed, looked a bit like *her*) in a burning tower. The prince had been climbing a vine to get to the princess's window (the vine also looked a bit like Lucas) but was now dangling from it, snoring loudly.

"Lucas!" The other O'Toole shook the snoring boy. "Wake up and finish the story."

"He *always* does this," Kip told Caley. "Last week he made a murder mystery, but just as the killer was about to be revealed, the detective began trimming a hedge and then fell asleep. I swear he's one-third human, one-third plant, and one-third sloth."

"That's speciest," said Lidia. "Sloths are often in torpor, which is different than sleep. Their metabolic rate and body temperature both drop, and brain activity is dramatically decreased, in order to conserve energy."

"One-third human, one-third plant, one-third dramatic drop in brain activity." Kip shrugged. "Works for me. Anyway, *I* just thought of a good story . . ."

Kip ambled up to the tapestry and started a story. It really wasn't much of one, just a dog chasing a squirrel, although Kip did manage a plot twist when the dog used an exploding acorn to stun the squirrel.

"Stupid squirrel," Kip said with a chuckle.

To Caley's surprise, Neive stormed off. Kip started to follow her, but Neive shot him a sharp look, her nose twitching, and he froze, watching her go, his head cocked curiously.

CALEY caught up with Neive in the palace gardens. A few clouds skudded by in the cool autumn afternoon, and ballerina blossoms curtsied at the girls as they passed.

"What's wrong?" Caley asked.

"I don't know why you hang out with Kipley Gorsebrooke. I think he's the densest boy in Erinath."

"Is this about his story?"

Neive glanced around warily. Groundskeepers were trying to herd the hippo-hedge out of a flower bed. Neive motioned to a greenhouse that resembled a giant glass fish near the edge of the gardens, and the girls walked there in silence.

"This is Master Pim's greenhouse," said Neive, opening the door for Caley. "He's the one who planted the gardens."

"I thought they were a thousand years old."

Neive shrugged by way of reply.

Caley looked around. Overhead, slits in the glass gently opened and closed, like gills, and a fine mist blew from tiny knotholes in the arched roots that spanned the roof. The greenhouse was full of the oddest plants and flowers. She began to sit on a wooden bench under a drooping willow with a curious crying face shape in the trunk.

"Maybe we better sit over *there* . . ." Neive led Caley to another bench farther away. "Can I tell you a secret?"

"Sure."

"Promise you'll never tell anyone?"

Caley nodded. "I promise."

A row of flowers with petals that looked like earlobes craned toward them. Neive clapped her hands loudly, and the earlobes quickly closed.

"I'm a squirrel."

"You mean . . . your baest?"

"Not exactly," Neive said. "It's complicated."

"That's cool."

"The squirrels made me promise not to tell anyone."

"I'll never tell." Caley shook her head solemnly.

"There's something else. It's hard to explain. My baest . . ." Neive gestured at herself, "is *this*."

Caley regarded her, puzzled.

"I was born a squirrel. I took a human as my baest."

"I . . . *think* I understand."

"*I* don't." Neive shook her head. "I've never met anyone else like me."

"What happened when you got it?"

Neive's large oval eyes narrowed as she stared into space. "I don't remember much. I was only two when they found me. They thought I was just some little kid who got lost in the Wandering Woods."

"How do you know you were a squirrel?"

"The squirrels told me. They tell me lots of things."

"Things like what?"

"Like . . . you were coming, and I needed to stay close to you. So I asked the duchess if I could be your maid."

"Neive, if the squirrels made you promise, aren't you going to get in trouble for telling me?"

Neive regarded Caley with an expression halfway between fear and defiance. "I don't know, but I wanted to. I trust you. I don't know why the squirrels told me to stick close to you," concluded Neive, "but I'm glad I'm your maid."

"But mostly my friend," said Caley. "Right?" she added nervously.

Neive smiled. "I've never had a royal friend before."

Caley smiled back. "I've never had a *friend* before."

CHAPTER EIGHT

The Wandering Woods

"So, do you think you're a new species of human, or do you think humans are a new species of *squirrel?*"

Caley regarded Neive intently in the mirror while Neive tried to brush her hair one morning.

Neive shrugged. "I wish I knew *what* to think—"

The brush snagged in Caley's amulet. Neive started to take it off, and Caley slapped her hand away and clutched it.

"Sorry!" said Caley, looking just as shocked as Neive. "I don't know why I did that! I don't take it off."

"Ever?" Neive asked.

Caley thought about this a moment and came to a surprising realization.

"I can never remember not wearing it."

"Is that kind of . . . strange?"

Caley took the amulet off and laid it on the dressing table.

"There. No biggie." Caley regarded the amulet. "I don't know why I even wear it. It's just an ugly old rock."

Neive began to comb Caley's hair again. "Where did it come from?"

"Who knows? I didn't even know where *I* came from until, like, a week ago. I only just found out who my mother was . . ."

Caley's eyes drifted over to the portrait of her mother.

"Do you think the amulet belonged to her?" Neive asked, following her gaze.

"I used to make believe it did. I have this dream where I'm living with my mother. I have a real home. But maybe I didn't deserve one. Maybe *that's* why she left."

"Why would you say that?"

Caley looked at Neive in the mirror. Should she tell her?

"I bring dead things back to life."

Neive stopped combing and stared, unblinking, back at Caley.

"Really?"

"Really. One time, I rescued a cricket from the pet store because it was going to be fed to a gecko. It was the only pet I ever had. Kind of fun, but, you know . . . a *cricket* . . . so not super engaging. The Gunch heard it chirping and flushed it down the toilet. That night a zombie cricket plague came out of the sewers and ate all her cashmere sweaters and skirts."

"Is that one of them?" Neive nervously eyed the ex-cricket in the cage.

Caley nodded.

"Another time I brought home an ivy I grew at school for Nature Studies. The Gunch tossed it in the trash because, she said, 'Plants need air and water, and who is going to pay for those?' Next morning, the whole orphanage was covered in ivy. They had to call the fire department to use the Jaws of Life to get it off the Gunch. Turned out it was poison ivy too. They never completely got rid of it."

"How do you know that was *you*?"

"I knew." Caley nodded. "I can always tell when it's going to happen because my hands start to burn."

"Burn? Like . . . actual fire?"

"Sometimes. And my amulet buzzes."

"Buzzes?"

"It vibrates—kind of like a warning, I guess. It's why no one ever wanted to adopt me. Like when they sent me to the Muirs. They had a son. Asher. He tortured his pets, and he made me bury them in the backyard. I could hear them screaming at night. I told the Muirs, who got me put on meds —which made the screaming worse. One day when I was burying a cat it started to claw out of its little cat grave. Then all the other dead pets did too. And they kind of messed up Asher. I got sent back to the Gunch."

Neive stopped brushing Caley's hair with a thoughtful expression.

"It sounds like they were bad people and bad things happened to them, so maybe the reason you can raise the dead is more like a force for good. In a weird, totally gross way."

"I never thought of it like that," said Caley.

Neive started trying to comb Caley's cobweb of curls again, but the brush snapped right in half.

"Don't worry about it," Caley told her. "I'll just tie it back or something."

"Use this . . ."

Neive lent Caley one of her barrettes, and the table the amulet was on suddenly toppled over. Before the girls could say anything, the rest of the furniture started shaking, and the portrait of Caley's mother almost fell off the wall.

"The castle!" shouted Neive. "We have to get out!"

A siren began to sound. The girls ran into the heaving hallway. Panicked students were racing from their rooms.

"Follow me outside!" The duchess appeared and began

herding everyone down a hallway. "Do not panic. And do not run. The aristocracy is never in a rush!"

Caley suddenly turned and raced back into her rooms.

"Where are you going?" called Neive.

"My amulet!"

Caley retrieved her amulet and set off again with Neive. Everyone else had disappeared. The hallway twisted into a pretzel, then began to bulge like a blocked hose. There was a feeling of intense pressure, like the moment before a hurricane hits.

Kip came sprinting toward them—he could sniff out wherever Caley was.

The hallway suddenly contracted. It was like being inside a burst balloon as a wild wind sent them flying out an archway that usually led to the academy courtyard.

Not this time.

Caley landed in some sort of woods. It was nearly dark, as if the sun had suddenly eclipsed. Withered trees reached into a purple sky, creaking and swaying in the wind like bones. A dense tangle of roots knotted the ground, slick with moss. Cold fog hung over everything. Caley's attention was drawn to a stone arch carved with animals. It looked ancient and didn't seem to lead anywhere.

Kip came hurtling through the arch from out of nowhere and landed face-first beside Caley.

"I've officially had it with the castle," said Kip, swiping dirt from his face as he got to his feet.

Caley stared around the fog. "Where's Neive?"

"Could be anywhere," Kip answered, gaping around. He saw the arch, and his expression fell. "We have to leave. *Now.*"

"Why?"

"This is the Wandering Woods. If Neive's here, she'll have

to find her own way out. And if anyone finds out *we've* been in here without permission, we'll be kicked out of the academy."

"But Neive might be lost. Or hurt. You said Gorsebrookes were born rebels."

Kip frowned. "Maybe if I had her scent . . ."

"This!" Caley pulled the barrette from her hair. "Neive lent it to me."

Kip sniffed the barrette. "A bit like . . . acorns." He set off with Caley, then grabbed her arm. "You can't come with me. The only time you're allowed in the Wandering Woods is to make the Unbreakable Bond. And then the only way out is to find your baest, or—"

"Or you wander in here forever," finished Caley. That's what Neive had told her.

"You don't have a baest." Kip shook his head. "It's too dangerous."

"We have to find Neive," Caley insisted, and she headed into the woods.

Kip shook his head ruefully and trudged after her.

"We're going to miss dinner."

Kip loped along, sniffing the air now and then. Nothing moved. Caley never imagined woods could be so still, so lifeless. It felt like a wax museum. And she had the feeling that while she hunted for Neive, something was hunting *her*.

"Did you hear that?" She stopped and looked around.

Kip turned to her blankly.

"Screams."

"What kind of screams?"

Caley knew the kind. She had been hearing them her whole life: the screams of dead animals. She pointed to a looming structure just visible through fog-shrouded woods. It was built out of the bone-trees, gnarled together. It reminded Caley of skeletons clutching at each other. The screams were coming from inside.

"What do you think that is?" Caley asked.

Kip regarded the structure unhappily. "Don't know. Don't *want* to know."

Caley set off toward it.

"We're not seriously going *in* there?" said Kip, looking mortified.

When they got to the structure, Kip motioned to a gap in the bone-trees, near the ground. They wriggled through. What they saw inside made the hair on the back of Caley's neck stand up. In the middle of a vast empty space stood a colossal machine. Enormous pistons and gears shook the earth. The heat coming off it made Caley's and Kip's faces shine with sweat. Ghostly, contorted creatures writhed above the machine in a dark vortex, being drawn relentlessly into it through a huge iron funnel.

"What are *those*?" Caley asked.

"Baests," said Kip, shaking his head in disbelief. "Of wolves, if I had to guess."

The machine shuddered, and from one end something rolled out, like a car on an assembly line. It was about the size and shape of a wolf, but its fur was made of needles and it had steel claws and teeth. Caley stared at the thing with a jolt of recognition. The wolf's yellow eyes blinked open, staring around in vacant ferocity, and then it let out a terrible cry, like an animal being born in pain.

"I've seen that thing before," said Caley, turning to Kip.

He was gone.

Caley wriggled out of the structure and stared around. To

her horror, she saw several mechanical wolves chasing Kip. His foot snagged on a root, and he fell with a cry. The wolves circled, their blade-like fangs bared.

Before she could think what to do, Caley ran toward Kip, and as she ran, something came at her from the depths of the dark woods—hurtling at inconceivable speed. It had no form. She *felt* it more than saw it. It was the feeling you get the second before you wake up from a nightmare: shapeless dread and doom descending. The instant it touched her she felt unbearable pain, like she had fallen into a frying pan.

Then everything went black.

Caley's breath returned to her with a juddering gasp, as if she had been drowned, and her eyes jolted open. The pain was gone except for a scorched sensation, like a bomb had gone off inside her. She stood in the middle of a charred crater like a meteor had landed. The wolves were incinerated into shadows, and acrid metallic ash clung to everything. Kip lay nearby. He sat up shakily, staring around in a vacant daze.

"What . . . happened?"

He wiped some burnt metal off his torn clothes, sniffed the air, and turned toward the forest.

Caley saw the tip of a squirrel tail disappear behind a tree.

Kip got to his feet and grabbed his ankle, groaning. "Can we please get out of here now?"

Caley began to help him toward the stone arch in the distance.

"WERE you attacked by a wolf, dear boy?"

Doctor Lemenecky examined Kip in the infirmary while Caley looked on. His glowing blue beard wriggled around his face like a wall of worms, and he started coughing so violently he almost fell over.

"Maybe you should see a doctor . . . Doctor," Kip said nervously.

"Everything's perfect. Practically . . ." Lemenecky responded.

He opened a medical bag and pulled out what looked like a large mechanical fish with a mouthful of titanium teeth. The teeth began rotating and roaring around like a chainsaw.

"My ankle's probably only broken," sputtered Kip. "I don't think it needs to actually come off!"

Lemenecky hacked off part of his beard with the chainsaw-fish, and his beard seemed to settle down.

"Now to fix that fracture. Feasibly . . ."

"Fix it feasibly . . . or feasibly fix it?" Kip gulped.

Lemenecky removed a vial of pink smoke from his bag and uncorked it.

"Breathe it in."

Kip inhaled the vial. Nothing happened for a moment; then the swelling and bruising in his ankle began to magically shrink.

"Amazing." He smiled. "Feels better already."

"Breath of Bone-Stitch." Lemenecky nodded. "My own formula."

Kip made a face and his body began shaking. He grabbed Caley's hand and squeezed down hard.

"Is he OK?" Caley asked.

"There are one or two side effects. A few kinks I haven't quite worked out yet. No need to panic. Possibly . . ."

Kip stopped shaking and his body went stiff.

"What's happened to him?" Caley asked, alarmed.

"Bone-Stitch is effective at joining bones together. However, it tends to join most everything *else* together as well while the affected part heals. Momentarily. Maybe . . ."

"Momentarily, maybe? Or maybe, momentarily?" said Caley.

Kip's skin began to take on the color and texture of marble.

"Is that part of the cure?" Caley asked.

"I may have miscalculated the dosage. But not to worry, I have an antidote. Somewhere. Sometimes . . ."

Lemenecky began rummaging through his bag again, but his beard pinned him to the ground and began to poke him mercilessly with a tongue depressor. Kip was turning to stone. In another minute, he'd be a living statue.

"Pink smoky bottle!" gasped Lemenecky, gesturing to his bag. "He needs to drink it. While he can!"

Caley found the bottle and emptied it down Kip's throat. In an instant, he was back to normal. Doctor Lemenecky bandaged Kip's ankle, then had another coughing fit and stumbled out as his beard overturned the contents of his medical bag over his head.

Caley looked down. Kip was still holding her hand. He turned red and let go, tearing off his tie, which was scorched and shredded from the attack in the woods.

"That was my good tie. Mom's gonna kill me. What happened, anyway? All I remember was those things from that factory attacked me. Then a bomb went off."

"Mr. Gorsebrooke."

They turned to see Duchess Odeli entering the infirmary.

"I understand there was some sort of wolf attack?" the duchess asked, staring at Kip.

"Not . . . exactly," Kip responded.

"Then perhaps you would tell me what *did* happen," said the duchess.

"We were in the Wander—"

"Wandering around the gardens!"

Everyone turned to see Neive hurrying in.

"Neive!" Kip and Caley said together, relieved to see she was safe.

"We were in the palace *gardens*." Neive turned to Caley and Kip with a leading look. "We *all* were."

"The *gardens*?" repeated the duchess.

"Yes . . . the . . . *gardens*." Caley slowly turned from Neive to the duchess.

"What were you doing in the gardens? During an evacuation order?" The duchess was staring holes through everyone by now.

"What were we doing in the gardens? During an evacuation order?" Kip repeated cluelessly. "Good question. Makes no sense—"

Neive elbowed his bandaged ankle.

"Ow!" Kip groaned.

"Sorry. Nervous twitch," said Neive.

"The castle . . . moved," Caley began haltingly. "And we all ended up there. And a hippo-hedge attacked me. Kip saved my life. Maybe I should knight him or something. Do they do that in Erinath?"

The duchess didn't look at all convinced by Caley's story and seemed about to ask more questions when the castle gave a little shudder, and she ordered Caley and Neive to return immediately to their quarters.

•

WHEN Caley got back to her rooms with Neive, she quickly shut the door behind them.

"Neive, why did you tell the duchess we were in the gardens?"

"We can't tell anyone we were in the Wandering Woods. Ever."

"Because of that factory making those . . . things?"

"Not just that. What else do you remember?"

"I went to help Kip, and there was some kind of explosion."

Neive stared back at her with a searching look, as if she suddenly didn't recognize her. "Athrucruth," she said finally.

Caley stared blankly at Neive.

Neive turned to the window. Night was gathering and rain had started to fall, a cold autumn drizzle that fogged the windows and seemed to seal in the castle.

"They tell stories about it," she began quietly. "To frighten children. 'Better be good, or the athrucruth will come . . .'"

"What's it look like?"

"Nobody knows. No one's ever seen one. It's supposed to be extinct. Long ago there were monsters here. This was the worst. And there's only one person who had its baest."

"Who?"

Neive kept staring out the window.

"Who?" repeated Caley.

Neive turned to her, her face pale.

"Olpheist."

"Is that why it attacked me?"

"It didn't attack you. I saw it. It made the Unbreakable Bond."

"The athrucruth is *my* baest? But . . . you said it's only the baest of Olpheist. So, does that mean . . ."

"You're *not* Olpheist, obviously." Neive shook her head. "There has to be some other explanation."

"Now we both have a secret," Caley said quietly.

CHAPTER NINE

Orocs

As if having an athrucruth inside you wasn't bad enough, the next day proved the worst in Caley's life (and that was really saying something). Her schedule had something new on it simply entitled 'Equidium.' Kip seemed obsessed with it, but Caley still had no clue what it was. The first-years were all told to meet in the courtyard, and everyone was talking back and forth excitedly when Caley arrived.

"I've been looking forward to this forever!" Kip told her, wriggling like an excited puppy (which technically he partly was). "You have to be thirteen."

"I can't believe this is finally the day," said Tessa O'Toole (or it might have been Taran—both twins had their hair in ponytails today). "I was so excited, I couldn't sleep."

"Me either," said Lucas Mancini (and *that* was really saying something).

A few more students hurried toward them, and Caley's heart sank. After a week of successfully avoiding Ithica Blight and her gang of tiara-topped twits, her luck had finally run out because there they were. This time, Ithica didn't even bother to bow to her. One of the Pingintees started to, but Ithica stepped on her foot.

The duchess headed in their direction, looking even sterner than usual.

"Follow me. Single file. Stay together. The Equidium is not a place you want to get lost in."

The duchess led everyone through an archway and down the steps of a long, twisting tunnel. They arrived at a heavy wooden door with the letter *E* carved into it and what appeared to be an enormous dragonfly. Everyone followed her into a stable that looked very old—even older than the rest of the castle. Every surface was worn smooth but well cared for, like a family heirloom that had been handed down. The stalls were so high Caley couldn't see the horses, but she heard odd-sounding shrieks coming from them.

"Into your armor. Quickly," announced the duchess, pointing to two changing rooms. "When you are ready, I will escort you in."

Everyone rushed into the rooms except Lidia Vowell.

"I'm sorry, Lidia," said the duchess, "but we do not have a species-fluid changing room here."

Lidia looked disappointed and headed in with the girls.

Inside the changing room stood rows of lockers with the students' names already on them in brass plaques. They opened them to reveal suits of armor inside. Caley opened hers.

It was empty.

"Oh, dear," said Ithica with fake concern. "I don't think they'll allow you in the Equidium in that sad old frock of yours."

Caley didn't appreciate Ithica's remark about her mother's clothes, but she didn't want to give her the satisfaction of knowing it.

Everyone began to climb excitedly into their armor. The suits were made of strong strips of interlaced roots reinforced here and there with crystals embedded between them, giving the armor an overall shimmering appearance. The helmets, with flowing rope-braided neck guards, were topped with a variety of carvings: antlers, bull horns, wings, fish fins, and animal heads. It reminded Caley of samurai armor (if samurai armor grew out of the ground). It looked pretty cool, and she stood there awkwardly as everyone admired their suits, trying to pretend she didn't mind not going to the Equidium (whatever *that* was).

A circle of tiara twits fawned over Ithica's armor. The wood was blond, like her hair, and the crystals were all huge and gold.

Neive hurried in breathlessly hauling a large cloth bundle with the Cross coat of arms on it.

"Sorry I'm late. Found this . . ."

Neive opened the bundle. Inside was a gleaming suit of armor, mahogany wood studded with green crystals. The helmet had the initials "C.C."—for "Catherine Cross"—carved on it, and it was crowned with a snarling cheetah's head.

The others regarded the armor admiringly. Even Ithica seemed momentarily impressed; then she turned her attention to Neive.

"One day a slave, the next a squire," she announced. "They'll be crowning stable rats next."

Ithica bumped past Neive on their way out the door, with the Pingintees following in a snigger-snorting clump.

Neive put Caley's helmet on her and nodded approvingly. "You look amazing."

•

KIP waited for Caley outside the changing room, munching on a sandwich. Everyone else had left with the duchess.

"They're pretty serious about the schedule here. We better catch up to the others." Kip offered Caley his chewed-up sandwich. "Got to keep your strength up for the Equidium."

Caley shook her head, and Kip shoved the rest of his sandwich into his armor and led her off.

"Thanks for waiting for me," said Caley. "I only just got my armor."

"That's a really good kit," said Kip. "I have this . . ." He gestured gloomily at his armor that was dull and full of chips and nicks. "My brothers all wore it before me. I look like an old laundry basket."

Caley was surprised to find her armor growing tighter around her.

"Kip . . . what's happening?"

Before he could answer, a figure stepped out from the shadows, blocking their way. It was the giant of a man Caley had seen behind General Roon in the Council Chamber—the one who looked like a lizard had been bred with a robot and fed through a trash compactor.

"Where do you two think yer goin'?" The enormous man glared down at them with his one good eye.

"The Equidium. Sir," replied Kip, not sounding like his usual carefree self.

"Yer not meant t'be wandering by yerselves. Things happen to people here. *Bad* things."

"It's my fault," said Caley. "I'm new and I don't know my way around. Mr. Gorsebrooke is taking me to the aquarium."

"Equidium," Kip corrected hastily.

The massive man stared down at Caley.

"I *knows* who y'are. Long-lost princess come home t'claim her kingdom." He leaned in to look at her closely. His breath smelled like death. There was no other way to describe it. "On your way then, little Highness. Into the Equidium. Some of 'em who goes in don't come out."

He hulked off, and Caley and Kip hurried on their way.

"Who was *that*?" Caley asked.

"The Scabbard."

"The Scabbard?"

"He's in charge of security, or something. They say he's part lizard. Been in more battles than anyone in Erinath. Supposedly killed in some of them too. Reptiles grow back limbs, so it kind of makes sense. Creepy, if you ask me."

"Sounds awful."

"Don't feel too bad for him. He's the meanest man in the kingdom. Just steer clear. I don't think he likes you. That's probably why your armor tightened. It does that if you're in danger."

Kip led the way through a vaulted hall. The walls were covered with portraits of students in armor.

"The Hall of Heroes." Kip gazed raptly around at the portraits. "That's Varl the Vanquisher. Captain of a three-time winning team. Most ever. And there's Osmond the Awesome. Only won the Equidium once, but it was so, well . . . *awesome* . . . they didn't even bother having it the next year because everyone was still partying."

"Kip, what actually *is* the Equidium?"

"The greatest thing ever!" replied Kip, hurrying up a sloping tunnel. "The rest of the academy is OK, but this is why I really wanted to come. My brothers brag about it endlessly— they all made teams—and now it's finally my turn. Even Dad was excited . . . other than telling me I should use this opportunity to take back the kingdom for the common people. I'm going to win it one day."

"Is it like training to be a knight or something?"

"Kind of. And at the end, there's the contest. But you have to make the team, and first-years hardly ever do. I'm the last chance for the Gorsebrookes. Imagine me winning. I'd be famous. And the family name would be restored."

Kip paused at a pair of armored doors at the end of the tunnel and turned to Caley, his jaw set.

"I'm going to do this."

He took a deep breath and pushed open the doors.

Caley was momentarily blinded as she stepped out into the sunlight. After her eyes adjusted, she saw she was in some sort of arena, like the Colosseum. Unlike the rest of the castle, this seemed to be made of petrified gray parchment with honeycomb-shaped openings above rows of stands. It looked a bit like a gigantic open-aired hornet's nest. In fact, she could swear she heard a faint buzzing coming from somewhere. Everyone was lined up at attention in their armor, and as Caley walked toward them with Kip, she felt a bit like a gladiator.

A seriously unprepared gladiator.

A man in military armor with a rhino-horn nose marched up to the students. Caley had seen him in the Council Chamber.

"I am Commander Pike, Master of the Equidium." The rhino-man's voice rumbled around the arena. "For a thousand years, on this sacred soil, each noble child of Erinath was cut from the womb of tenderness and mercy to be bathed in the blood of sacrifice and pain and born anew as Equidium competitors. Train hard, fight hard, and you will be victorious. Give in to the coward's way and bring shame and dishonor to yourself and your family."

Caley noticed Kip blanch a bit.

Pike turned toward an iron gate that slowly began to rise, its sharp teeth wrenching from the arena floor. The class craned their heads to try to get a glimpse of what was inside the darkened tunnel. Everyone seemed terrified and thrilled at the same time.

"What if I can't ride one?" Lucas asked. "Dad's already disappointed about my baest."

"Be proud of whatever you are," said Lidia, who was having a bit of trouble fitting her helmet over her elk horns.

"Besides, I don't think orocs eat shrubs," jeered Ithica.

"Kip, what's an oroc?" Caley asked.

No sooner had she said this than she heard the sound of claws on concrete, and from out of the tunnel burst creatures beyond Caley's wildest dreams. They looked like horse-sized prehistoric dragonflies. Their tear-shaped heads had huge multifaceted eyes and horned antennae. Their sleekly muscled bodies were covered in fine, fibrous coats in a variety of shades from foam white to onyx black, many shot through with iridescent patterns and streaks. Long, glowing fibers were arranged in a spiky line down their necks, almost like a horse's mane. Their four legs were barbed and boney, ending in clawed feet. Their torsos tapered into long tails nearly the length of their bodies ending in a variety of shapes: forked, wedged, notched, and fanned, like bird feathers. As soon as they were free of the tunnel, they each unfolded two pairs of dragon-like wings that shimmered in the sun. They lifted straight up into the air like helicopters and began circling the arena, splitting the air with their high-pitched, almost insect-sounding shrieks.

Everyone stared, some looking stunned, some looking euphoric, and others looking like they just wanted to run away and hide.

"*That's* an oroc," said Kip, gawking saucer-eyed at them.

As Caley stared at the amazing creatures swooping and swirling above her, the most powerful sensation came over her. It wasn't fear, or awe, or anything like that. It was a feeling so strong and so deep that she would never in her life forget it. The moment she set eyes on the orocs, there was only one thing she wanted to do more than anything she had ever done before.

She wanted to ride one.

"These orocs have been domesticated, but I *warn* you," Pike said, eyeing the students gravely, "an oroc is never fully tamed until it has its rider." He hoisted a scroll and read. "Kipley Gorsebrooke."

Kip gulped so hard it sounded like he'd swallowed his tongue. As he began to walk to the center of the arena, it looked like his knees were going to give way.

"Looks like the orocs will get an early lunch," Ithica cackled to the Pingintees, who were trying to look brave though Caley could see their pudgy pink lips quivering.

Kip stood in the middle of the arena, squinting up through the slit in his helmet visor at the orocs.

"How do you choose one?" Caley asked Lidia.

"You don't choose an oroc; it chooses *you*."

A single oroc dove through the pack at Kip.

"Steady!" one of the O'Tooles called to Kip.

"Show no fear!" added the other O'Toole.

"Silence!" shouted Pike.

Kip didn't move (whether out of bravery or because he was frozen stiff, it was hard to say). The oroc stopped inches from his face and hovered, its four wings beating with a sound like giant hummingbird wings. Still, Kip didn't move, but his eyes were darting back and forth behind his visor, looking like they'd rather be anywhere other than in his head seeing this.

"What happens if the oroc doesn't choose him?" Caley asked.

"I don't think they'd let anyone actually . . . die," Lucas replied weakly.

The oroc landed, folding its wings and thrusting its long, glossy snout into Kip's stomach so hard it knocked him on his back; then it gobbled up the sandwich that had popped out of his armor. Kip shoved the oroc's snout away and sprang back to his feet indignantly, swiping oroc snot from his armor.

"That was my snack, you great goobery beast!"

The oroc seemed momentarily surprised; then it reared onto its hind legs, let out a shriek, and beat its wings so furiously it almost blew Kip over again. He managed to stay on his feet and stared back at it with a defiant look. The oroc shook its head several times, gnashing its teeth and pawing the ground, then eventually settled down and kneeled. Kip climbed clumsily onto its sloping back, which made a perfect saddle. As soon as he sat, the oroc unfolded its wings and launched like a rocket, with Kip hanging on to its glowing mane for dear life.

A few students began to clap, and Lucas shouted, "Way to go, Kip!" but a look from Pike silenced everyone. The oroc did a loop around the arena, and Kip gave everyone a cheeky wave —which was a mistake because the instant one hand was off its mane, it immediately rolled without slowing down, sending Kip dropping like a sack of stones to the arena floor. His armor instantly tightened, and he bounced once then didn't move.

"He's hurt!" cried Lidia.

Pike held out a hand for everyone to stay put. After a moment, Kip's armor loosened again and he sat up, looking stunned but OK. He gave a weak thumbs-up and returned shakily to the others as a few kids clapped him on the back.

"Princess Ithica Blight," Pike read from his scroll.

Ithica strode past Caley. If she was scared, she wasn't letting anyone know it. She stood in the middle of the arena, raising her visor to scan the orocs as if daring one to come down. Nothing happened for a moment, and her smug smile slipped a bit. A large oroc with a jet-black coat dove at her. For a moment Caley had the happy thought it would carry Ithica off to its nest—or wherever orocs lived—and feed her to a bunch of little orocs, but after some more shrieking and beating of its wings, it landed in front of Ithica and kneeled. Ithica climbed on its back, and the oroc rose into the air and swooped around. Caley had to admit it was a pretty decent ride. Ithica managed to land her oroc and got back in line, accepting the congratulations of the tiara twits with a bored look that seemed as fake as the rest of her.

"I don't see what all the fuss is about," Ithica sniffed. "And orocs smell worse than boggers. I'm going to have mine hosed down and perfumed."

One by one, the others were called by Pike and each was able, somehow, to get an oroc, except Evegny Pooner, who had an antelope baest and was beginning to develop hooves for hands. Lidia Vowell protested to Commander Pike that they should find an oroc and let *it* ride Evegny—to which Pike just snorted that the Equidium was no place for "alternative thinking."

Lucas Mancini somehow managed to fall asleep on his oroc, which even seemed to impress Pike momentarily.

"Princess Caley Cross," Pike announced.

As she made her way to the center of the arena, Caley was thinking that everyone else probably knew a lot more about the oroc situation than she did (zero), and certain tiaraed twits would no doubt be delighted if she fell flat on her face . . . or worse. But for some reason, none of that mattered. In fact, the feeling she'd had when she first set eyes on the orocs was stronger than ever. She wanted to ride one. She *would* ride one. For the first time in her life, Caley felt like she belonged right where she was, doing exactly what she was meant to be doing.

The orocs were circling overhead. Maybe she could pick one out. A green one to match her eyes would be cool. Caley raised her visor to see better, and as soon as she did, they began shrieking. It wasn't the same sort of sound they had been making before. This was more like the noise crows made when a strange bird attacked their nest. It sounded *angry*. Her armor grew tighter. The next thing she knew, the orocs dove at her, one after the other, beating their wings and snapping their teeth. Caley tried to remain motionless, as she had seen others do. Maybe it was some kind of test. Out of the corner of her eye, she noticed Pike drop his scroll and begin to run toward her. Something was wrong. Very wrong. Her armor was so tight now she could barely breathe. She felt a thud on her shoulder. An oroc had tried to bite her! Another one bit, then another, and soon they all began to swarm her. Her armor was fending off the attack—for now—but she huddled in a heap on the ground, shaking with fear. It was funny, she thought, how quickly you could go from wanting something with all your heart to being scared to death of it.

(But not "ha-ha" funny.)

Stable hands came spilling out of the tunnel, but they couldn't get close to the frenzied orocs. Suddenly, they scattered as a dark shape burst through them and heaved Caley onto its shoulders. The Scabbard, swinging a spike-studded club, batted the orocs away as he hauled her into the tunnel, yanking the iron gate down behind them. He dropped her roughly to the ground, wiping the blood from a gash across his face where he'd been bitten, which had already begun to close up.

"Thank you," Caley managed.

"Can't let high borns get gutted in the Equidium," grunted the Scabbard. "Not if I wants to keep my job."

He spat out one of his baked-bean teeth and stalked off, leaving Caley shaking in the dirt.

CHAPTER TEN

The Darkness

Caley ran, still in her armor, from the Equidium all the way to the greenhouse on the edge of the gardens. She sat on a bench and began to sob. She couldn't remember the last time she had. There had been so many good reasons to (*see *Caley's life*), but she could never remember crying.

Until now. Until the orocs.

A puddle grew beneath her riding boots, and Caley realized with a shock her eyes were gushing like a waterfall. For a moment, she thought she might drown in her own tears.

"Weepy willow."

The little old fox-man from the Council Chamber had suddenly appeared behind her. He pointed his staff at the willow tree Caley sat under—the one with the crying face in its trunk. She saw that its eyelike knotholes were also gushing water.

"Planted it myself. I find a good cry now and then helps clear the head. Or at least the sinuses." He pulled a handkerchief from a pocket in his gardener's overalls and handed it to Caley. "I believe yours may be sufficiently drained."

The willow stifled a few sniffs and stopped crying.

"Perhaps we should take a walk? I'm Pim. I feel we've met before . . ."

Pim peered at Caley with his astonishingly bright orange

eyes a moment, then began to stroll through the greenhouse with her. Several small furry-looking berries leaped off a bush and went splatting to the ground.

"Leaping lemming berry bush. Complete failure, I'm afraid. They always jump just before you can harvest them. Oh . . . there's one left. Catch it!"

Caley managed to catch the berry.

"Try it," encouraged Pim.

She bit it . . . and immediately spat it out.

"It tastes like an old battery!"

Pim shrugged. "Just as well they're impossible to harvest. Isn't nature wise?"

Caley saw another plant that seemed to have a bunch of little red glowing buttons for flowers.

"I call that 'sunny surprise,'" said Pim. "Press one."

She did, and it gave her whole arm an electric shock.

"Ow! Why didn't you tell me that was going to happen?"

"It wouldn't be much of a surprise then, would it?" Pim smiled.

"What's the point of growing these?" Caley asked with a frown. "Seems like a serious waste of time. Most flowers and plants are either pretty to look at or you can eat them. Yours are just silly."

"The world is full of serious things. And I usually find them to be far more of a waste of time than my flowers and plants. I always do one silly thing before teatime. You might try it. But I assume you're here about the nuts."

"Nuts . . . ?"

"The squirrels have not buried a single nut this year so far as I can tell." Pim stroked his long gray whiskers thoughtfully. "What do you think it means?"

"That . . . it's going to be a short winter?"

"Or never-ending." Pim gazed out the greenhouse at the forest that bordered it. "The squirrels know, but they never tell. Of all the creatures, squirrels have never made the Unbreakable Bond with humans. Which is a pity, because I believe squirrels would have many interesting things to share with us. I find it's often the most seemingly insignificant creatures that have the most important parts to play. Perhaps you could ask about the nuts if you're ever talking to one."

"I don't talk to squirrels," Caley said quickly.

Pim regarded her with his twinkling eyes. They seemed to burn right into her brain, so Caley made herself stop thinking about Neive. She had promised not to tell anyone about her baest. Her thoughts swung back to the orocs, and she felt another tear roll down her cheek, though they had walked quite a way from the willow by now. Pim removed a trowel from a pocket in his overalls and began to pry a gnarled rust-colored weed from a flower bed.

"Most people dislike weeds. But they are just as useful as any other living thing if you bother to get to know them."

Pim pried on the weed some more. It appeared to be fighting back against him. One of its roots grabbed his trowel.

"This, for example . . ." he grunted, wrestling with the weed, "can easily destroy an entire garden in a single day. Every plant has a defense. A rose has its thorns, ivy its poison, but they are nothing compared to this. I call it 'fearfew' because it fears few things . . . even gardeners!"

The fearfew grabbed Pim's arm and began dragging him down into its widening hole as Caley watched with growing alarm.

"On the other hand," gasped Pim, "chop it up and sprinkle

it on some salad, or brew it in a tea, and a person becomes just as fearless as fearfew!"

"Master Pim!" Caley shouted into the weed hole that was now so deep all she could see was the point of his frayed straw hat.

"Animal cracker?"

Pim had popped up behind her with a clump of fearfew in his hand. He grabbed his hat before it disappeared into the hole and pulled a box of animal crackers from another of his pockets, which seemed capable of holding anything.

"It is forbidden, of course, to transport goods from Earth to Erinath," he winked mischievously, "but I *do* love these. Major Fogg brought some back for me when he brought *you*."

Pim gobbled up a cracker and gave one to Caley.

"Now if you'll excuse me, I should probably trim that willow. It's getting quite out of hand." He wiped a tear from his eye with a handkerchief, wrapped the fearfew in it, and handed it to Caley. "Oh, and would you mind bringing this to Doctor Lemenecky? He may find some use for it."

"**DID** you see Gorsebrooke?" Ithica Blight's mocking voice rang out. "I thought he was dead after that oroc threw him."

"I went first," said Kip. "I should get a medal."

"Because your *name* was called first," chided Lidia Vowell.

Caley's classmates were in the stable, admiring their orocs. Caley slipped past them into the changing room where Neive was waiting. She gave Caley's shoulder a sympathetic squeeze and helped her out of her armor.

"You'll get an oroc next time."

Caley nodded woodenly, but she knew there wouldn't be a

next time. She could still feel the terror in the pit of her stomach from when the orocs attacked her—and the humiliation as she was hauled out of the arena in front of everyone. She handed Neive the handkerchief Pim had given her. Neive regarded it, puzzled.

"It's fearfew," said Caley. "Can you give it to Doctor Lemenecky?"

Caley headed out of the changing room with Neive, hurrying quietly past the others, hoping no one would notice her.

"Lucas, you're probably the only person ever to sleep through their first oroc ride," one of the O'Toole twins pointed out.

"They'll write songs about it someday," said Lucas, patting his oroc.

"Lullabies," said the other O'Toole with a grin.

Everyone laughed, their faces still flushed with excitement from the Equidium.

"Anyone could fall asleep on *Lucas's* oroc," said Ithica. "It's so gangly and spotty, like Lucas. I've studied the breeds. Mixed breeds have dull temperaments and lots of horrid spots and streaks." She gestured to her oroc. "Mine's all black. Solid colors mean pure bloodlines. I'll have to come up with a suitable name for him."

"How about Nightmare?" suggested Kip.

The orocs suddenly began stomping and shrieking, and Kip noticed Caley and called across the stable to her. "Caley! You OK?"

Caley turned to Kip and tried to paste on a smile. The others were staring at her now, grim-faced as if they were dealing with someone who just had a death in the family.

"Not everyone gets their oroc the first try," Lidia said gently.

"Seems even orocs hate earthlings," said Ithica.

"Take that back!" Neive got right up in Ithica's face.

"You may go." Ithica snarled at Neive.

The Pingintees immediately lumbered up beside Ithica, while Kip went and stood next to Neive.

"She doesn't have to do what *you* say," Kip told Ithica. "You're not in charge. Princess Caley is."

"*She's* not in charge of anything." Ithica's cold blue eyes narrowed at Caley. "She's not from here, and she's not a real princess. Even her own mother didn't want her."

Caley's hands began to turn bright red, and her amulet started to buzz. Neive immediately pulled her out of the stable.

"She's not worth it," said Neive.

THE following day, Caley checked her schedule on her way to the academy, and her heart sunk. Equidium was the first class. Even the business with the athrucruth wasn't as distressing as the thought of seeing orocs again. The duchess was already in the courtyard, organizing students into single file to lead them into the stable.

"Duchess Odeli," Caley started as she hurried up to her, "I can't go to the Equidium. I might have Crohn's disease. Or it could be conjunctivitis. Cholera . . ."

"I see," said the duchess. "You should probably go to the infirmary. I'll send for Doctor Lemenecky—"

"Never mind," Caley said quickly, "I'll live!"

Caley slunk to the back of the line behind the others as they headed into the Equidium. *Anything* was better than Doctor Lemenecky!

As soon as she entered the stable, the orocs began scratching their claws against their stalls and shrieking. Caley dashed into the changing room. Neive was waiting for her beside her locker.

"I can't deal with this." Caley shook her head.

"I was thinking," said Neive in a low voice. "I wonder if the orocs are freaked out because you're a you-know-what."

"Athrucruth?" whispered Caley.

Neive nodded. "Orocs are sensitive to their rider's energy, and a you-know-what has a *lot* of that."

"So what am I supposed to do?"

"I don't know," said Neive. "But you can *do* this. At least try one more time."

Caley tried to smile. Her hands were shaking so hard she could barely put her boots on.

THE class stood at attention before Commander Pike in the arena as Caley slunk to the end of the line. Pike turned to Caley.

"Princess Caley, we will attempt again to find an oroc for you." Pike nodded to the stable hands, who headed into the tunnel leading down to the stables. Caley instantly felt sick. Pike turned to a long wooden chest.

"While we wait for the orocs to be brought up, we will begin fire-sword lessons."

The class exchanged excited looks as he opened the chest to reveal what looked like a row of sword handles made of polished stone. Pike picked up one of the handles. Instantly, a bright red electric flame shot from the end of it.

"I've always wanted to hold a real fire-sword," Kip said to Caley. "My brothers never let me even *look* at theirs."

"Each of you, collect a sword," ordered Pike, "and form a circle."

There was a mad dash to the chest.

"One at a time!" shouted Pike.

Once everyone was in a circle with their sword, Pike told them to activate them.

"You will need to concentrate on starting the flame," instructed Pike.

A few kids managed little sparks; some shot out feeble flickers, like broken bug zappers. One of the Pingintees got a pretty decent electrified flame going and almost burnt her own nose.

Pike frowned. "It helps if you hold the handle *away* from your body."

Ithica's fire-sword began to glow with a flame about the size of a garden snake. By her expression, you'd have thought she'd discovered fire all by herself.

Kip squinted and managed a pretty decent flame.

Caley was pleased to be able to create a glowing flame about the length of her forearm. Her mood quickly sunk, however, when she heard the shriek of orocs echoing in the tunnel beneath the arena.

"Swords away for now," Pike called. "Princess Caley, step forward."

Caley couldn't seem to move. She'd heard of people frozen with fear and decided this is what it must feel like. (*Unpleasant. Very.)

"Caley . . ." Kip gave Caley a gentle nudge.

"I can't ride an oroc," Caley told Kip miserably.

The orocs began to fly from the tunnel. In a moment they would see her, and she felt sure that this time no one could save her.

"FIRE!" someone shouted.

The chest containing the fire-swords was burning, the flames threatening to spread up the parchment-like walls of the arena. Pike spied Kip standing beside the chest, flaming fire-sword in his hand.

"Oops," said Kip with a sheepish look. "I was putting my sword away, and it went off in my hand. Guess I concentrated too much."

Stable hands raced to put out the fire, and Pike ordered everyone out of the arena. Class was done for the day.

KIP caught up to Caley and Neive as they emerged from the Equidium tunnel into the academy courtyard.

"What's going on? Why can't you ride orocs?"

Caley and Neive traded looks but said nothing.

"I think I deserve to know why I just risked getting thrown out of the Equidium," Kip persisted.

Caley let a few students pass and glanced around to make sure no one could hear them.

"Kip, do you remember what happened in the Wandering Woods?"

"I was following the acorns."

"Acorns?" Neive repeated.

"You smell like acorns to Kip," Caley explained.

Kip blushed a bit. "Then we saw that factory . . . the mechanical wolves attacked me . . . and a bomb went off. That's all I remember."

"*I* was the bomb."

Kip stared at Caley perplexedly.

"It's my baest. I didn't ask for it or anything . . ."

"You don't choose your baest. It's the animal part of your nature. So, this baest of yours . . ."

"It's called an athrucruth."

Kip gaped at Caley like she had just grown an extra head. "Athrucruth? AWESOME!"

He slapped Caley on her back so hard she almost fell over.

"Kip . . . *shush!*" Neive eyed a few students heading across the courtyard.

"An *athrucruth!*" Kip lowered his voice. "I never even *heard* of anyone getting an athrucruth! It feeds off the darkness of its host. The legends say they can get so powerful they can swallow a planet. No wonder orocs freak out around you . . . you're the most dreaded predator ever!"

"Which means I'll never get to ride an oroc," Caley said. The thought of this materialized as a painful lump in her throat.

"Wait a minute . . ." Kip was slowly realizing something. "The athrucruth is only supposed to be Olpheist's baest. So, this may not be exactly . . . awesome . . . because if you have an athrucruth . . . does that mean you're . . . no offense . . . Olpheist?"

Neive glared at him. "You're really unbelievable."

Kip scratched his long nose thoughtfully and regarded Neive. "And another thing. *You* were in the woods. What's *your* baest? Are you an athrucruth too?"

"None of your business," snapped Neive.

She stalked off, and Kip instantly bolted after her. Neive wheeled around, stopping him in his tracks.

"Why are you following me, weirdo?"

Kip stared at her, his head cocked and his hair bristling. Neive's nose twitched; then she set off again.

"Cat." Kip stared after Neive and made a low growling sound. "Bet *that's* her baest."

Caley wasn't listening. She was thinking that if athrucruths fed off darkness, she had more than enough of *that* to go around. It was bad enough making zombies. Now, whatever terrible thought entered her head might end up snacking on planets. The Gunch always called her a demon.

Well, maybe she was right.

CALEY spent the rest of the day in her bedroom. And the next. And the days that followed. Neive brought her meals, but they didn't talk much about anything. What was there to say?

As for Kip, whenever he came by all he wanted to do was talk about athrucruths. He always had some new fact he'd dug up on the Web. Kip burst into her rooms one afternoon and announced, "Athrucruths may have a substance like sulfuric acid in their blood but way more powerful. It can ignite hydrogen molecules and turn air into fire. Never try to stab one . . . not that you could see it coming!" Another time, he had sketched a picture of what he thought an athrucruth looked like (a giant blob of burning tar with teeth everywhere that was eating Erinath). Finally, Caley told Kip not to visit her anymore because she might be molting.

One morning, there was a knock on her door.

"Kip, stay away!" Caley shouted. "I'm going to burn a hole right through the castle!"

"I certainly hope not, Your Highness." It was Duchess Odeli. "The castle has feelings too. I can't imagine it would appreciate being scalded."

Caley let the duchess in.

"Do you have a fever?"

"Not exactly," answered Caley. "But I *do* feel uneasy. It may be water on the brain. Or walking corpse syndrome . . ."

"You're not attending class."

"No."

"Or the Equidium."

"Do I have to?"

"It is the duty of a future monarch to take part in the life of her kingdom. To better understand her realm."

"But this *isn't* my realm." Caley scowled. "I was brought here, and I didn't even have a choice."

It suddenly occurred to Caley she had spent her whole life wishing for her life to change, and now that it had, she wished it *hadn't*.

"May I?" the duchess asked, eyeing a tea tray.

"It's probably cold," Caley answered. "Neive's bringing a fresh pot."

The duchess poured herself a cup and took a sip. Caley noticed her hand was shaking.

"An old wound," the duchess said, catching Caley's look. She sat beside her and stared at her in her hawklike way. "No matter where we come from, or where we find ourselves, the only choice we often have is what to do about the choices we do *not* have."

Caley stared back at the duchess, puzzled.

"I mean to say that I believe a terrible darkness is coming, and you have been brought here for a purpose. Despite the grave circumstances of your life, you have survived. I believe your *true* life, your . . . destiny . . . is only just beginning."

"I'm pretty sure I'm not who you think I am."

"If I may make a suggestion, you can hide away, or you

can, as I believe the saying in your world goes, 'Suck it up, Princess.'"

The duchess curtsied and let herself out.

Caley sat there thinking about what the duchess had said. She was wrong. No matter what had happened to Caley—being orphaned, living with the Gunch, the foster homes, zombies, orocs, and now this thing with the athrucruth—she *had* sucked it up. She was a world champion suck-up. In *multiple* worlds, it turned out.

And what if the terrible darkness was *her*?

Neive arrived with the tea tray and set it down beside her.

"I brewed something special today."

Caley regarded the tea tray. On it was the fearfew root Master Pim had given her.

"It's Equidium this afternoon," said Neive. "I thought you could use something stronger."

She poured a cup and held it out to Caley. Caley hesitated, staring at Neive, who nodded, and then she took the cup.

CHAPTER ELEVEN

Fearfew

"Loosen your grip! Let your mind control the oroc, not your hands!"

Commander Pike was instructing Ithica Blight, who flew unsteadily around the Equidium on her oroc while the class waited on theirs for their turn. Ithica did her best to look bored to bits, but it was clear she was struggling to stay on.

"To control your oroc, control your thoughts," Pike told the class. "Think only of what you want it to do. Let your energy flow from your fingers through its mane. Everything in your head should be empty."

"In that case, Ithica should be the best rider in history." Kip smirked.

Ithica got her oroc flying straight and even managed a little loop around the arena before she came back down. A few tiara twits clapped politely while the Pingintees hooted as if she had just landed on the moon.

"Commander Pike, I need an oroc to ride."

Everyone turned from Ithica to Caley as she strode into the arena in her armor.

Caley felt calm yet lit up inside at the same time. That first sip of fearfew tea had surged through her brain like a wave, washing away her worry. Everything seemed brighter, clearer.

Her thoughts—usually so many and so merciless!—were barely a whisper now, and the space between them felt free with possibility.

Pike nodded to the stable hands, who ran into the tunnel. A few moments later, the orocs flew out. They circled over Caley, but it didn't look like any of them were even interested in attacking her this time. Caley raised her visor. No reaction from the orocs. Pike gazed up at the orocs with a frown.

"It doesn't look like they're in the mood to choose a rider today," said Pike.

"Orocs hate earthlings, like I said."

Caley heard Ithica's taunting voice and the Pingintees snigger-snorting. A sharp look from Pike quickly silenced them.

A splitting shriek made everyone look up. A shape descended from the sky, scattering the other orocs, and the most ferocious-looking oroc Caley had ever seen appeared, brilliant white with a metallic green blaze on his nose and a fan-shaped tail.

"That's a wild oroc. Where did it come from?" Pike turned to the stable hands, who looked as confounded as he did.

The fierce oroc swooped over the arena with another shriek, its large, multifaceted eyes flashing furiously at everyone. The class struggled to steady their panicky orocs.

Caley didn't move. Not from fear—a different feeling flooded through her: excitement. The wild oroc dove straight at her, then hovered so close his beating wings blew her helmet off and sent her staggering backward on her heels, sending up a cloud of dust that had everyone covering their eyes. Ithica mimed having her helmet blown off, and Caley could see Kip through the dust, shaking his head at her as if to say, *Don't!*

Everyone else just stared in horror.

The oroc stabbed his snout toward Caley, baring his teeth. She could feel his hot breath on her face. She was surprised to see his eyes were green, like hers. He glowered at her challengingly, mirroring back her unblinking stare. She held her hand out slowly. She wasn't scared at all. He jerked his head back with a skittish shake. Her hand reached closer . . . and patted his nose. It was surprisingly soft. He tucked his head and calmed his wings, then kneeled on his forelegs as if inviting her. Without thinking, she swung up on his back, gathering his glowing mane in her hands. The instant she touched him, Caley felt a powerful current surge through her body; then she took a breath and softly spoke a word:

"Up."

The oroc shot into the sky and began to fly around the arena. The base of his four wings rotated, allowing him to dart and drift, rise straight up, drop down, or hover like a hummingbird, and so incredibly fast it made Caley gasp. She clenched her legs around his muscled flanks as he soared with effortless power. The wind whipped her face, and she realized she hadn't put her helmet back on. She didn't care. As she flew up into the clouds, it felt like she could do anything.

It felt like heaven.

Kip let out a whoop and high-fived Lucas. The Pingintees pointed with awed expressions, as if they were watching fireworks.

Ithica glared around at everyone, and Caley saw a flame flash from her fire-sword, right in front of Lucas's oroc. It shot into the air, spooked, Lucas and all. Lucas was so terrified he fell fast asleep in his saddle and turned into a lily.

"Mr. Mancini, come down here at once!" ordered Pike.

"LUCAS! WAKE UP!" shouted Lidia Vowell.

Lucas woke with a start that sent him tumbling right off his oroc. He seemed so freaked out he couldn't decide whether to be Lucas or a lily. He kept changing back and forth from a plant to a person as he plummeted to the ground.

"He's going to die!" cried one of the O'Toole twins.

"Someone *do* something!" screamed the other twin.

Stable hands came running with a net, but it was clear they would never reach Lucas in time.

"Dive!" Caley instructed, tightening her grip on her oroc's mane. He went lunging toward Lucas, fast as a lightning strike. It was all Caley could do to hang on. The oroc swooped under Lucas, skimming so close to the ground his wings sent up a froth of dirt and dust. Caley knew she would only have one chance to catch Lucas, who was a lily again. With one hand holding onto the oroc's mane for dear life, she reached out the other, her fingers grasping for a petal. The oroc landed in a long skid, his wings furiously back-beating to slow himself. When the dust settled, everyone saw Caley holding the lily. The lily shook itself back to being Lucas, relieved but red-faced to find Caley clutching him tightly in her arms. The class raced over. There were cheers, and Kip called Caley a hero.

"Princess Caley."

It was Pike.

"Well done." Pike nodded curtly.

AFTERWARD, in the stable, everyone gathered around Lucas, who seemed to be none the worse for his ordeal.

Kip turned to Caley, his face beaming. "You rode an oroc! Even though you're an athrucr—"

"Earthling!" Neive cut him off, kicking Kip's ankle.

"I thought your twitch was in your *arm*," squawked Kip.

"Earthlings riding orocs," Ithica drawled to the tiara twits. "I suppose it *is* entertaining watching aliens perform tricks."

Kip peeled off his gloves, turning to Ithica.

"I saw what you did."

Ithica pretended to ignore him. She shoved her helmet at her squire, who handed her her tiara.

"You spooked Lucas's oroc," Kip persisted.

"Why would I do that?" Ithica snapped back.

"That's easy," answered Kip. "You can't stand someone else getting all the attention. Especially Caley."

"I'd be careful making wild accusations to your superiors, Gorsebrooke. I could order you to sweep stalls the rest of your miserable mutt life."

Kip looked like he was about to say something really nasty to Ithica when Caley came between them and stared straight into Ithica's icy eyes.

"If you ever do anything like that again, *I'll* order your little tiara melted down to make oroc shoes."

Ithica's mouth made a shape like Caley had just shoveled manure in it. Then she screwed her face into something resembling a couldn't-care-less look and affected the world's tiniest bow to Caley . . . then kept on bending to wipe some invisible dirt from her boot, so it wasn't *technically* a bow, but Caley didn't feel like standing up to Ithica Blight anymore. She just wanted to run outside and scream with delight.

She had ridden an oroc!

"Fearfew," Caley said to herself with the faintest smile, and she strode into the changing room with everyone staring after her.

•

AFTER that, things seemed to settle into a more or less predictable pattern. Each morning, the wooden finches in the rafters in Caley's bedroom woke her up with their song, and the eyelid windows blinked open. She liked to linger in bed and identify as many scents from the gardens as she could before she had to get up. This morning she smelled lemon cough drops, freshly baked bread, and a hint of skunk from a black-and-white-striped flower Master Pim had probably planted— for what reason (serious, silly, or otherwise) she couldn't begin to guess. Then she checked Bee-Me. Her profile now included a picture of her and her oroc.

Neive would arrive and try to help her comb her hair, which always left them breathless and half-buried in broken brushes. No matter how many showers and hot oil treatments, Caley's cataclysmic curls always had the last laugh. By then she was usually late and racing to the dining hall for breakfast. The duchess would inevitably appear from out of nowhere and remind her, "Royalty is never in a rush. It is up to the kingdom to catch up to *you*."

Caley and Kip always ate at a table near the back of the dining hall with Lucas. Caley was supposed to sit at the front with Ithica and the tiara twits but (for obvious reasons) didn't.

Classes were as crazy as ever. In science, everyone's marble planets were growing. Kip's looked like a chewed-up tennis ball, and the teacher was concerned he was gnawing on it (which Kip denied, but he *was* part dog). Lucas's planet was a bit flattened because he kept falling asleep on it. Tiny life-forms were beginning to appear on everyone's worlds, and Lucas's was full of semi-squished, fully annoyed bed bugs (which made sense if anything did). Ithica's planet was, according to Ithica, "Already the #1 most royal." It was blindingly gold, and its microscopic life-forms all wore little tiaras and bragged about the size of their mountains. Caley's planet was populated by cricket-like creatures munching happily on an ocean of moss. It was really awesome, she thought, because she had never been allowed to have pets and now she had an entire *world* full of them (although there were not supposed to be pets in Erinath, so Caley called them 'inhabitants').

Animals and Botanicals class was canceled. Apparently, Doctor Lemenecky was ill. On her schedule for Know Your Baest, Caley had written, "AVOID!!" (*see *athrucruths*).

The last class Wednesdays and Fridays was Equidium, and Caley couldn't wait for that. She had never really looked forward to anything in her life before (*see *Caley's life*), but as soon as she began the long walk down the tunnel to the stable and smelled the intoxicating barn blend of musty hay and old wood, her heart beat faster. She would climb quickly into her armor with help from Neive, take a sip of the fearfew root tea she kept in a jar in her locker, and hurry to the stalls. Each stall now had a plate inscribed with the name the students had given to their oroc. Kip had chosen "Arrow" because his oroc flew fast and true. Lucas's was "Dream" (what else?). Lidia refused to name her oroc because she said orocs should not have to conform to human behavior. The identical O'Toole twins named their orocs (also, fittingly enough, identical) "Torrent" and "Tornado," and not even the O'Tooles seemed to know which was which.

Ithica named her big black oroc "Shadow." Her parents (supposedly the richest royals in the kingdom) gave her a fancy throne-like saddle to put over the oroc's back, even though orocs didn't normally wear saddles. The saddle was gold with her obnoxious family crest (a giant crown held by two fire-breathing bazkûls) plastered on it.

As for Caley, she named her oroc "Fearfew."

Commander Pike would usually lead a variety of drills. There was lots of sparring with fire-swords. Caley managed to keep her flame about the width of a garden hose unless she had to spar with Ithica, in which case both their flames would get red-hot and huge until Pike decided they shouldn't spar together anymore.

Then there was jousting, which was a lot like the old-fashioned kind where two riders rode at each other, but with fire-lances. Like fire-swords, you controlled the lances with your mind. It was usually the bigger, stronger kids who did well because the big stone handles of fire-lances were heavy. The enormous Pingintee cousins were also nearly impossible to knock off their orocs (once you managed to haul them *on*). Kip told Caley that if you got better, you could make the fire-lances pierce armor.

"Looking forward to that," Kip said, eyeing Ithica.

What Caley really looked forward to was free ride. After class, everyone got to ride their orocs around the arena wherever they liked. A sort of invisible bond was said to deepen between oroc and rider over time. Soon, Caley found that Fearfew knew where to go almost before she thought it. She clutched the glowing mane-like fibers on his neck, her energy flowing to him from her fingertips, and off he went. Just as often, however, Fearfew would bolt off in some random direction, snorting with secret delight as Caley caught her breath, her arms wrapped tightly around his neck just to stay on. She could feel the powerful creature's heart beating in his veins and was sure he could feel hers, pounding with a thrilling mix of excitement and fear. She couldn't decide if he enjoyed these haywire aerials or was really trying to throw her. Fearfew didn't seem afraid of her, but she felt he wasn't exactly at ease with her either. It was usually a struggle to get him out of his stall and into the arena. He would often stubbornly refuse to come when she called and would stare back at her with his intense green, mirrorlike eyes, as if to say, *Don't think we're friends now. I'm watching you.*

Each student was responsible for his or her oroc's care. Ithica tried to get the Pingintees to do her chores, telling Commander Pike, "I'm a princess. Why should I do bogger work?" Pike just handed her a broom and walked away, shaking his head and muttering something about inbreeding not being a good idea for orocs *or* humans.

Caley *loved* everything to do with orocs, including stable work. She delighted in taking a big, soapy brush to Fearfew and scrubbing away the sweat and salt from his sleek body. She groomed his iridescent white coat until it shone. She'd sometimes spend a whole hour just combing his mane, which was also white with metallic streaks of green, like his blaze. She felt a twinge of sadness whenever she left the stable, but the smell of oroc always slightly clung to her, which lifted her spirits.

As she got dressed one afternoon at her locker, Caley tugged absently at her amulet. Maybe at long last, her good luck charm was actually working, because for the first time in her life she felt happy.

ONE afternoon, as the class led their orocs into the arena, Commander Pike announced a new training routine. Major Fogg was standing at attention beside something that looked like a cross between one of those machines that shoots tennis balls and a miniature elephant. A faint buzzing sound was coming from it.

"Today we are going to practice trapping," explained Pike. "Each of you get a snagger."

There was a bin filled with pitchforks with the middle prong missing. Everyone got one, and Kip (who seemed to know a bit about snaggers) made an electrified glowing net appear from the ends of the prongs.

"My brothers used to catch me with their snaggers when I was little," Kip told Caley. "Never let me try them, of course."

Everyone waved their snaggers around, making various-shaped nets appear, like big bubble wands. Apparently, you could control the nets with your mind and make them any size or shape you could manage.

"Mount up!" ordered Pike, and then he marched off, snapping a salute to Major Fogg. "I leave the class in your hands, Major."

The class climbed onto their orocs while Major Fogg flicked a few switches on the elephant thing, which began to vibrate slightly. Puffs of smoke pooted from a trunk-like tube on it.

"Right-e-o. This new invention of mine should keep the process running smoothly this year," said the major. "The smoke keeps the venowasps nice and peaceful, and the tube can suck them back in if necessary."

"They carried off my cousin Lyndon last year." Lucas gulped. "Found him a week later, covered in boils the sizes of tennis balls."

The major fiddled with the controls on the elephant. The buzzing from it grew louder, like some really angry hornets were trying to get out.

"Kip, what's a venowasp?" asked Caley.

The elephant wobbled a bit, and from its tube flew a black-and-yellow-striped creature the size of a giant wasp, covered in shiny scales that looked like solar panels, with bladelike wings. Its head was glowing bright red like a miniature Christmas tree bulb.

"Awww . . . cute buggy wuggy!" Pansy Pingintee held out a stubby finger to let the thing land on it.

The bug stabbed Pansy's finger with its stinger. The goliath girl dropped to the ground with a thud, foaming at the mouth and shaking spastically. Everyone stared, stunned, except Ithica, who was laughing at Pansy. Stable hands raced in with a stretcher and wobbled off under the strain of the ponderous Pingintee.

"*That's* a venowasp," said Kip.

A few more venowasps flew from the elephant's tube, and everyone immediately put their helmets on and urged their orocs into the air.

Caley sat on Fearfew, unsure what to do.

"Catch one," called Kip, flying off, "if you can!"

It was crazy hard and totally scary trying to catch a venowasp. They were lightning fast—even faster than orocs. Even if you did manage to get near one, snagging it was almost impossible. Caley almost caught one, but it disappeared in midair.

"Camouflage!" Kip swooped past Caley. "Venowasps have amazing defenses!"

Apparently, their scales could change color to match whatever was around them, making a venowasp appear to vanish.

A venowasp zipped past Caley's head, and someone's snagger swiped at it. Caley rolled Fearfew to avoid getting hit and spotted the venowasp right below her. She flicked her snagger and, to her amazement, found the creature in her net buzzing furiously.

"You caught the first one!" Kip gave Caley a thumbs-up.

"Princess Ithica caught one!" Petunia Pingintee whooped.

Ithica was trying to look unimpressed with herself, but Caley could see the corners of her perma-puke scowl were quivering, trying not to turn into a giddy grin. The two exchanged stares and streaked off after venowasps, their snaggers flying.

Major Fogg's elephant invention began to swell alarmingly, then its tube belched out a bunch of angry venowasps that attacked the class. Fortunately, their armor kept everyone from getting stung, but it was still terrifying, and kids were mostly trying to get as far as they could from the nasty bugs.

"Remain calm!" Major Fogg shouted. "Just a bit of bother!"

Several venowasps linked up like a snap-together toy to form one huge venowasp and carried him right out of the arena.

"Or a bit bigger than a bit . . ."

"Another defense," Kip called to Caley. "Venowasp scales are magnetic, and they can link up to—"

"Kip! Look out!" cried Caley.

A venowasp swarm appeared out of midair behind Kip, linking up to latch onto him.

Caley instantly swung her oroc under Kip's, disappearing from view, then swooped back up behind the venowasps and caught them in her snagger with one quick flick of her wrist. Kip waved back at her with relief.

Another cloud of venowasps buzzed by, and Caley set off after them, swinging her snagger. Her arm was surprisingly strong (probably from all the mopping, scrubbing, raking, painting, ditch-digging, and log-splitting for the Gunch). Fearfew seemed to enjoy catching venowasps as much as Caley, and he was also incredibly nimble, reacting to the speedy creatures often before Caley could even see them. Soon her snagger was full of the things. The others had hardly caught any, except for Ithica, whose snagger was also full. Caley had to admit Ithica rode well (which for some reason made her dislike her even more).

Eventually, all the venowasps were caught. Stunned kids were sitting on the ground, nervously checking their armor for stray venowasps. Commander Pike came storming out of the tunnel gate, stable hands in tow. "Turn off that thing!" he barked, pointing at the major's elephant invention, which was just shuddering now like a landed fish and making a feeble groaning sound.

"And someone find Major Fogg!"

AFTER the class, Ithica stood in the middle of a circle of tiara twits in the stable, trying (unsuccessfully) not to look incredibly pleased with herself.

"Princess Ithica caught fifteen venowasps," fawned a twit. "It's probably a record!"

"Princess Ithica, you should try out for the Equidium team," flattered another twit.

"I *would*," Ithica said, as if eating worms were more appealing. "But it would distract me from my royal responsibilities."

"You mean being a giant pest?" asked Kip. "Caley caught seventeen, and I bet that *is* a record."

"I *could* have caught more," Ithica shot back, "but I stopped. It was boring. *Equidium* is boring. Mindless entertainment for the masses. Like Gorsebrookes."

"You'd never try out because you'd never make a team in a million years," Kip told Ithica. He turned to Caley. "But *you* would. You're a natural."

A few kids nodded, and someone called Caley "a born trapper."

Caley shrugged uneasily. All this talk of teams reminded her of gym class, where no one would pick her. Not picked last, mind you—picked *never*. Was that even legal?

Ithica must have noticed how uncomfortable Caley looked because she pivoted her perfectly prim nose toward her and said, "I'll try out if *she* does. Or are you chicken?"

"That's speciest." Lidia Vowell shook her head. "Chickens have numerous predators, so they have evolved enhanced protective instincts."

Before Caley could say anything, Kip pointed at her. "She'll try out. Then we'll see who's chicken—I mean, who has enhanced protective instincts."

There were cheers for both Caley and Ithica, and everyone headed into the changing rooms. Caley noticed Ithica had an alarmed look, like she'd just volunteered to jump off the roof of the castle.

Which made Caley wonder. She suddenly realized she still had no idea what the Equidium actually was. Kip hadn't explained anything to her other than it was some sort of contest.

"Kip . . . what exactly happens in the Equidium?"

CALEY watched Kip position objects on the billiards table in the common room as a few kids looked on.

"Equidium rules are simple." Kip positioned eight chess pawns on the table. "Eight teams. Players qualify during trials to play for their ancestral houses. Gorsebrookes have all been on the House Cross Cheetahs. The Cheetahs and the House Blight Bazkûls are the powerhouses."

"Cheetahs and Bazkûls have won more than all the others houses combined," Lucas explained with a nod.

"Each team has seven players: five defenders . . ." Kip placed five darts on the table, "a tracker . . ." he placed a pair of binoculars ahead of the darts, "and the trapper." Kip plunked a wastebasket on the table.

"I don't think Princess Caley should be represented with a wastebasket," said Lidia. "It's inappropriate."

"Trappers catch things like wastebaskets do," explained Kip.

Lidia replaced the wastebasket with a hair scrunchie, and Kip continued.

"All the team needs to do is track the queen, defend against her venowasps, and trap her. The team that traps the queen wins."

"Queen?" Caley was getting more confused by the minute.

"The queen venowasp," replied Kip. "She migrates to her breeding ground once a year to lay her eggs, at the first frost. It's the only time she leaves her nest. Even then, you can't always catch her. Then it's a pretty lousy year. Venowasps buzzing around everywhere . . ."

"One venowasp doesn't seem so bad," said Caley. "I just caught seventeen."

"Nope. Not so bad." Kip smiled agreeably. "Of course, those were pygmy venowasps. Also, the queen is . . . bigger."

"How much bigger?"

"Umm . . . about the size of your average bazkûl," Kip muttered.

"The size of a . . . *dragon*?" asked Caley in disbelief.

"Stinger the length of a fire-lance." Lucas shuddered.

"But nothing at all like an *actual* bazkûl," Kip said quickly, eyeing Caley's blanching face.

"What *is* it like?" asked Caley.

"Umm . . . worse . . . ?" Kip offered.

"Last year the queen stung one of the defenders," said Lucas. "He still has to be fed through a tube—"

Kip shot Lucas a look, and he stopped talking.

Caley regarded Kip with disbelief. "And *you* said I'd try out?"

Kip shrugged sheepishly. "But on the plus side, simple rules."

CHAPTER TWELVE

Trials

"**K**ipley Gorsebrooke is the *densest* boy on Erinath."

"He just thinks I'd be a good trapper," said Caley.

Caley and Neive were headed to the dining hall when they noticed a cluster of kids around the doors. Commander Pike had posted a sign-up sheet for Equidium trials. Ithica Blight had entered her name under the Bazkûls, with lame little tiaras dotting each *i*. Under the Cheetahs, Caley was alarmed to see her name.

"Who did this?" Caley turned to Neive, who seemed just as surprised.

Kip ambled up with Lucas Mancini.

"Are you excited to try out for the Equidium?" Kip asked Caley.

"She didn't even sign up for it," replied Neive. "Someone wrote her name down."

"*I* did," said Kip.

Neive gave Kip the look she always gave him (disbelief).

"Why did you do that?"

Kip gave Neive the look he always gave *her* (dense).

"She said she would if Ithica did."

"*You* said she would," countered Neive.

Lucas began yawning. Conflict always made him fall asleep.

Kip turned to Caley. "Wouldn't worry about it. First-years hardly ever make teams. There hasn't been one in years."

"Athold Murkinblok on the Brunswick Bulldogs," said Lucas sleepily. "He was stung by the queen and lost control of his bladder. Forever."

"So now Caley's not good enough to make the team?" Neive glared at Kip. "She can make it if she wants to. She's—"

"An athrucruth!" Kip nodded excitedly.

Fortunately, Lucas had fallen asleep on his feet.

"Would you *stop* saying that?" Neive snapped. "I was going to say she's a good *trapper*."

"A natural." Kip nodded again.

Neive and Kip exchanged looks. They seemed as upset about agreeing with each other as they usually did about *not* agreeing with each other.

Lucas woke up with a start and blinked around nervously.

"Did someone say 'athrucruth'?"

COMMANDER Pike stood in the middle of the arena as the Equidium hopefuls entered with their orocs. Parents watched anxiously from the stands. Caley led Fearfew in. Kip was already standing beside Arrow, looking nervous but determined. Lucas trudged by with his oroc, Dream, looking like he was going to his beheading.

"My dad said I had to sign up. To build 'character,'" Lucas told Caley. He waved weakly up at the stands to a man in a meticulous mustache and military uniform sitting stiffly beside a thin woman with a nervous face who vaguely resembled an ostrich. Lucas's mom waved back worriedly, but his father just sat there with his arms crossed stiffly in front of him.

The coaches came jogging out wearing tracksuits and whistles, looking like every gym teacher Caley had ever seen (way too energetic for anybody's good and vaguely angry).

"Candidates, to your groups. Quickly!" ordered Pike.

Everyone assembled in groups. The trappers all seemed to know each other from last year's teams. They hugged or high-fived dramatically, spoke in too-loud voices, and seemed impossibly happy, like the kids Caley used to see on the first day in every new school she went to—the ones who seemed to live in a different world than her. Now that she *was* living in a different world, she was disheartened to discover some things never change.

Ithica waved. Caley was so surprised she started to wave back . . . then saw Ithica was actually waving to the Pingintees, who were thumping toward the defenders. They were by far the largest in their group aside from Ben Bruin—a brawny third-year boy with a bear baest and a serious beard—so they'd probably make their team, Caley figured (if their orocs didn't collapse and die under the weight of them first).

"Trials will last three days," Pike announced once everyone had settled into their groups. "The coaches will be scoring you for their house teams. Results will be posted Sunday before dinner. Good luck to all."

Commander Pike blew a whistle, and the trials began. Stable hands hauled something covered in a tarp toward the trappers. Major Fogg marched briskly behind it in his signature beret and khaki jumpsuit.

"Right-e-o, straight to business!" The major yanked off the tarp, and everyone flinched. But it wasn't another venowasp-filled elephant; it appeared to be a mechanical octopus on a rotating stand, its arms loaded with small clay discs.

"Mount up! Snaggers at the ready!" ordered the major.

The trapper candidates hopped on their orocs and activated their snaggers.

"Speaking of snaggers," the major went on, "as some of you may know, I hit a bit of a snag with my venowasp trainer . . . or a bit bigger than a bit. So we'll use this until I can get the bugs worked out. Ha! Bugs! Venowasps! Little unintended pun there."

A few kids groaned.

"This should do the trick. Simple device. Nothing can possibly go wrong."

The major yanked a lever, and the octopus apparatus began to rotate. He gave a cheery thumbs-up to everyone, and an octopus arm grabbed his hand. It began to spin around wildly with him, then shot him straight out of the arena like a cannonball.

"Turn off that blasted gadget!" Pike came running with the stable hands. "And someone find Major Fogg!"

Eventually, they got the disc launcher working, and the trappers began flying around on their orocs, trying to catch them in their snaggers. Caley noticed a boy atop a powerful blue oroc. He had attached a rope to the handle of his snagger that allowed him to whirl it around like a lasso. He was fast and catching a lot of discs. Ithica was also catching a lot. Caley wasn't. Every time she went for one, someone (usually Ithica) cut her off or thumped into her oroc. In fact, everyone was bumping and banging around like some sort of crazy car rally. It had to be cheating, but Pike didn't say anything. After about forty-five minutes, he whistled for everyone to stop and counted discs, announcing the totals. The boy with the blue oroc had twelve, and Ithica had ten. They were in the lead.

"Caley Cross . . . zero," announced Pike.

Ithica smirked so wide it looked like she might bust her braces.

The parents streamed down from the stands, and everyone stood in animated clusters discussing the trial. Caley began to lead Fearfew back to the stable, passing Lucas, who was with his parents.

"You did very well, dear," Lucas's mother was saying. "You tried hard."

"He caught *one*," his father grumbled. "Why sugarcoat it? The boy just isn't cut out for anything active. Why do you think he's a bloody *plant*?"

Lucas glanced around miserably as nearby kids and parents looked away, pretending not to hear. Caley gave a sympathetic smile to Lucas as he trudged off after his parents. She knew what it felt like to be humiliated (*see *Caley's life*). She felt pretty humiliated herself since she had come in dead last.

"Hullo."

Caley turned, surprised to see the boy with the blue oroc walking lankily toward her.

"I never caught any my first day of trials either," said the boy. "Too nervous."

He removed his helmet. He had short, dark, curly hair and an easy smile. Caley thought she recognized him from Bee-Me, but she wasn't sure. For some reason, her face felt flushed. Maybe she had overheated in her armor. Might be heat rash. Or hives. Diphtheria?

"Ferren." The boy held out his hand to shake.

"Caley."

"I'm always nervous at trials," the boy went on. "The thing

to remember is that so is everyone else. And don't let them knock you around."

"Doesn't seem fair."

"All's fair in the Equidium. Think venowasps fight fair? They'd just as soon sting you in the back. You're fast. Handle your oroc well. But there's more to being a good trapper."

"Like what?"

"You need to fight back."

"Fight back?" Caley repeated. That would be a first.

"Ferren!"

They turned to see Ithica beelining over with her parents in tow. Caley could tell right away they were Ithica's parents because they had the same perma-puke expressions as her that seemed to scream, *I'm richer than you; I'm royal-er than you. Now crawl off and die.*

"You know my parents, of course, the duke and duchess," Ithica twittered to Ferren in the bilious bird-song voice she used whenever she was particularly pleased with herself (almost always).

Another woman in a tall tiara and too much eye shadow that made her look like a hungry magpie inserted herself into the middle of the group, beaming at the Blights.

"Isn't it marvelous our children are competing together? A chance for our families to become even closer!"

Ferren looked uneasy. "This is my mom," he told Caley.

Ithica pointed at Caley to her parents. "That's the earthling I've been telling you about."

Ithica's parents gave Caley a small, stiff nod and marched off. It was pretty clear what Ithica had been telling them (nasty, horrible stuff).

"Ta-ta, dear parents." Ithica limp-fish waved at the Blights.

"Shall we all go for tea?" Ferren's mother asked as she followed fawningly after them.

"I didn't know you were *that* Caley," Ferren told Caley. "I normally bow to princesses."

"Please don't," insisted a blushing Caley.

Ithica wheeled from her departing parents and wedged herself in between Ferren and Caley like Caley wasn't there at all.

"A few of us are getting together for a little trials kick-off soiree in my rooms after dinner." Her smile evaporated as she eyed Caley. "Invitation only."

"I need to regrip my snagger," replied Ferren. "Enjoy your 'soiree.'"

He gave a sweeping, over-the-top bow to Caley, winked, and sauntered off.

"Come by later if you can!" Ithica called frantically after him.

The Pingintees plodded up, gazing moonily at Ferren.

"I don't think he wants to," said Pansy.

"It doesn't take *that* long to re-grip a snagger," added Petunia.

"Morons." Ithica glared at her cousins and race-walked to catch up to Ferren.

"Can we still come to the soiree?" Pansy called after her.

"What's a 'soiree'?" Petunia scratched her ponderous pink head.

"Moron. It's a place you go and swear at commoners," replied Pansy, clumping off with her cousin.

"What did A Bit Glitchhi want?" Kip had wandered over, staring over at Ithica.

"To make everyone's skin crawl?" Caley shrugged.

"There's my mom." Kip waved at a pleasant-faced roundish

woman wearing an overcoat that seemed to be sewn from a field of wildflowers. She hugged Kip and gave him a kiss, leaving a big red lipstick smear on his cheek.

"That was exciting today, dear. Well done."

"Thanks. Mom, this is Caley."

"*Princess* Caley." Kip's mom curtsied to her. "I'm Mary Gorsebrooke. Kipley can't stop talking about you."

Caley noticed that now *both* Kip's cheeks looked like they had lipstick on them.

"Your father sends his love. I'd better be getting back to put dinner on. Kipley, are you catching a cold? Your face is bright red. Princess Caley, I hope to see you again soon."

Mrs. Gorsebrooke curtsied to Caley again and headed off.

"Didn't know you knew Ferren Quik." Kip nodded over at Ferren heading into the tunnel with Ithica.

"I don't. We just met. He's trying out for trapper too."

"Almost won it for the Cheetahs last year. Tracker let him down. How did you do today?"

Caley eyed Ithica and Ferren disappearing together into the tunnel.

"I think . . . I need to fight back."

THE second day of trials was almost over, and when Caley looked in her snagger, it was empty again. She had never hit or bumped (or barely talked back to anyone) her whole life and couldn't seem to start now, even against Ithica, who kept slamming into her and stealing any disc that came close. When Commander Pike blew the whistle, Ferren was in first place, followed by Ithica. Caley was solidly last. Pike announced that tomorrow, Friday, was the final day of trials, and that if anyone hoped to make a team, they had better give it their best shot.

Back in the stable, Caley yanked her helmet off and handed it to Neive.

"One more day. I wish it were over."

"No luck?"

The girls turned to see Ferren sauntering over.

Caley's face felt flushed again.

Definitely diphtheria.

"So what's the game plan for tomorrow?" asked Ferren.

"No plan. I'm not a fighter."

"Me either. That's why I let my animal nature do the work."

"Animal nature?"

"My baest. You need to use its energy. It's the only way to win. Mine's a panther. Fast reflexes. Also, quite aggressive when it goes after its prey."

Ferren fixed his dark eyes on Caley, and she had to look away before the diphtheria completely melted her face.

"I don't think I want to use *my* baest," said Caley, staring at her riding boots. "It's . . . pretty wild."

"The wilder the better, Your Highness." Ferren made another ridiculously elaborate bow to Caley and headed off, giving Neive a little swooping bow as well.

Caley noticed Ithica staring at her. The look Ithica gave her seemed even more murderous than usual.

NEIVE escorted Caley back to her rooms, grinning nonstop.

"OK, what's so funny?" Caley asked.

"Ferren Quik."

"What *about* him?"

"Tall, dark, handsome. Perfect name too: 'Quik.' He moves fast."

"He's just trying to help me."

"Or your 'animal nature.'" Neive was still grinning.

"He's not interested in me like that," Caley insisted.

"He's supposedly going out with Ithica Blight. At least that's what it says on her Bee-Me."

Caley's brow furrowed.

"What if I *did* use it?"

"Use what?" said Neive.

"My baest. I mean, shouldn't I at least know *how*? What if it just pops out, or whatever, and then, you know . . ."

"Eats the planet?" Neive frowned. "Kip is exaggerating. I *hope . . .*"

"But maybe I should talk to Master Aramund. I wouldn't tell him about me being a you-know-what."

"Just be careful," Neive cautioned.

CALEY knocked on the door to Aramund's class. No reply. She was about to head off when the door swung open by itself. The jungle was there, but she couldn't make out much because a dense white smoke hung over everything. She was thinking Aramund must have left for the day when she spotted him, in his peacock robe and cap, hunched over a fire. He rose and bowed to her, gesturing for her to sit beside him.

"You have come to me about your baest."

Caley's eyes drifted to the stone fire pit, which was carved with ghostly animals. Aramund stared into the smoke of the fire intently, as if watching an invisible play.

"Here we reveal what is hidden within us. The spirit realm."

Caley could hear Aramund's voice, but he had disappeared into the smoke. The smoke formed an image of the Wandering Woods, the moaning bone trees reaching into the purple sky like skeleton hands through the frozen fog. Seeing it again made Caley shiver.

"But . . . you've *been* in the Wandering Woods," said Aramund in an astonished tone. "You must tell me—which baest did you receive?"

His voice seemed to be hypnotizing her. Caley's body began to feel strangely weightless, drifting like the smoke images.

"Don't you know?" she asked.

From the smoke, a shape began to materialize . . . every bad dream forming into the shape of Caley's darkest imagination . . . the athrucruth!

"A mouse!" Caley managed to gasp. "Just a mouse."

The smoke vanished into a wisp. Aramund was gazing at her with a vexed expression.

"A mouse," he finally said, nodding.

"I came to ask you . . . how do I control it?"

"Your baest is your deepest nature," Aramund replied. "It is what drew it to you to form the Unbreakable Bond. You can summon it anytime, but beware. To tame it, you must tame yourself. There are those who become seduced by its power and are consumed like a fire consumes its fuel . . . leaving only ash."

The fire sputtered. The smoke turned black and formed into one of the mechanical wolves from the nightmarish factory in the woods. Caley noticed that Aramund's expression had turned as black as the smoke.

"Soon, we must all choose . . . which nature will rule us?"

Aramund turned from the fire, bowed to Caley, and walked into the jungle.

•

"I think Aramund knows about my baest," Caley told Neive as she climbed into her armor.

It was the final day of trials, and the mood was tense. The usual jokey buzz had given way to a kind of grim seriousness. Caley took a sip of fearfew tea and headed out from the changing room with Neive.

"Can you trust him?" Neive asked.

"Trust who?" Kip was waiting outside the changing room.

"I went to see Master Aramund," said Caley, her voice hushed.

"About your athrucruth?" Kip blurted out.

"Stop saying that!" hissed Neive.

"Might be good to do more than *say* it," said Kip. "The Cheetahs would definitely win with a you-know-what."

They noticed Ithica Blight with Ferren Quik. Ferren saw Caley and looked like he was going to head over when Ithica grabbed him by the arm and led him off, grinning and chattering at him like she had just adopted a puppy.

Caley turned and walked back to her locker, grabbed the jar of fearfew tea, and took another sip . . . a very long sip.

MAJOR Fogg started the octopus disc launcher, and the trappers urged their orocs into the bright blue autumn sky. The discs started zipping around, and everyone began banging and bumping. The coaches were watching everyone (well, *almost* everyone . . . they'd stopped watching Caley the first day).

A disc zipped by Caley's head, and she steered Fearfew after it, flicking out her snagger. She almost caught it when . . .

WHAM! Something hit Fearfew. Caley grabbed his neck and just managed to hang on.

It was Ithica, of course.

Ithica crashed her oroc into Fearfew again, and he shrieked. One of his wings was crumpled a bit, like a paper lantern. He landed, shook it out, and pawed the ground, furious. Caley felt a red-hot stab across her body as if she had been wounded too. She stared up at Ithica, who leered at her and flew off. The sky suddenly grew dark with storm clouds, and it began to pour, black sheets—black as Caley's anger. Lightning ripped across the arena, and with it, a shock-current filled her body with something she had never felt before: a feeling of raw, furious power. A word came to Caley, unexpected as the sudden storm. She didn't need to speak it—Fearfew sensed it and bolted back into the air, then dropped so rapidly Caley's stomach was in her throat. Ithica was about to grab a disc when Caley flew past, whipping her snagger violently. It snapped Ithica's snagger in half, and her helmet popped off with the impact. Ithica stared at it, stunned like it was her own head tumbling to the ground.

Caley arced Fearfew around, her eyes fixed on Ithica, and spoke the word out loud.

"Attack."

It was as if everyone were moving in slow motion. The world was a blur yet very still at the same time. Caley flew Fearfew into Ithica, nearly knocking her off her oroc, then began hammering into the other players, catching every disc, her snagger a streak in her hand. All anyone else could do was try to hang onto their orocs or just fall off limply in her wake, like rag dolls.

After an instant (but it could have been an hour), Pike's

whistle blew and the discs stopped flying. The next thing she knew, Caley was standing beside Fearfew, his muzzle flecked with foam, his chest heaving. She hauled off her helmet and stared around. The other trappers were slumped in the mud or leaning against their orocs in the pounding rain, looking a bit like drowned rats. The coaches regarded Caley with a surprised expression and scribbled something in their clipboards. Caley looked down at her snagger.

It was full.

Ithica was being helped out of the arena by the Pingintees. Her armor looked like it had been in a car crash, and her fancy gold saddle with the ridiculous family crest was covered in mud. Ithica turned to Caley with a look Caley had never seen on her face before: fear.

"Impressive." Ferren was walking toward Caley, shaking mud from his hands. "You might have beaten my record, but Pike blew the whistle. Looks like you found that animal nature of yours."

Over Ferren's shoulder, Caley saw Ithica disappear into the tunnel. Whatever happened, that look on her face almost made the whole miserable trials worthwhile.

And that dark, electrifying feeling of power.

CHAPTER THIRTEEN

One Day

"Was it the you-know-what?" asked Neive.

"I think so." Caley nodded.

After the trials, all Caley wanted to do was bury herself in her rooms and hide from everyone and everything to do with the Equidium. Neive ordered snacks, and a parade of servants began delivering pastries and fruit on silver trays. Caley regarded the mounds of treats but didn't feel hungry. There was a deep unsettled sensation in her body, like some sort of wild animal had made a nest in it, rearranging everything.

Kip suddenly burst in. "They post the teams Sunday!" He helped himself to some lemon tarts. "But try not to think about it."

"That's exactly what Caley is doing," said Neive. "And please, come right in without knocking and help yourself to anything you see."

"What happened with you?" Kip asked Caley. "I saw you banging everyone around. Was it the athrucruth?"

A few servants eyed them nervously.

"Thank you for visiting Her Highness." Neive began herding Kip toward the door. "It would be most excellent if you could leave now."

"Oh, I almost forgot the reason I came by." Kip squirmed

free from Neive and turned back to Caley. "My parents want to invite you for the holiday this weekend."

"Holiday?"

"One Day. Don't you have it on Earth?"

"I've never even had a *holiday*."

"Anyway, Mom's making a pudding."

"Can Neive come?"

"It's not a *large* pudding," added Kip.

"I don't want to go," said Neive.

Kip grabbed another tart on his way out. "It'll help take your mind off the teams—" He craned back at Caley before Neive slammed the door in his face.

Neive turned to Caley. "Kipley Gorsebrooke—"

"Is the densest boy in Erinath. I know." Caley nodded. "But he *is* trying to look out for me. He walks me to class every day."

"He's a dog, and dogs are loyal. *Dense* . . . but loyal."

NEIVE and Caley waited outside the castle for Kip the next morning after breakfast. The duchess had insisted Neive go with Caley to visit Kip's family, informing her, "We cannot have princesses of the realm visiting the countryside without being properly attended. Who knows how rural folk run their estates these days? What if you were served from the right instead of the left? It's situations like that which foster the complete unraveling of society."

So really, who could argue with that?

They spotted Kip trotting toward them, his backpack overflowing with food.

"Brought a little snack for the trip. Mom's already complaining she doesn't have enough food and it's not fancy enough for royalty, Dad's complaining about the monarchy, and my brothers are complaining about having to dress up on holiday. Should be fun!"

Caley regarded the castle, surprised by what she saw. Compared to the day she arrived, it looked a thousand years older. Its fish-shaped turrets and towers were shedding their scalelike shingles, and you could see holes right through its root-walls. There were guards clunking around in boxy red armor with helmets that had tiny little slits. They reminded Caley of walking mailboxes. The mailbox-men were checking everyone coming and going from the castle (mostly "non-persons," Caley noted).

"We'll take a worm," said Kip.

He led them down a set of stairs to what looked like a subway station, except there were no tracks. Caley often wondered how everyone got around in Erinath (aside from carriages with harried horses). There were signs everywhere with dire warnings from the Sword:

STAY SAFE! REPORT SUSPICIOUS ACTIVITY
IF YOU'RE NOT US, YOU'RE THEM!

While they waited, Kip chewed on some mixed nuts and checked his bee.

"Look at this . . ."

Kip's bee showed a report from the Sword. Another "non-person" attack, along with a sketch of the assailant described by the victim. Everyone exchanged surprised looks. It looked like one of the mechanical wolves from the Wandering Woods.

Before anyone could say anything, the station shook and a giant wormlike creature came rumbling down the tunnel. Kip dove into the side of the worm, disappearing into it as if he'd jumped into jelly, followed by Neive and Caley. Caley found herself suspended inside the worm, like a marshmallow in mousse. Kip mumbled an address through a mouthful of nuts. The next thing she knew, Caley felt like she was being spun around in a blender, though her body did not appear to be moving at all. When everything unscrambled, she found herself beside Neive in the middle of a farmer's field next to a surprised cow.

A moment later, Kip tumbled out of nowhere and landed beside them. He stared around at the empty field.

"Never give worm destinations with your mouth full. Good to know. We can walk from here."

AFTER a short hike, they arrived at a big, rambling cottage in the country, surrounded by a well-tended garden dressed in autumn colors. Like all houses in Erinath, it looked like an overgrown mushroom covered in bits of worn glass and shells. It had a mossy roof with a lopsided belvedere that made it seem like it was wearing a jaunty hat. The cottage was dotted with spore-like additions, helter-skelter as if it had barely been growing fast enough to hold its inhabitants.

"Better not say anything about the attack," Kip advised as they approached the cottage. "Dad will insist it's a government plot and try to storm the castle. Lunch will be ruined."

"Your concern is overwhelming," replied Neive.

The door swung open, and the Gorsebrooke family came tumbling out. Four boys were directed into line by a short, barrel-chested man in crinkled tweed pants, jacket, and cap. He had jowly jaws and droopy eyes and reminded Caley of a Saint

Bernard. Kip's mother, wearing an amazing dress that seemed to be made from a field of poppies, gave Kip a kiss, leaving a big red lipstick mark on his cheek.

"Lovely to see you again, Princess Caley." Mrs. Gorsebrooke curtsied to her.

"Please, just call me Caley. And this is Neive."

"Neive's a servant," said Kip. "She's not having pudding."

The boys all regarded Neive, their heads cocked curiously, their hair bristling, the exact same way Kip always looked at her. Neive's nose twitched back at them.

"Allow me to introduce my family," said Mrs. Gorsebrooke. "This is my husband, Robert."

"Welcome," said Mr. Gorsebrooke. "Kipley talks about you nonstop."

The rest of Kip's face turned lipsticky.

"And this is the pack." Mrs. Gorsebrooke gestured at the boys, who ranged in age from seventeen to twenty. "Riley, Kirby, Henry, and Garby."

They all had the same long noses as Kip, and their clothes were just as rumpled.

"Please come in." Mrs. Gorsebrooke smiled at Caley and Neive. "You must be famished from your journey."

"We only left twenty minutes ago—" Neive began.

"Starved!" Kip cut in, and the Gorsebrookes clambered into the cottage, with Caley and Neive following along in their wake.

"It's nice to have all our boys home for the holiday," said Mrs. Gorsebrooke, "and two beautiful girls in the house, isn't it?"

Kip's brothers glanced at Caley and Neive and exchanged grins . . . which made Caley and Neive turn a bit lipsticky too.

The big rambling cottage was cozily furnished with overstuffed furniture that seemed slightly chewed on with a layer of fur over everything, although Caley didn't see any dogs.

Mrs. Gorsebrooke beamed at Caley. "We have not entertained royalty since your dear mother left. I was her lady-in-waiting, you know. We had the honor of hosting her on three occasions."

"*Two*," corrected Mr. Gorsebrooke.

"Three if you count the time we had tea in the village," said Mrs. Gorsebrooke, leading everyone to the kitchen, where a wide wooden table was laden with food. "Please sit here, Princess Caley." She patted a chair at the head of the table. "And Neive, here beside the princess."

"Oh, no, I have to serve," protested Neive, "and from the *left!*"

"Nonsense," Mr. Gorsebrooke said sternly. "You'll eat with us. There are no servants or masters here. No high born or low. We don't observe artificial hierarchies in the Gorsebrooke household—"

"Mr. G," Mrs. Gorsebrooke shot her husband a warning look, "no politics at the table."

Caley eyed the table. There were steaming heaps of pasta and potatoes, vegetables of every kind, an enormous roast that appeared to be made from beans, countless bowls of dips and sauces, and platters of cheese and fruit, all heaped so high Caley could barely see anyone sitting across from her.

Mrs. Gorsebrooke turned to her. "I apologize for the meager lunch and the humble condition of things in general."

"The state confiscated everything we owned." Mr. Gorsebrooke scowled.

Mrs. Gorsebrooke shot her husband another look, and he removed his cap and bowed.

"On this One Day," began Mr. Gorsebrooke, "we give thanks for the generous bounty Erinath has provided and remember that all living things arise together, as one, bound in harmony, unity, and equality. No royals or commoners, no—"

"Thank you, Mr. G," interrupted Mrs. Gorsebrooke. "The food is getting cold."

The Gorsebrookes dove into the meal like a pack of hungry wolves, barely seeming to breathe. Miraculously, it disappeared in almost no time. Caley and Neive had hardly begun eating when Mrs. Gorsebrooke began removing dishes.

"That's the appetizers out of the way. Garby, please help me clear room for the main course."

"I understand you're trying out for the Equidium along with Kipley," Mr. Gorsebrooke said to Caley, "and you're a first-rate trapper."

"First-rate," Kip repeated.

"It would be quite an achievement," Mr. Gorsebrooke went on, "two first-years making the team. The Gorsebrookes have been House Cross Cheetahs for generations. The older boys all made the team in their final years, but no wins. Do you think we have a chance?"

"Definitely!" Kip nodded enthusiastically. "Especially because Caley is an athruc—ow!"

Neive had kicked Kip under the table.

"A cow?" Garby asked. "Is that your baest?"

"Kip has a sore ankle." Neive glared at him.

"It *was* doing fine . . ." Kip glared back.

"Speaking of baests," said Mrs. Gorsebrooke, carrying more food to the table, "the Gorsebrookes have also all been trackers, like Kipley. Riley is a beagle, Kirby and Henry are both bassets, Garby's a spaniel, and Mr. Gorsebrooke is a Saint Bernard."

"Almost won the darn thing the year I competed," said Mr. Gorsebrooke, "but I had hay fever. Couldn't smell a blessed thing. Anyway, paws and tails crossed this time."

"And of course, Kipley is a mutt, bless him," said Mrs. Gorsebrooke.

"But mostly bloodhound," corrected Kip. "Ninety-eight percent."

"They all have *dog* baests," Neive whispered to Caley as the Gorsebrookes began to make more mounds of food disappear into their mouths like a magic act. "Explains a few things . . ."

When the meal was done (seven courses by Caley's count, but she was so stuffed by the fifth her brain couldn't add anymore), Mrs. Gorsebrooke stood up and announced, "I hope everyone saved room for dessert."

"*Dessert?*" Neive groaned to Caley.

"THROW the ball!"

Garby handed Caley a chewed-up tennis ball, and Kip and his brothers trotted to the other side of the yard. After lunch, everyone had gone outside to "work up an appetite for tea."

Caley spent the better part of an hour throwing the ball for the Gorsebrooke boys. They raced after it, and whoever caught it brought it back to her. It looked like they could go on doing this forever, and Caley's arm felt like it was going to fall off.

Suddenly, someone shouted, "Squirrel!" Neive curled up into a ball, and the boys went chasing after a squirrel that scurried up a tree. Then they stood there staring up at it, tongues hanging, looking frustrated.

"Stupid squirrels," murmured Kip.

"Dumb dogs," murmured Neive.

•

AFTERWARD, everyone sprawled on couches in front of a roaring fire, playing card games while Neive helped Mrs. Gorsebrooke bring out hot cocoa and what appeared to be dog biscuits.

Caley stared around at everyone's faces, flushed and happy from playing outside, chatting easily about this and that, and a thought came to her. This is what a real family must be like (aside from the dog biscuits). No burnt toast for breakfast, slave labor for lunch, and locks changed on her room in the dead of winter for dinner. She felt an odd tinge of bitterness. Why had her mother abandoned her to that?

"Princess Caley, may I show you something?"

Mrs. Gorsebrooke was standing in the doorway to the kitchen. She led her to a greenhouse attached to the back of the house, bursting with rose bushes in every color imaginable.

"They're beautiful," said Caley.

Mrs. Gorsebrooke picked a few petals. "These are clothes-roses."

"How do you make the different fabrics and designs?"

"It all depends on what you feed them." Mrs. Gorsebrooke began opening tins from a shelf neatly lined with them. "I use Dandelion Dust if I want a nice sheen." She sprinkled some yellow dust from the tin on a rose, instantly turning it gold. "Or Moon Meadow for a warm glow." From another tin, she removed a dried blossom that shone like a little moon and crumpled it over a rose. It began to glow magically. "The styles I create by careful pruning." She fetched a pair of delicate silver sheers. "Neive tells me your clothes are a bit out of style."

"No, I love them," Caley insisted, shaking her head.

"I grew all your mother's clothes-roses."

Mrs. Gorsebrooke deftly trimmed a purple and white rose into the shape of a dress.

"Would you like to try it on?"

Caley nodded eagerly, and Mrs. Gorsebrooke handed the rose to her. She blew on it, and it began to shimmer over her school uniform, which vanished and was replaced by a flowing white dress, cinched at the waist with a purple ribbon that seemed to be made of the finest lace, dotted with tiny purple buds. It was almost weightless. Caley did a quick twirl. The fabric floated around her like a suddenly surprised field of butterflies.

"Teatime."

Kip poked his head in the greenhouse. He froze, staring at Caley.

"Do I have something on my face?" asked Caley.

Kip snapped out of it. "Mom, can you grow me a few school ties?"

"What do you do with them, Kipley?" Mrs. Gorsebrooke shook her head, perplexed. "You seem to go through one a week."

Kip gave a weak shrug and hurried off again.

Mrs. Gorsebrooke adjusted the ribbon around Caley's dress and stood back admiringly. Caley was surprised to see her wipe a tear away.

"You're the spitting image of your mother."

"What was she like?"

Mrs. Gorsebrooke began to put away her tins, an odd look on her face. "We played together as children. Then I was her lady-in-waiting, but I don't feel I ever truly knew her. There was always something about her that wasn't of this world. She would talk to things only she could see, and she was gone a lot. No one ever knew where she went. And then one day . . ."

"What?" pressed Caley.

"She disappeared for good. Not long after her parents were killed. The king and queen were on a carriage ride in the country. The authorities claimed it was a wolf attack. Only the horse survived. Cedric, I think his name was. Or Cecil."

Caley's eyes widened.

"Things changed after that. With your mother gone, the Council took over. Or, should I say, General Roon, and his frenzy against 'non-persons.' Odious term. A lot of people don't agree with what is happening, and there have been violent protests. My husband led one with the academy faculty. That's why he was fired. I worry about Kipley. He's a lot like his father."

Mrs. Gorsebrooke stared out at the garden, bathed in the golden glow of late afternoon, then turned back to Caley.

"What I *do* know about your mother was that she was kindhearted but tough as a thorn. A lot like you, I suspect. And I'm positive she must have loved you deeply. She never would have left here, left *you* . . . unless she had a very good reason."

Mrs. Gorsebrooke plucked a dying rose and put on a smile. "Brighter days ahead now that *you're* here. Shall we join the others for tea?"

IN the living room, the Gorsebrookes were devouring mounds of little sandwiches and slurping tea. Neive sidled up to Caley when she entered.

"They're eating. *Again!*"

Kip sprang up when he saw Caley.

"Want to see something?"

Kip led Caley and Neive into a small library off the living

room. Caley suddenly realized she hadn't seen any books in Erinath before.

"These are Dad's," said Kip. "Pick one."

Caley noticed a book with an oroc on the spine and took it from the shelf. She opened it randomly to a page about the variety of tail shapes.

"Read it." Kip nodded encouragingly.

Caley read the description beneath one of the illustrations: "The fan-tailed oroc is one of the most graceful flyers, using its wide tail as a fifth wing."

To her surprise, as she read the words, the image of the fan-tailed oroc came alive, like a hologram. It soared off the page and around the library, gliding and swooping between the shelves.

"It's a look-book," explained Kip.

"An unbound one, at that."

Everyone turned to Mr. Gorsebrooke entering the library.

"That is to say, not connected to the Web and censored. They'd burn these too. If they knew about them," he added with a wink.

"Dad used to teach history at the academy," said Kip.

"No use for history anymore." Mr. Gorsebrooke frowned. "Not when you make up your own."

Caley regarded the book in her hand a moment thoughtfully, then turned to Mr. Gorsebrooke.

"Do any of your books have something about my mother in them?"

Mr. Gorsebrooke shook his head. "Sorry. Not that I've read."

Caley nodded resignedly and began to put the book away. The oroc flew back and took its place on the page as she closed it.

Mr. Gorsebrooke made a reluctant grumbling sound and removed reading glasses from a pocket.

"But as you will be queen one day, perhaps you *should* know something of our history. Our *real* history. Not the lies General Roon spreads."

He closed the door firmly and located a book on a top shelf. The others joined him around the fire, pulling their chairs closer as he opened a page and began to read.

"'Before time was measured, a great kingdom arose in Erinath.'"

Caley saw a kingdom appear above a map of Erinath, green and pleasant.

"'Living things evolved together in an intelligent and benevolent Oneness. Baests were born, and nature bound with technology for the good of all. It was a Golden Age. But a shadow was growing.'"

Caley watched as cities and factories spewing smoke dimmed the sea and sky and spread like spilled ink, closing in around the kingdom. It reminded her of where she used to live —a poisoned place.

"'In the Gray Land, Olpheist—a dark magician—twisted the minds of men to believe the kingdom was plotting to use the power of baests to exterminate their empire of ashes. From the depths of the earth, he raised foul things, long dead, and set this army of shadows against all who stood in his way.'"

"You mean . . . zombies?" asked Caley. "On Earth, we call them zombies. But they're not real. Except for a few frogs . . . crickets . . . an ivy or two . . ." Caley's voice trailed off uneasily.

Over the book, shadowy monsters swarmed toward the kingdom.

"'But there were those who resisted. A few, noble-hearted

and brave, joined together to defeat Olpheist and send him to the Black Gate.'"

Mr. Gorsebrooke closed the book, took off his glasses, and turned to Caley.

"That is the history I taught before General Roon replaced it with the speciest version *he* believes—in which baests are our ancient enemies and we are again under attack."

Caley, Neive, and Kip exchanged a wordless look.

Mr. Gorsebrooke rose to put the book away. "They made me stop teaching, but you can't keep a Gorsebrooke on a leash."

"Born rebels," Kip agreed.

"What do *you* believe?" asked Caley.

Mr. Gorsebrooke's fingers lingered on the spine of the book a moment before he pushed it into place on the shelf and turned to them.

"The interesting thing about history is that it has a habit of repeating itself until its lesson is learned. In this case, I believe . . . dark days are ahead."

"And *I* believe you better help me set out more food if you don't want our guests going home hungry, Mr. G."

Mrs. Gorsebrooke was standing in the doorway, her arms crossed. Everyone made their way out of the library.

"I'm in the doghouse again," Mr. Gorsebrooke muttered.

AFTER tea, the Gorsebrookes lined up outside the cottage to say goodbye.

"You must come back soon." Mrs. Gorsebrooke hugged Caley and Neive. "And please make sure Kip eats properly. He gets distracted by so many things. He has a very active mind."

"Yes, it's quite *dense*." Neive nodded.

Mrs. Gorsebrooke handed Kip a basket stuffed with snacks "for the journey home," and everyone waved as Caley, Neive, and Kip set off for the worm station. The Gorsebrookes all shouted, "Happy One Day!" and began howling at the rising moon.

As they walked along the dirt road, Kip was talking nonstop about the Equidium. If he made the team—which he definitely probably would—and won—which he definitely probably would —the Gorsebrooke name would be restored to its former glory and his dad might even be able to go back to the academy. Which would make his mom happy because she was pretty tired of his dad ranting about government plots all the time.

"I think you'll make it," Neive said to him.

Kip regarded her like he was waiting for her to say something sarcastic, but Neive just nodded reassuringly.

"Thanks," Kip said, breaking into a hopeful smile.

As for Caley, she was thinking about what Mrs. Gorsebrooke had told her. What had caused her mother to leave? She had the growing feeling that whatever it was, it had something to do with Olpheist.

CHAPTER FOURTEEN

Warm-ups

As soon they got back from the Gorsebrookes, Kip made a beeline for the dining hall.

"How can he be hungry again?" Neive held her stomach and groaned at Caley.

But for once, Kip wasn't thinking about food. There was a nervous knot of kids outside the dining hall, jostling to see the Equidium list Commander Pike had posted. Everyone leaned in for a look, either jumping for joy or slumping off like they'd like to die. Kip squirmed his way through, then let out a loud whoop.

"I MADE IT! I MADE THE TEAM! I CAN'T BELIEVE IT!"

Kip hugged the nearest person—who happened to be Neive; he instantly let her go when he saw who it was, hugged her again anyway, then turned to Caley, grinning from ear to ear.

"And so did *you!*"

Caley squeezed her way to the list. She saw Kip's name under the House Cross Cheetahs, along with Ferren Quik, who had been named captain. Her name wasn't on it.

"Ferren Quik is the trapper." Caley turned to Kip, puzzled.

"At the bottom," Kip said, pointing at the list.

Caley noticed another group titled "Substitutes." Under the Cheetahs' team, she saw her name.

"I'm a substitute?"

"Every player has a sub. If someone drops out or gets injured or something, you're in. You train with the team and everything. You'll be a lock to make it next year!"

"Congratulations."

Caley turned to see Ferren smiling at her.

"You're my captain's pick. Each team gets one. Don't let me down, teammate."

Ferren gave her a pat on the back.

"I won't let you down either," said Kip, smacking Ferren heartily on his back. "*Teammate!*"

Ferren—who had almost been knocked over by Kip's enthusiastic smack—gave him a thumbs-up and sauntered off.

Kip turned back to Caley. "We need nicknames."

"Nicknames?"

"All the players have them. I'm thinking 'K-Dog' because, you know, I'm part dog, and 'K' for 'Kip.' What would yours be?"

"How about 'World Swallower'?" suggested Caley.

Kip regarded her thoughtfully.

"She's *kidding*, Kip," said Neive.

AFTER the teams were announced, a kind of Equidium fever gripped the castle. Everyone wore team scarves, and Bee-Me buzzed with photos of their favorite players. Caley noticed a lot of girls had Ferren Quik as their screen savers—even if they weren't Cheetahs fans. In science, Caley's class decorated their planets in their favorite team's colors. Lucas Mancini (Cheetahs: red and gold) put his planet in a bed of ice so the leaves all started to change from summer to autumn colors, which Caley thought was pretty clever. Ithica Blight (Bazkûls: black and blue) dyed her oceans those colors, which made her planet look like it had a giant bruise. There was endless intense discussion about the weather. The queen venowasp left her nest to breed at first frost, and the nights were getting colder.

Practice began after class that Wednesday, and the coaches joined their teams. A big blubbery man in a starched military uniform with tusk-teeth and whopping whiskers that looked like a cat had landed on his lips waddled toward the Cheetahs' squad.

"It's old 'blood and tusks,'" groaned Kip. "He's been the Cheetahs' coach *forever*."

The walrus-like coach cleared his throat loudly—the sound was like a bathtub draining—and fixed everyone with a steely stare.

"I am Sergeant Major Mandrake. I am here to train you for the Equidium. Although nothing can prepare you for what is to come. Death! It stares you in the face! All you can do is stare back and say, 'Dismember me, disembowel me, disintegrate every drop of me, I am ready for the ultimate sacrifice!'"

"Real motivator." Kip winced.

Mandrake's gaze fell on Caley.

"Who are you?"

"Caley Cross."

"You're that princess from another world." He stared at Caley as if he had just spotted a two-headed goat.

"I'm only a princess on this world," replied Caley.

She wasn't trying to be funny, but a few of the other players chuckled.

"I've *heard* about earthlings." Mandrake's nostrils made an unimpressed snorting sound. "Animal killers. I'm *watching* you." He ordered everyone to start warming up and waddled off to sit in the shade.

Ferren turned to Caley. "Coach is old-school. He'll change his tune once he sees how good you are. But you need to work on your technique. Let's start with your grip."

Ferren took Caley's hand to show her how to hold her snagger properly. Caley felt her face get hot, the way it did whenever he was around.

There were several bright flashes, and she noticed a throng of reporters with bees taking pictures of them. Caley instantly jerked her hand away.

"Don't worry about the press," said Ferren. "And if they ask you anything, just say, 'There's no *i* in *team*' and 'We just need to catch one venowasp at a time.'" He took Caley's hand again. "Focus on practice, and you'll be fine."

FOLLOWING warm-ups, the teams were sorted into squads and began scrimmaging against each other. Mandrake—who seemed to have taken an immediate dislike to Caley—ordered her to fly around on Fearfew pretending to be a venowasp while everyone tried to catch her. Kip kept swooping over and shouting, "Can you believe this? We're on an Equidium team! It's a dream come true!" Caley was thinking it was a good thing none of *her* dreams ever came true (*see *Olpheist*, etc.), but if she ever *had* a decent dream, this wouldn't be it (pretending to be a venowasp). Fearfew, as always, seemed to sense her mood because he fluttered around like a lost moth, easily getting snagged by one team or the other until Mandrake blew his whistle to end practice for the day.

Caley headed back to the armory after rinsing Fearfew down. A horde of reporters were interviewing players, with bees snapping photos. Ithica Blight had made the Bazkûls as trapper along with the Pingintees, who had been selected as defenders. Ithica was surrounded by reporters, pretending her hardest to look uninterested in all the attention, answering questions in her usual too-bored-to-bother voice.

"We're going to win, obviously, because I'm the best trapper. People said that as soon as I was chosen for the team."

"*We* said that." Pansy Pingintee nodded dully to the reporters.

"As soon as Princess Ithica told us to," added Petunia.

A woman with dazzlingly white teeth and slicked-back helmet hair interviewed Kip.

"They call me 'K-Dog,'" Kip was telling her.

When the woman saw Caley, she practically shoved Kip aside, darting toward her, trailed by a sea of flashing bees.

"Princess Caley!"

The woman seemed so excited that Caley looked around to see if there was another Princess Caley who was *actually* exciting.

"I'm Trixi Thistlewhip, and I would *love* to interview you for *Trixi Tells*. I'm sure you read it."

She thrust a glossy glowing leaf at Caley. The cover had a photo of Ithica Blight and Ferren Quik with a heart around them and a big question mark in the middle with the headline:

"ROYAL ROMANCE ON THE ROCKS!?"

Before Caley could say anything, Trixi put her arm around her, tugging her so close their cheeks squished and smiling for the bees buzzing frenziedly about their heads. Caley never thought anyone could have so many teeth. Could people in Erinath have sharks for baests?

"We're here with Princess Caley for a *Trixi Tells* exclusive! It has been a whirlwind since you arrived," Trixi trilled without appearing to breathe. "Mystery girl from a faraway world. Future queen and now substitute on the Cheetahs Equidium team. What a journey it must have been from what I understand were humble origins . . ."

"If by 'humble,'" Caley replied, feeling a little dazed, "you mean 'used garbage bags for winter boots . . .'"

"A delightfully dark sense of humor!" Trixi tittered to the bees. "And that *hair*. So *red*! Curls, curls, curls! Do many Earth girls have hair like you?"

"A few . . . witches?" Caley shrugged.

"Well, *you're* certainly a 'Red Menace.'" Trixi lowered her voice conspiratorially. "Your mother, Queen C, of course, was also shrouded in scandal. Vanished under mysterious circumstances. Would you say you're a bad girl too? A royal rebel? A puckish princess?"

"A puckish princess?" repeated Caley. What did that even *mean*?

"And Erinath's most eligible bachelorette. Anyone in the romantic picture? You've been seeing a lot of Prince Ferren."

Caley glanced—red-faced—over at Ferren, who was also being interviewed.

"There's no *i* in *team*," Caley said robotically.

"Teammates . . . and maybe *more*?" Trixi turned back to the bees. "They were spotted together in the Equidium looking every bit the item!"

"He was just helping me with my snagger," sputtered Caley. (That sounded weird.) "I mean . . . we were warming up!" (That didn't sound any less weird.)

Trixi shark-smiled at the bees. "There you have it, royal

watchers, straight from the oroc's mouth. Trixi tells *you* things are really *heating up* in the Equidium!"

Trixi skittered off again, trailed by flashing bees, leaving Caley blinded and breathless.

AS Caley headed across the academy courtyard on her way back from practice, she noticed kids huddled on benches, reading leaves and talking animatedly. They glanced up as Caley passed, and there was a lot of whispering.

"If it isn't the 'Red Menace,'" Kip grumbled when he saw Caley.

"What are you talking about?" asked Caley.

Kip thrust a leaf in front of her.

Caley groaned. "Oh no . . ."

It was a copy of *Trixi Tells* with the headline:

"EQUIDIUM HEATS UP!"

The front page featured a photo of Ferren holding Caley's hand with the subtitle: "RED MENACE SNAGS PRINCE CHARMING!" Caley flipped through the leaf, her face getting redder and redder. There were endless pictures of her and Ferren!

"She made all that up," said Caley. "No one's . . . snagging anyone."

This elicited snickers from nearby kids.

"I don't care about your stupid royal romance," Kip fumed. "It's about the team. You're being a headline hog."

"Hogs are not greedy." Lidia Vowell shook her head. "They have adapted into highly versatile omnivores to survive challenging environments."

"There are others on the team, too, you know." Kip

flipped the story to a tiny article at the back that included interviews with the rest of the House Cross team, entitled "Princess Caley's Equidium Posse," and he pointed to a name. "She called me 'K-*Frog*.'"

A few kids made croaking sounds, and Kip crumpled the leaf.

"So long as they got *your* nickname right, 'Red Menace.'"

Caley glanced around the courtyard and suddenly realized every single kid was reading the ludicrous leaf. Ithica was staring at her like she wished she could stab her to death with her icicle-eyes.

"I'll just tell people the truth," said Caley.

"That would be unwise, Your Highness."

Duchess Odeli had materialized behind them. Kip almost fell off his bench, he was so startled.

"If I may offer a word of advice, for someone in your position it is preferable to remain above the common fray. Personal feelings are better left to the proletariat. Your best—and *only* —response is to smile and wave."

The duchess float-fluttered off again.

"They should make her wear a little bell or something. You could have a heart attack." Kip regarded the departing duchess, then turned back to Caley. "Anyway, good advice. Smile and wave. Can't get into trouble with that. But if you *do* speak to any reporters, maybe you could mention it's 'K-*Dog*.'"

"Kip . . . that stuff about me and Ferren Quik . . ."

"Like you said," said Kip, "all made up. Right? And like the duchess said, you can't have personal feelings. *None* of us can. I mean, only because we can't have any more distractions before Equidium."

•

UNFORTUNATELY, there was nothing *but* distractions after that. At Equidium practice the next day, Caley was dismayed to see the stands filled with reporters, all shouting questions at her and Ferren. Bees were flashing everywhere, trying to get pictures of them together.

The team was divided into squads, as usual, battling each other with their fire-swords and lances, with Caley as the venowasp. No one could hear the commands with all the shouting, and a bee flashed right in front of Ferren's oroc, momentarily blinding it. It collided in midair with someone's oroc, their wings got tangled, and Ferren was thrown. He sat up, then bent over in obvious pain, clutching his chest.

Coach Mandrake shoved through the players gathering around Ferren and turned to Caley. His tusk-teeth were quivering so much, they looked like they would leap right off his face.

"I warned you, earthling. You're out!"

"HE can't just kick you off the team," said Neive.

Neive, Caley, and Kip were on their way to the infirmary to visit Ferren after dinner.

"Maybe now people will stop making a big fuss," said Caley. "I never wanted to be on a team in the first place."

"Then why did you sign up?" asked Kip.

Neive eyed him with her usual look (disbelief) as they entered the infirmary. A nurse finished putting a compress on Ferren's chest.

"Visiting hour is over in five minutes," the nurse informed them sternly, wheeling a hospital cart away.

Kip gave a wave to Ferren. "There's been some confusion about my nickname. It's not 'K-*Frog*'—"

Neive butted between Kip and Ferren. "We actually came to see if you were OK."

"Busted my rib, but I'll live," said Ferren. He tried to give a thumbs-up but winced in pain. "Problem is, no one can find Doctor Lemenecky."

"What are we going to do without a trapper?" asked Kip. "The Equidium is going to happen any day now. There's freezing temperatures forecast for the weekend.

"We *have* a trapper." Ferren was looking at Caley.

"She was kicked off the team," said Kip.

"Coach Mandrake's got no choice but to put in the sub," said Ferren. "It's that or the Cheetahs forfeit."

"But I haven't even practiced," said Caley. "I've been pretending to be a venowasp."

"You're as good a trapper as me," Ferren insisted. "Just do what you did during the last day of trials."

"I'm not sure I should do *that* . . ." said Caley uneasily.

"You mean the you-know-what?" asked Kip.

Neive glared at him warningly, but Kip's attention was somewhere else, his eyes widening. The others followed his gaze.

There was frost over the windows.

CHAPTER FIFTEEN

The Equidium

When Caley woke up the next morning, a thick layer of frost coated the palace grounds. The flute-flowers blew a shivery reveille, and shrub-monkeys hooted at each other's frozen goatees. As she made her way to the dining hall, everyone was talking back and forth breathlessly, wearing their team scarves.

The Equidium was starting.

"Caley! Where are you going?"

Kip was hurrying past with the Cheetahs team.

"Breakfast . . . ?" replied Caley.

"No time. We need to get to the arena and suit up."

"Kip, I'm not on the team, remember?"

"You, there."

They turned to see Coach Mandrake waddling up to Caley.

"As the substitute . . . and now *only* trapper, I have no choice but to reinstate you onto the team. I know we have had our differences in the past, but I want to make it clear that I have absolutely no faith in you and this will likely end in unparalleled slaughter."

Mandrake waddled off again.

"Inspiring words, sir!" Kip called after Mandrake; then he

turned to Caley. "Back on the team! It's gonna be great. Hope we don't die."

NEIVE was waiting in the stable for Caley when she entered with Kip. The usual jokey banter was replaced with a penetrating silence as players suited up in their armor. It reminded Caley of the patients in the Gunch's medical dramas who were about to undergo some life-threatening operation.

Ithica Blight fixed Caley and Kip with a mocking look.

"Here comes the Cheetahs. Mutts and subs."

The Pingintees tried to snigger-snort, but they were so nervous they just choked a bit.

Caley headed into the changing room with Neive. Her hands were shaking as she retrieved the glass jar from her locker.

It was empty.

"Neive . . . is there more of this?"

Neive shook her head. "That was the last of it."

Caley instantly turned and ran out of the stable.

"Where are you going?" called Neive. "Caley! The Equidium is starting!"

CALEY raced to the greenhouse on the edge of the palace gardens.

"Master Pim! Master Pim!"

He was nowhere to be seen. Caley heard faint music coming from somewhere and noticed a toadstool-shaped cottage on the edge of the nearby forest. Maybe Pim lived there. She raced to the cottage. A sign above the small round door read:

ERASMUS E. PIM, ESQ. RING BUZZER.

An arrow pointed to a flower with a red button in its middle growing out of the door. It looked suspiciously like the "sunny surprise" flowers in Pim's greenhouse that gave electric shocks. Caley grabbed a stick and pressed the button with it—and the flower squirted water in her face. The door swung open, and Pim was standing there, giggling merrily.

"That's a rude way to welcome guests," said Caley, wiping her face.

"Not as rude as an electric shock. So things are looking up!"

Caley followed Pim into the cottage. It was round and cozy, like a fox's den. A small rocking chair sat next to a fireplace with a softly boiling teakettle hanging above it. There was a straw bed with a worn flower-patterned quilt covering it. A tidy writing desk sat beneath a window with a view of Castle Erinath in the distance.

"You're just in time!" Pim shouted above the music. "We're having a party!"

"*We?*" asked Caley, peering around. "There's no one else here."

"*I'm* here. And so are *you!*"

"But . . . I only just got here."

"My dear girl, you should stop living in the past. It will only confuse you."

Pim danced with surprising agility, considering how old he seemed. Caley shuffled around a bit, just to be polite (and to see if there might be some fearfew root lying about). She was surprised to see the music coming from an old record player like people had on Earth. It was powered by some sort of motor attached to a glowing bazkûl-breath gem.

"Major Fogg brings me back things from your world now and then," said Pim, boogying past the record player. "I don't think the Council would approve. People often fear what they don't understand. But I find if you take the time to get to know something, you might discover a lot of good in it. Your music, for example. In Erinath we have a lot of marches and fanfares. Not much fun to dance to." Pim held up a faded album cover. "Have you heard of the Beatles? I had a cousin who had a beetle baest. Couldn't hold a tune, mind you . . ."

Pim danced around some more, singing along with the song—something about a barber showing photographs.

"Master Pim, I need to ask you something!"

"Have you been noticing the squirrels?"

"The . . . nuts?" said Caley. "Sorry, I haven't found out anything about that."

Pim turned off the music and gazed out the window at the castle with a serious expression.

"This is more troubling. Many of them make their home in the castle, and they are leaving."

"Uh-huh. Do you have any more fearfew?"

"Fearfew?" Pim turned to Caley.

"The root from your greenhouse. I need more."

"Whatever for?"

Caley took a deep breath, and the words came spilling out.

"I love orocs, but there's something inside me that makes them want to attack me, which makes me scared of them . . . but I really wanted to ride one . . . so I've been drinking fearfew tea so I can ride Fearfew—the oroc, not the root—it's also my oroc's name . . . and I need more because I'm on an Equidium team, and it's starting now—"

Pim held up a hand for Caley to stop.

"I'm sorry, but I composted the last of it last week. Not to mention it was plain old gardener's bane. Looks very much like fearfew. The root, not the oroc. I really should have my eyes checked."

"Then . . . why did it work?"

Pim shrugged. "How should I know? I'm just a gardener."

Caley slumped into the chair opposite Pim.

"Then I'll never ride Fearfew again. The oroc, not the root."

Pim plopped himself down in his rocking chair next to Caley, rubbing his knees gingerly.

"Orocs are fascinating creatures. Once they choose a rider, they never choose another. It would be terribly sad if Fearfew—the oroc, not the root—lost his rider, because despite how wild they appear, they *do* seem to enjoy being ridden. Although in my opinion, it is the *oroc* who is really in charge. But that is a discussion for another day. You will be late for your Equidium."

Pim sprang up and opened the door for Caley, who trudged out with a sigh.

"Oh, and please, have some . . ." He pulled a few animal crackers from one of the bottomless pockets of his overalls. "For the road."

Caley shoved the crackers in a pocket and set off from the cottage.

"Are you good?" called Pim.

"Am I . . . good?" Caley turned back to him. Every time Master Pim looked at her with his piercing orange eyes, she felt like she was getting x-rayed. *Was* she good? Or was she an evil, dark, planet-eating, apocalypse person?

"A good trapper," said Pim.

"Oh! I don't know. Maybe . . . ?"

To her surprise, Pim flung on a Cheetahs' team scarf.

"Go Cheetahs! Oh, I know it's just a foolish tournament, but it's jolly exciting. So long as no one dies. Do let me know if you hear from the squirrels."

THE stable was empty when Caley returned. The stomping and cheering of the huge crowd in the arena shook the dust from the ceiling. Caley sat dejectedly on a bench beside Fearfew's stall, her head in her hands.

"Caley!"

Neive was hurrying toward her.

"Where were you? They're introducing the teams!"

"I went to see Pim. There's no more fearfew root. It wasn't even fearfew to begin with."

"But it worked, didn't it?" said Neive. "And maybe you don't need it anymore."

Caley turned and opened Fearfew's stall. He immediately began shrieking and snapping at her, and she slammed the door shut.

"Or I one hundred percent *do*." Caley shook her head hopelessly.

"Get into your armor," said Neive. "I'll lead Fearfew up to the arena. Maybe he'll calm down. We'll think of something. You can't miss the Equidium!"

CALEY entered the arena. The stands were crammed with thousands of spectators. Everyone was waving banners and flags. The teams were marching past the Royal Box, where Chancellor Abbetine, General Roon, Duchess Odeli, and others were seated. Everything was being projected on a giant screen floating above everyone, like one of those jumbotrons in sports arenas (except this one was made of about a million electrified bumblebees). The teams were displayed on the jumbotron (or *bumble*tron, decided Caley) as their supporters sang their song.

> *Blight Bazkûls, noble, royal,*
> *To our House forever loyal!*
> *We shall win with strife and toil,*
> *Your blood will spill upon this soil!*

The other teams trooped past as their songs rang out—all of which basically promised to annihilate or otherwise destroy their opponents. Caley slipped into line with the House Cross Cheetahs.

"Where were you?" asked Kip, looking relieved.

Before Caley could answer, Chancellor Abbetine got up to speak, his face projected over the bumbletron.

"Welcome to the Equidium. To the teams, good luck and may you return victorious. I believe we are set to begin."

An expectant hush fell across the arena as everyone's attention turned to the matrix of honeycombed openings above the stands. There was a buzzing sound, faint at first, like mosquitoes in a tent. It grew louder until the entire arena began to vibrate. The players quickly lowered the visors on their helmets.

"Kip . . . what's happening?" said Caley.

In answer to her question, Kip pointed wordlessly to the honeycombs. Venowasps began pouring from them; *thousands* of them, big as birds, hovered above the crowd like a humming, hungry thundercloud.

Caley realized with a sudden shock that the Equidium arena was one gigantic venowasp nest.

From a deep, dark honeycomb opening at the very top flew the biggest, baddest-looking venowasp Caley had ever seen. It was the size of a car, with barbed mandibles that looked like they could tear through a tank, a bulging belly—which Caley supposed was full of nasty little venowasp eggs—and a curved stinger the length of a fire-lance, sparking out zaps of electricity like a downed power line.

"The queen," breathed Kip, looking awestruck and horrified at the same time.

"She's a big one this year," Mandrake said, shaking his head. "Can't see anyone surviving this."

"He really needs to work on his leadership skills." Kip grimaced.

The queen hovered above the arena, staring down at the players like an eagle eyeing mice. She clicked her mandibles with a sound like slashing swords, sending everyone scrambling for their orocs. The venowasp swarm instantly snapped together around the queen like a giant construction set. As they did, their bodies changed to the color of the sky, making the mass of them seem to vanish as they flew off.

"Mount up!" shouted Ben Bruin. The Cheetahs' bearlike lead defender had been named replacement captain.

Caley craned around and saw Neive holding Fearfew. She began to head over, but her legs seemed to have been turned into chewing gum. Everyone was glued to the bumbletron, where a little weasel-faced man in a bad toupee and loud plaid sportscaster's blazer began commenting in rapid-fire.

"Good afternoon, Equidium fans, I'm Chuck Clutterbuck! Eight teams, one big bug. The rules: simple . . . there *are* none! Catch the queen and stop her from laying her eggs because if she does, better bust out that bug spray! The queen is ready . . . the players are ready . . . the fans are ready . . . so let's get . . . BUZZZYYY! A lot of storylines we're following in this year's Equidium. Bazkûls with three rookies, an Equidium record. At starting trapper, riding Nightmare, Princess Ithica 'Terror-in-a-Tiara' Blight!"

The bumbletron showed Ithica mounting her oroc with her usual "couldn't care less" look, like she was going shoe shopping.

"Blight looking composed. With her, two first-year defenders: Pansy and Petunia 'The Poundin' Pingintees.'"

The Pingintees appeared on the bumbletron as several stable hands struggled to heave them onto their orocs.

"Cheetahs also with their share of rookies," Clutterbuck continued. "At starting tracker . . ." he stared down at some notes, "Kipley 'K-Frog' Gorsebrooke."

Kip appeared on the bumbletron, yanking his helmet off and glaring.

"It's 'K-*Dog*!' Come *on*!"

"Of course, the big story of this Equidium, Cheetahs' trapper Ferren Quik a late scratch. Stepping in, from Earth, standing maybe five foot three, weighing . . . probably not a whole lot, I'm guessing: Princess Caley 'The Red Menace' Cross!"

A bee buzzed up in Caley's face, which was then projected, fifty feet tall, on the bumbletron, as she stood there frozen in place.

"Cross!"

Coach Mandrake was flapping his flipper-like hands frantically at Caley to shoo her along. "What are you waiting for? Mount up!"

The other teams were flying out of the arena after the venowasps. Caley took a deep unhappy breath and headed toward Neive, who was holding Fearfew. As soon as she got near, the oroc started snapping at her. It didn't help that Mandrake was screaming, "Hesitation is death!" and ten thousand spectators were staring at her.

"Cross . . . taking some time getting on her oroc . . . not exactly sure what the holdup is," Clutterbuck said over the bumbletron. "Coach Mandrake absolutely livid on the sidelines. He's pretty much livid *everywhere*. Very passionate individual."

Kip rode over to Caley. "We have to go!"

"You're not helping," Neive told Kip, trying to hold Fearfew from Caley.

"Why is he trying to bite her?" asked Kip.

"I can't do this," said Caley. "Maybe one of the defenders can be trapper."

Kip sniffed the air. "Snacks!"

"You're thinking about food *now*?" Neive shook her head. "Unbelievable."

Kip jumped off Arrow, reached into Caley's armor, and pulled out a few of Pim's animal crackers. Fearfew immediately began snapping at them.

"He wants *these*," said Kip, tossing a cracker to the oroc, who gobbled it up and immediately seemed to calm down.

Caley and Neive exchanged amazed looks.

"See? I don't always think with my stomach." Kip affected an insulted tone—then gobbled a cracker, jumping back on his oroc. "I missed breakfast." He shrugged. "And probably lunch, at this rate."

Caley climbed up on Fearfew, and Neive handed over her snagger with a nod of encouragement. She grasped onto Fearfew's mane, feeling the familiar electric jolt course through her body.

"Can we *go* now?" Ben Bruin had ridden over.

The Cheetahs flew out of the arena in formation and soon caught up with the other teams. Caley scanned around, trying to catch a glimpse of the venowasp phalanx, which only appeared when a passing cloud was reflected against their scales.

"She's moving low and slow," Ben Bruin called around to the team. "Loaded down with all her eggs. That's the good news."

"What's the *bad* news?" asked Monty Ottley, one of the Cheetahs' defenders.

No sooner had Monty said this than . . . BAM! An oroc smacked into him.

Caley saw that opposing teams were trying to knock each other off their orocs, swinging their fire-swords and lances around violently.

"Why is everyone fighting each other?" shouted Caley, ducking as a riderless oroc flew past her head. "Aren't we trying to catch the queen?"

"The queen's not going anywhere in a hurry," replied Ben Bruin, fending off an attacking defender. "She's smart. She knows we'll tear each other to pieces before we even get to her!"

"That seems stupid," said Caley.

"This is the sensible part!" shouted Kip, ducking the firelance of a Bazkûl player. "Fighting the queen is *really* stupid!"

Caley went zigzagging around on Fearfew, avoiding the other players, most of whom were much slower, especially the defenders, who were all huge and heavily armored and seemed content to just bash each other about. Players were dropping like flies. Caley noticed Ithica had positioned herself safely between the Pingintees. You couldn't budge a Pingintee off an oroc (once you managed to get one *on* it). The two ginormous girls were swinging their fire-lances and snigger-snorting every time they sent someone flying.

"Smack him again, Lumpy!" Ithica was barking orders to her cousins. "Come on, Dumpy, you can hit harder than that!"

"She's heading for the tunnels!" someone yelled.

Caley caught a glimpse of the venowasp swarm headed toward the cliffs beneath the castle. The queen was appearing, bit by bit, as venowasps flew off, like someone peeling an orange.

"They're leaving the queen," said Kip.

"Is that good?" asked Caley.

Before Kip could answer, the venowasps appeared, like little jet fighters, bearing down on the players. It was a full-on attack.

"I'm going to say *not* good!" Kip cried.

"Porcupine formation!" shouted Ben Bruin.

The team quickly got into a defensive formation, Caley in the middle, Kip in front on the "nose," tracking, and the defenders around the perimeter. There were only three left now: Ben Bruin, Monty Ottley, and a huge fifth-year boy who looked like he had a gorilla for a baest. Their fire-lances poked out from behind their shields, making them all look a bit like a porcupine.

Monty Ottley cried out in pain. Several venowasps had linked together and carried off his helmet while another stung his neck. He slumped over his oroc, shaking and foaming from the mouth.

"Stay together!" cried Ben Bruin. "Hold your positions! Steady! Steady!"

Aside from Monty Ottley, the venowasps had a tough time getting through the players' armor and started stinging the orocs instead. While the stings didn't seem to affect orocs the way they did humans, it did make them *really* angry, and they began bucking and barreling in midair. The team formations quickly fell apart. Players panicked, and more than a few bolted as fast as their orocs would take them.

"Charge!" ordered Ben Bruin.

The other teams all seemed to have the same idea, and everyone charged at once. The venowasps immediately stopped attacking and flew back to protect the queen. The remaining players desperately tried to fight their way through them, flailing their fire-swords, sending venowasps dropping to the ground like flies hitting bug zappers. The queen began to burrow into a cave on the side of the cliffs.

"We'll never find in her in the tunnels!" Ben Bruin called to the team.

He urged his oroc straight at the queen, leveling his fire-lance. The queen spun from the cave, her massive mandibles snapping Ben's fire-lance like a twig. Ben was flung from his oroc and landed heavily on the hillside, looking dazed but alive.

Caley and Kip landed their orocs at the base of the cliffs and stared around. They were the only ones left from the Cheetahs. A few players from the other teams were chaotically trying to organize themselves as the queen began to burrow back into the cave.

"Any more of those crackers?" Kip asked, turning to Caley.

Caley fumbled around her pockets and found an animal cracker. Kip dumped it into his glove and speared it onto Ben Bruin's broken fire-lance, which had landed nearby.

"Go, Arrow!" Kip urged his oroc into the air.

Caley stared, mystified, as Kip flew straight at the queen, dodging venowasps. He aimed the fire-lance and heaved it with all his strength. It lodged in one of her wings. She spun around frenziedly, her mandibles slashing at Kip. He managed to dodge the deadly jaws and landed again near Caley.

"What was that all about?" said Caley. "You could have gotten killed!"

Kip swung down from Arrow, and his armor, which had a great gash from the queen's mandibles across it, fell right off him.

"That's the end of this useless kit, and good riddance. Think I'll wear a trash toad to the next Equidium. If I survive *this* one. Follow me. I'll explain later!"

Kip began to scramble up the cliffs. Caley threw her helmet off with a puzzled look and followed. When they reached the cave entrance, Kip motioned in the direction of the players who were making their way in, the trackers stopping and listening every now and then and staring uncertainly into the murk.

"The other trackers' baests are all hawks and owls and things like that," said Kip. "Good for seeing and hearing, but the tunnels are dark and the queen's here to lay her eggs. She won't be buzzing around flying. You won't hear or see her. And that's where K-Dog comes in." He pointed at his long nose. "I'll follow the scent of that cracker."

"Kip . . . you're brilliant!"

The two headed into the cave. They reached a series of tunnels all leading off in different directions. They could hear the footsteps of players echoing around faintly. Kip sniffed the air and chose a tunnel that descended deeper and deeper into the earth. As they rounded a bend, the last light filtering in from the cave entrance disappeared. They were now in total darkness. Kip drew his fire-sword, making a little flame at the end of it.

"Once we find the queen, I'll have to put it out," he said in a hushed voice. "She hates bright lights. Lives in her nest in complete darkness and only leaves to lay her eggs here. It's one of the reasons her drones surround her, aside from the camouflage. Keeps it nice and dark for her. Clever creatures, venowasps. Horrible . . . but clever."

They followed the tunnel deeper under the earth. The air became moist and foul. Kip's nose wrinkled in disgust. He held up his sword to reveal they had emerged into a huge cavern tangled with immense dark taproots giving off a faint bluish glow and slowly writhing. It reminded Caley of the legs of an enormous stepped-on spider.

"We must be right under the castle," Kip whispered. "Those are the main roots." He sniffed the air again. "I know that smell . . ."

A hacking cough made them turn. Kip raised his fire-sword to provide more light. To their surprise, they saw Doctor Leme-necky in a corner of the cavern. He drank the contents of a vial. His beard glowed bright blue and began to spasm as if it had been electrocuted. It attached itself to one of the castle's roots, and the glow spread to the root.

Caley and Kip exchanged confounded looks, but there was no time to think about what they had just seen because a scraping sound snapped their heads in the direction of a huge shadowy silhouette burrowing into the floor of the cavern. They could make out giant wings with a fire-lance impaled in one.

It was the queen.

"She's laying," Kip said, his voice hushed.

He silently sheathed his sword. Now the only light came from the roots that seemed to be glowing even brighter than before and twitching violently. Kip and Caley began to pick their way toward the queen, across the tangle of twisting roots that formed the cavern floor. Caley took a deep breath and activated her snagger. Her hand was shaking so badly it took her three tries to make a little net that she was sure couldn't catch a fruit fly.

"Think of it," Kip whispered excitedly, "two first-years capturing the queen. It's never been done before. We'll be famous. They'll write songs about us—"

They heard a low moan and turned to see Pansy Pingintee lying rigid on the ground, foaming at the mouth.

Kip leaned over her and shook his head. "A venowasp must have bit her. She'll be all right. I feel bad for the venowasp . . . biting a Pingintee. They must taste *terrible*—"

A fire-sword suddenly stabbed from the darkness and sent a jolt through Kip, who buckled in a paralyzed heap, his eyes rolling back in his head. Ithica stepped out from the shadows. She poked Kip with her sword again, and he groaned feebly.

"What do you think you're doing, Ithica?" asked Caley.

"Winning the Equidium. Thanks for leading me to the queen. I can take it from here."

Pansy groaned and lifted her head. Ithica poked her with her sword, sending out an electric zap, and Pansy flopped back.

"And stay down this time."

"*You* did that to her?" said Caley.

"Can't have anyone else taking credit, can I?" Ithica twirled her fire-sword lazily, admiring the glow it was giving off. "I've been getting pretty good at this. I figure I can do

more than stun someone." The flame on her sword grew
brighter. She inched the tip of it toward Caley. "I could say the
queen stung you. Guess *I'd* be a queen, too, one day, instead of
you. As it should be."

"Bright . . ."

Kip was struggling to speak, his eyes fluttering wildly in
his head.

"Of course, I'm bright, dumb mutt," replied Ithica. "'Blight
the Bright.' That could be my new nickname."

Caley felt her armor tightening around her. The queen
rose up from behind Ithica, her fire-sword shimmering in the
venowasp's immense mirror-black eyes. Ithica caught Caley's
horrified expression and slowly turned. Her pasty face turned
even pastier as she froze, dropping her sword.

"She hates . . . bright . . . lights," Kip managed to gasp.

The queen shot across the cavern at Ithica, her mandibles
slashing viciously. Ithica managed to snap out of it and transformed into a cobra, slithering off into the darkness. The
queen instantly turned her attention to Kip, who was desperately trying to get to his feet. She spun around, raising her fatal
stinger as he lay helpless beneath her.

"GET AWAY FROM HIM, YOU BIG UGLY BUG!"

The words erupted from Caley in a monstrous voice she
didn't recognize. Something seismic jolted her bones and
seemed to vaporize her from the inside out. She was now a
dark swirling mass lunging straight for the queen, faster than
thought. The queen's giant stinger stabbed spastically, but it
was useless against the onslaught that enveloped her like an
atomic cloud. A snagger streaked from the explosion, its net
expanding to trap her, Caley's hand materializing on the other
end.

Kip slowly got to his feet, staring wide-eyed at Caley, who was standing beside the trapped queen, breathless. He shook his head slowly, a look of awe spreading across his face.

CHAPTER SIXTEEN

Invitations and Investigations

Cross Cheetahs, glorious and ancient,
Never lost nor o'ertaken!
Noble House, o now awaken,
Crush our foes, obliterate 'em!

Caley and Kip, along with the House Cross Cheetahs (those not in the infirmary) were gathered with their fans in the common room to celebrate their Equidium victory. Everyone was arm in arm, singing the team song over and over again, each time louder than the last. Then they'd yell, "Red Menace! K-Frog!" hug each other, raise a glass of stout-berry beer, and start again. Kip didn't even look upset about the nickname—his face was fixed in a giddy grin halfway between euphoria and disbelief.

Coach Mandrake sat in an armchair cradling the Equidium Cup, muttering about what a miracle it was that everyone wasn't killed the way they played. He was trying to look upset about it all but wiped a tear when he gazed at the cup.

Lucas Mancini ran in with a stack of leaves, and everyone gathered round to read them. They all featured pictures of Caley with the queen venowasp trapped in her snagger and various sensational headlines:

."STUNNER EQUIDIUM FINISH!"

"CHEETAHS CONQUER!"

"PRINCESS CALEY SNAGS WIN FOR THE AGES!"

Lucas began reading *Trixi Tells*, which featured a picture of Caley riding Fearfew.

"'The plucky little princess from another planet pulled off one of the biggest upsets in Equidium history, overcoming numerous distractions leading up to the big tourney.'"

"Trixi Thistlewhip was the biggest 'distraction' of them all," said Kip, as Lucas read on.

"'Princess Caley, looking savage but stylish in her mother's ancestral armor, managed to capture the queen—and our hearts—with only Kipley Gorsebrooke by her side.'"

Everyone cheered and started singing again.

"This is the happiest day of my life." Kip beamed at Caley.

Caley beamed back. She felt happy too. But there was another feeling, even stronger. Her body was still tingling with the aftereffects of the athrucruth that had taken over her in the cavern, and that feeling of dark, limitless power. It seemed the wild animal that had made a nest inside her had moved in for good.

The common room began to shake. The evacuation siren sounded, and mailbox-men clanked in, ordering everyone to get out of the castle as quickly as possible.

EVERYONE gathered on the lawn, watching anxiously as the castle convulsed. A few of the bat-like balconies fluttered off into the gathering dark, looking like they'd finally had enough. Colonel Chip Chesterton's beaver-baest squad were racing around with headlamps, trying to shore up the various parts of the building that were threatening to collapse.

"Have you seen Neive?" Caley asked Kip, scanning around.

Kip shook his head. "And this time I am *not* looking for her."

Caley stared at the agitated castle a moment.

"What do you think Doctor Lemenecky was doing in that cavern?"

"Maybe that's where he sleeps." Kip shrugged. "Or . . . grows . . . or . . . whatever he does."

"And now the castle's going crazy," said Caley. "That's strange, don't you think?"

"He *is* the Animals and Botanicals teacher," replied Kip. "He was probably trying to cure whatever's wrong with it."

Caley nodded, unconvinced.

Kip's hair bristled. Dark shapes were moving across the castle: squirrels, hundreds of them, scurried down the trembling walls and into the nearby forest.

"What's with the squirrels?" said Caley.

The all-clear siren eventually sounded, and everyone headed back to the castle.

Neive came hurrying up.

"Where were *you*?" asked Kip.

"I have something for you to give to Master Pim." Neive placed an object wrapped in a leaf in Caley's hand.

"What is it?" said Kip.

"None of your business," replied Neive, hurrying off again.

Kip cocked his head, his hair bristling, as he watched her go.

"*Definitely* a cat."

•

CALEY found Pim puttering around in his greenhouse.

"Congratulations on your Equidium victory today." Pim smiled. "I'm happy you and Fearfew reunited. The oroc, not the root."

"Thanks. He liked your magic crackers."

"Magic?"

"They worked just like fearfew. The root, not the oroc."

Pim pulled a box of animal crackers from a pocket in his overalls and handed them to Caley.

"In that case, please have the rest."

"I have something for *you*. From . . . a friend."

Caley handed over the leaf-wrapped package. Pim opened it, and she saw it was some kind of tree nut. Pim's eyes narrowed on it a moment; then he turned to Caley.

"Will you walk with me? Chilly, but no snow yet. A pleasant enough evening for a stroll."

The two walked together in silence through the winding pathways of the gardens. The trumpet flowers blew a fanfare to the rising moon as the ballerina blossoms in their tulip tutus curtsied to it. Pim stopped before a row of overhanging yews that magically parted to reveal a hidden grove.

"My secret garden," said Pim, entering the grove with Caley. "I find it a good place to think. Or to *not* think."

The garden smelled of evergreen and (strangely) soup. Pim picked a yellow berry from a bush that was growing on the bank of a pond and handed it to her.

"Try it."

Caley regarded the berry warily. Pim nodded encouragingly, and she bit into it. To her surprise, it tasted like squash soup. It was even warm.

"It's a ponderberry. My own breed." Pim smiled proudly.

"Ponderberries taste like whatever you think about." He popped a berry in his mouth, then spat it out loudly. "Pardon me. I was thinking I should have worn warmer socks."

Caley noticed Pim was turning the nut over in his hand distractedly.

"Master Pim, what does it mean?"

"It is a message from our friends, the silent squirrels. It says, 'The castle is dying. We shall not return.'"

"How can a castle . . . die?"

Pim carefully wrapped the nut up again, placing it in his pocket.

"The castle, as you may be discovering, is no ordinary structure. In fact, it is a nen."

"A . . . what?"

"The rarest and most long-lived of beings. A nen castle is the sacred center of Erinath. Energy flows to and from it, connecting and protecting everything in its vast network of roots." Pim's face grew solemn as he gazed toward the castle lights glimmering above the yew-tops in the darkening distance. "Though for how much longer, I cannot say."

"I saw Doctor Lemenecky under the castle. My friend Kip thinks he's trying to save it, but . . . I'm not sure."

Pim kept staring at the castle. "The doctor is himself a nen. A very young one, perhaps only a few hundred years old. He has cared for the castle since his arrival here, not so long ago. If something malicious is happening, dark forces are at work."

"Olpheist?"

Pim began to poke around the ponderberry bush with his staff.

"I think he's looking for me," Caley went on urgently. "I think—"

"Caterpillars love these berries." Pim plucked a caterpillar from the bush. "I cannot say what they think of when they eat them. I find caterpillars nearly as difficult to understand as squirrels, although I suspect they think about their feet a lot, having so many of them."

Caley's shoulders slumped. As usual, Pim didn't even seem to be listening to her. Or at least the mention of Olpheist didn't appear to alarm him.

"They would happily devour every single berry if they could," Pim went on, "but the bush knows this and it releases poison into the berries when it senses a caterpillar. Not enough to kill it; just enough to give it a bad tummy ache. You see, the bush needs this particular species of caterpillar because when they become butterflies, they pollinate its blossoms. Sometimes, however—perhaps the winter was unusually warm and there were many caterpillars in the spring—the bush would be forced to make so much poison it would kill the caterpillars. Then the bush would die as well. No soup for you."

Pim carefully placed the caterpillar back on the bush.

"It is the way of the One."

"The One?" asked Caley.

Pim turned to the moon's bright reflection in the pond.

"Everything in the ocean of galaxies—the caterpillar, the bush, the berries, the poison—is connected in a great and delicate balance within the One."

He poked the water with his staff, and the moon's reflection rippled apart.

"There are those, however, who see only *two*: good and evil, black and white, me and you. I think every destructive act —or even unkind word—happens when you see the One as two. Don't you?"

The ripples reached the edges of the pond, the water stilled, and the moon came together again.

"There are protectors of the One. They are known as the Watchers. Olpheist was once a Watcher. But he turned against the Order." Pim's voice was suddenly bitter. "And very nearly destroyed us all."

A passing cloud eclipsed the moon's reflection into darkness.

"He was finally defeated and sent to the Black Gate. For an endless age, he remained there. But he escaped." Pim stroked his whiskers thoughtfully a moment. "Around the time you were born, come to think of it."

"How did he escape?"

"Only a Watcher can open a Gate."

"But . . . I opened one."

Pim regarded Caley intently, his orange eyes twinkling in the night like two tiny suns.

"What does Olpheist want with *me*?" Caley met Pim's gaze. "I'm just an ordinary girl. Except . . . I raise the dead. And I have an athrucruth baest."

Did she just say that out loud? Those X-ray eyes of Pim's! If he heard, his face revealed nothing. He set off again with Caley.

"Do you know why I call it a secret garden?" Pim said after a moment.

Caley shook her head.

"My Eavesdrop-Daisies love to listen. They draw secrets out."

Caley looked at the flowers and realized they were all ear-lobe shaped, and each one turned toward them as they passed.

"Oh, don't worry." Pim pointed his staff at some delicate blue flowers with fuzzy black centers growing here and there.

"The Forget-Me-Lots never let them remember a thing. Forget-Me-Lots grow wild in the gardens. Nearly as obnoxious as fearfew. The root, not the oroc. Be careful not to spend too much time around them, or you will lose your mind. Quite literally."

Caley wasn't thinking about Pim's flowers. She was thinking about Olpheist.

As if he were reading her thoughts again, Pim's face grew solemn. "Olpheist is searching for something."

"What?"

"Something, perhaps, that could return him to full power."

"Can't *you* stop him?"

"I'm just a gardener."

Pim led Caley out of the garden, and the yew trees joined their branches to conceal it again. He stopped and turned to her.

"Be careful. There are more than flowers with ears in Erinath. The castle will protect you from Olpheist. He cannot enter it. Not while it stands."

Pim suddenly raised his staff, sending out a burst of light, igniting the fireworks flowers along the path leading back to the castle.

"Stay on the path. Stay in the light. Oh, and do watch out for the Forget-Me-Lots."

He ambled off, popping a ponderberry in his mouth, then made a sour face.

"I was just thinking, *I hope I don't step in any oroc manure on the way home.*"

Caley saw a crow fly unevenly from a nest in a nearby pine tree, dodging the fireworks reflecting off its metal wing.

·

"**SO**, the nen is supposed to protect Caley from Olpheist, but the squirrels or caterpillars or something are killing it, and Caley is poisonous."

Kip regarded Caley and munched thoughtfully on some grapes. They were huddled in the common room with Neive. The Equidium celebration had resumed after the evacuation, but it was late and the last partyers were straggling out, singing random snatches of the Cheetahs' song.

"*She's* not poisonous," Neive told Kip. "Pim's berries have poison to protect *them*. The squirrels are leaving the castle because it's dying, and . . . weren't you listening to anything she said?"

"But Caley *could* be poisonous," Kip persisted, "because there's poison in the blood of an athrucruth—"

"My head is literally going to explode!" Neive almost screamed.

"Athrucruth?"

Everyone turned, alarmed, to see a fern in an empty beer glass turn into Lucas Mancini.

"Lucas, what were you doing in there?" said Kip.

"I must have fallen asleep during the party." Lucas yawned. "Too much excitement, I guess. And stout-berry beer," he added.

"It's a good thing he wasn't a spy." Neive turned to Kip. "Were you also not listening when Caley told us that Pim said she should be careful?"

"Did I hear something about the castle?" Lucas scratched his hedge-hair nervously. "The research I did for my Animals and Botanicals project determined the castle is rotting. And it's getting worse."

"What if Olpheist is killing the castle somehow?" asked Kip.

"Actually, that kind of makes sense," said Neive.

Neive and Kip regarded each other. Caley couldn't tell if the surprised looks on their faces were because they were agreeing with each other or because they weren't *more* surprised they were agreeing with each other.

"What are you young people doing here at this hour?"

The duchess was standing behind them, her arms crossed, an angry look on her beaky face. Kip was so startled he spat out some grapes, and Lucas instantly turned back into a fern.

"It's past curfew. To your rooms, immediately. And no more flaunting rules. Next time I catch any of you where you are not supposed to be, there will be serious consequences."

The duchess set off, clucking to herself like a hen who'd just found a fox in her nest.

"How much do you think she heard?" whispered Kip, staring after her.

"Maybe we should tell the duchess what we know," suggested Neive. "Maybe she can help."

"I'd like to know what *she* knows." Caley frowned. "A crow with a metal wing was spying on me, all the way back on Earth, and I just saw it here."

"No one knows what her baest is," said Kip.

"She also knew about the Gunch, right?" Caley turned to Neive. "How could she, unless she was there?"

"It's obvious," declared Kip. "The duchess is Olpheist's spy. I bet she knows his whole plan. Maybe even how he's killing the castle."

Neive looked dubious. "I don't think the duchess is a spy. Anyway, how could we find out?"

Kip turned to the fern in the beer glass, a smile slowly spreading across his face.

"Send a spy to catch a spy."

•

"TO what do I owe this unexpected visit?"

The duchess opened the door to her room the next day to find Caley, Neive, and Kip standing there.

Kip nodded encouragingly at Caley, and she held out the fern in the beer glass to the duchess.

"I wanted to thank you for everything you've done for me since I got here."

"How thoughtful," said the duchess, taking the glass.

"Make sure you water him. *It!*" Kip blathered.

Neive began to yank Kip by his tie out the door.

"Watch the tie!" Kip yelped.

"Your Highness, would you remain with me a moment?" asked the duchess.

She closed the door behind them and placed the plant on her desk next to a large stack of glowing leaves, handing one to Caley.

"Invitations," said the duchess. "I wanted to give you yours personally before they went out to the general population."

Caley read the leaf out loud, and as she did, each bright gold word sparkled.

Duchess Odeli hereby invites you to a formal Investiture Ball for her Royal Highness, Princess Caley Cross.

The 11th full moon of the year, 7 p.m. sharp.

Great Ballroom, Castle Erinath. Formal attire.

"I'm going to be . . . invested?" asked Caley.

"Now that you are settling into your duties, it is time for you to be formally installed as princess." The duchess regarded the fern. "And *I* shall find more suitable accommodations to install this little plant in."

The duchess headed out with the fern, and Caley followed.

As soon as the duchess was out of sight, Kip and Neive sprang out and hustled her off between them.

"It's all going according to my plan," said Kip.

"What's that?" Neive was staring at the leaf-card in Caley's hand.

"An invitation to an 'Investiture Ball,'" replied Caley.

"There hasn't been a royal ball in *ages*," said Neive. "The last one was for your mom, I think."

"I heard about it from *my* mom," said Kip. "They had a coronation cake the size of a haystack."

"It'll be *the* event of the season." Neive smiled.

Caley and Neive regarded each other excitedly.

Just then, the castle gave a shudder—almost knocking them off their feet.

"Let's hope the castle's still standing by then," added Neive, steadying herself.

"Or no cake," Kip pointed out, nodding.

"Or no *Caley*," said Neive.

CHAPTER SEVENTEEN

Birds and Bees

News of the Investiture Ball spread like wildfire and seemed to light up everyone along with it. No one could talk of anything else. Many kids (and more than a few adults, Caley observed) walked around with the duchess's leaf tucked in a pocket or clutched in their hand, fearing to lose their precious invitation.

"I heard Major Fogg is doing fireworks for the ball," Kip announced at breakfast. "Last time he made a thirty-foot fire-breathing bazkûl that burned down part of the gym. It was *epic*."

Ithica Blight strode in with the Pingintees flanking her and stopped near Caley's table.

"How tedious . . . a ball," Ithica announced to no one in particular in a loud voice so that everyone, in particular, could hear. "I'm sure it will be a night to *forget*."

"Do you see what she did there?" Pansy grinned dully at Caley. "Princess Ithica said a night to *forget* instead of *remember*."

"Because she hopes it'll be a bust," added Petunia. "Because she doesn't want you to be a more important princess than her."

Ithica jabbed a manicured nail into the Pingintees' flabby flanks, prodding them along in front of her.

"If they were any bigger or any dimmer," Kip said, shaking his head, "we'd all be in danger of being sucked up into them like black holes."

"Did Lucas find out anything about the duchess?" asked Caley.

"Oops," replied Kip. "I forgot to get him."

Everyone stopped eating and stared at Lucas Mancini, who was making his way into the dining hall. His hair—which usually looked like a windswept shrub (which it technically partly was)—had been trimmed into a bunch of poofy balls and buzz-cut rings like you'd see on a prize poodle. He slunk into his seat embarrassedly next to Kip.

"What did you find out?" Kip leaned close to Lucas.

"Nothing," said Lucas. "The duchess spent hours addressing ball invitations, then she . . . trimmed me."

Little ripples of laughter spread across the dining hall. Lucas tried to smush his poofs down.

"I think the duchess was onto me," Lucas continued. "Never saw her turn into a crow or anything. I was stuck there all night. I'm so tired I could—"

Lucas fell asleep face-first in a plate of pancakes.

Kip absently removed Lucas's face from the pancakes and gobbled one, studying the class schedule with a perplexed look.

"What is it?" said Caley.

"Dance lessons?"

THERE were waltz lessons in the gym each morning leading up to the ball. The girls were in giggling groups and the boys in grim-looking gangs, glancing glumly back at them. Lidia Vowell was standing in the middle looking agitated (but awesome, thought Caley) with her elk horns dramatically encircled by hair buns.

"What's going on?" asked Caley.

"Classic gender dynamics," replied Lidia. "The boys want to

dance with the girls, but they're terrified, so they're pretending they don't care. The girls want to dance with the boys, but the boys look like they don't care, so the girls are acting like *they* don't care. Of course, some girls want to dance with girls, and some boys with boys, but they're all just as freaked out. I don't see what all the fuss is about. *I'd* rather dance with a giraffe."

"A *bogger* is the only thing that would want to dance with *you*," said a sneering Ithica, cueing the standard snigger-snorts from the Pingintees.

The door to the gym burst open, and Duchess Odeli float-fluttered in with Major Fogg.

"Good morning, students," announced the duchess. "We have one week before the ball to prepare you all to waltz properly. Major Fogg has kindly agreed to help me demonstrate."

"Right-e-o! Nice to see you all!" The mole-like major blindly saluted a rack of basketballs.

Wooden cherubs on the ceiling holding harps and horns began to play a waltz. The duchess grabbed Major Fogg and started to swing him around. They resembled an overgrown crow dancing with a blind mole. All the while, the duchess kept up a running commentary.

"And . . . one . . . two . . . three. Gentlemen lead by stepping out with their left foot and rotating to their right. One . . . two . . . three. Ladies follow on their right foot to the previous position, turning to the right as well. Ladies, be as soft as a lark landing on a willow branch. One . . . two . . . three. Gentlemen, hold your partner tightly and release lightly, like a bee gathering honey."

This elicited a lot of embarrased chuckles from the class and eye-rolling from Lidia.

"One . . . two . . . three. The lady steps in front of her right foot with the left, continuing her turn to the right."

The duchess stopped and turned to the class. "That is the beginning of the waltz. Any questions?"

Everyone raised both hands desperately.

"It's easier to learn when you're doing it," said the duchess. "Each of you choose a partner."

The boys looked at their feet, and the girls looked at each other. No one moved.

"It's going to be a long week," Lidia noted with a sigh.

AFTER the initial excitement of the ball announcement, the students settled into a kind of uneasy stalemate. The girls moved in inseparable little clumps, like jungle explorers afraid to wander off the path, while the boys bunched together solemnly, exchanging curt words as if preparing to march off to war. There were numerous side stares and lightning fast look-aways between the two groups if anyone caught anyone else's eye. A flurry of postings flooded Bee-Me: girls making kissy faces together, acting like they were having the time of their lives and didn't need anyone to go to the ball with; boys riding around on orocs, holding fire-swords with ridiculously large photo-enhanced flames.

Caley and the girls were gathered in the common room after class.

"I can't take this anymore," said Tessa (maybe?) O'Toole, shooing away her bee in mid–kissy face. "Someone needs to ask someone."

"Risky," responded Taran (maybe not?) O'Toole. "It's like being the first to land on the moon. Once someone does it, everyone follows. But if you miscalculate, it could set the whole program back."

The girls stared over at the boys, who were pretending to be very engaged in a game of Erinath-style snakes and ladders (real ladders and snakes, with a moat thrown in for good measure), but you could tell they were distracted because most of the time they were sliding back down on the snakes into the moat with embarrassed glances at the girls.

"They're not going to ask us," declared Evegny Pooner (antelope baest). "We'll have to make the first move."

"I'm not sure I *want* to ask any of them," said Lidia, "despite the refreshing gender power reversal. They're all kind of ridiculous."

"What about Ben Bruin?" Evegny asked, gesturing to the big bearlike boy.

"He's always flicking his hair," said another girl. "Probably has brain damage by now."

The girls turned to Ben Bruin, who noticed them and flicked his hair with a violent jerk that sent him sliding backward down a fifteen-foot python into the moat.

"One waltz with him and you'd be permanently whiplashed," said an O'Toole.

"What about Lucas Mancini?" suggested the other O'Toole.

The girls looked at Lucas, who was fast asleep, dangling from a ladder.

"He *does* have dreamy eyes," remarked Evegny.

"When they're *open*," added Amalia Tweedy, a second-year girl.

"He *is* the most species fluid of the lot," said Lidia.

Lucas woke up with a start, saw the girls looking at him, instantly turned into a bright red poinsettia, and tumbled down the ladder into the moat with a loud splash.

"He just got a lot more fluid." Amalia grinned.

"Kipley Gorsebrooke?" asked whichever O'Toole it was.

"I think he likes *you*," the other O'Toole said to Caley. "He's always following you around like a lost puppy."

"He *is* part dog," replied Caley.

She glanced over at Kip, who caught her looking and just missed getting bitten by a snake before sliding off into the moat, where a dozen or so boys were flailing around.

Afterward, everyone watched tapestries. The girls made up stories with princesses and princes romping around various castles, while the boys made up an Equidium battle against bazkûls, with lots of flames and exploding stuff.

"Classic gender dynamics," noted Lidia with a frown.

"**WHO** do you want to go with?"

Neive was helping Caley pick a clothes-rose for dinner.

"Who would want to go with *me*?" asked Caley.

"Seriously?" said Neive. "You're heir to the throne. You're funny . . . in a dark sort of way. And pretty."

Caley looked at Neive like she was crazy.

"Ugh!" Neive groaned in exasperation and twirled Caley to the mirror. "*Look!*"

Caley studied herself. Her hair didn't look half bad, and she realized she had put on weight since arriving in Erinath because her shoulder blades weren't poking out like little chicken wings. She actually looked pretty good. She adjusted her amulet in the mirror. It seemed shinier than usual, almost like a real piece of jewelry.

"And have you checked your Bee-Me?" Neive went on. A bee instantly buzzed in front of them. "Show Princess Caley."

The bee projected Caley's home page. Her profile picture

had hundreds of honeycomb emojis (which, she guessed, in Erinath stood for "likes").

"Every boy in the kingdom will be lining up to ask you to the ball," said Neive.

"Who should we go with?"

"*I* can't go." Neive shook her head. "The ball is only for nobles."

"This kingdom has a lot of stupid rules. I guess I could go with Kip."

"Kip? Kipley *Gorsebrooke*?" asked Neive, as if she didn't recognize his name for a moment.

"He's the only friend I've ever had, besides you."

Neive snapped the clothes-rose box shut quickly. "You'll probably have to go with someone of similar rank. Another stupid rule. You better hurry. Dinner is starting."

AFTER dinner, Caley, Neive, and Kip slipped out of the castle and made their way through the palace gardens. The sun was setting earlier and earlier, and it was almost pitch-black on a moonless night when they reached Pim's secret garden.

"It's the perfect plan," said Kip. "Can't believe I didn't think of it before." He held up a vine he was carrying. "Lucas climbs up to the nest, the duchess turns into a crow, and he has a bird's-eye view of everything she's up to. Genius!"

"Until we get caught outside the castle after curfew," said Neive.

"Is this it?'" Kip stared up at a pine tree with Caley, who nodded. He placed the vine on the trunk, and it wrapped itself around it and slowly began to creep toward the crow's nest.

There was a loud rustle from the gardens. Everyone froze,

expecting to see the duchess. In the gloom, they could make out two fat shadows, digging around. There was no doubt who it was.

"The Pingintees," whispered Kip.

The colossal cousins spotted them and stomped off into the night.

"What are they doing out here?" asked Neive.

"Rooting for truffles?" suggested Kip.

"We better get back before they tell someone they saw us," said Neive.

AS they made their way back through the castle to their rooms, the evacuation siren began to wail. The castle was convulsing like it was having a heart attack. Everyone raced around trying to find a way out, but the hallways were heaving and weaving so violently, you couldn't tell which end was up or down.

"It's a bad one!" cried Kip. "We have to get out of here!"

The three began to run, but the hallway suddenly rose then dipped, like a roller coaster, tossing them straight at the ceiling. The instant before they slammed into it, it disappeared, and they somehow landed in an entirely different part of the castle. The convulsing had stopped. It was dark, and the air was foul.

"That smell . . ." Kip's nose was wrinkling.

When their eyes adjusted to the gloom, they were surprised to find they were in Doctor Lemenecky's lab. A stinking blue haze hung over everything.

"This is about the *last* place I want to be." Kip swallowed, peering around the spooky lab.

Doctor Lemenecky appeared through the fog, filling a vial

from a copper cauldron emitting the blue haze. He didn't seem to notice them, and Kip was about to say something when—

THUMP!

Everyone jumped as a giant boot kicked the door open.

It was the Scabbard, holding a torch.

Caley, Neive, and Kip backed into the shadows, holding their breath. The Scabbard's one eye scanned around the haze, fixing on Lemenecky.

"What is the meaning of this intrusion?" demanded Lemenecky.

"No one's seen you lately, Doc. Thought I'd come by, make sure yer OK."

The Scabbard spoke in a soothing tone, like a veterinarian about to put down a pet. He dipped a metal finger into the cauldron, tasted it, then spat it out loudly.

"You been a naughty little splinter. I better take this."

He began to heave the cauldron up onto his mountainous shoulders.

"NO!" screamed Lemenecky, grabbing one of the Scabbard's arms. "I'm putting a stop to this evil once and for all!"

With a swipe of his rake-hand, the Scabbard sent the stump-like doctor flying across the lab into a shelf. The giant jar containing the slugdevil came toppling down and shattered at Kip's feet.

"Close your eyes!" Kip screamed at Caley and Neive.

The Scabbard's huge head snapped in the direction of the sound, and he held up his torch.

"Who's there?"

Kip kicked the slugdevil as hard as he could toward the Scabbard. The creature's burning pinwheel eyes riveted on the Scabbard's, instantly stunning him. He toppled like a tree, shaking the lab. The slugdevil immediately latched itself around his leg and began oozing its way toward his head.

"Run!" cried Kip.

They ran out the door just as the castle gave another heave, tossing them into the air like popcorn. When they landed, they found themselves outside a wall of the castle, which was looming above them in the darkness.

"I don't know who I feel worse for," said Kip, trembling with relief and adrenalin, "the Scabbard or that slugdevil. I wouldn't want to eat the Scabbard's brains. But this proves what I've been saying all along; Doctor Lemenecky's trying to save the castle. And now we know the Scabbard's trying to stop him. Which means he's working for Olpheist."

Neive turned to several Eavesdrop-Daisies that were listening intently.

"Kip, keep your voice down!"

"Oops," said Kip, but then he kept going, too full of excitement to stop himself. "Bit of luck we ended up in the lab. Now we know the scariest person in the kingdom is working for the evilest person in the universe or wherever, and the castle that's supposed to protect Caley from him is probably doomed." His face fell. "Actually . . . that last part is probably not so lucky."

"I don't think it's luck." Caley shook her head slowly. "I've never had much of that. I think the castle sent me to Doctor Lemenecky's lab, just like it sent me to the Council Chamber, and the Wandering Woods to get a . . . you-know-what. I think it's trying to protect me, somehow."

Everyone gazed up at the castle. As if on cue, it gave a faint shudder.

"But how can we protect the *castle*?" asked Neive.

"Don't worry," Kip said confidently, "Lucas will find out who the crow is, and then we'll find out the rest of Olpheist's plan."

They heard a flutter of wings, and everyone turned to see a crow that had been staring at them from the roof of the castle fly off unevenly, its metal wing glinting in the moonlight.

"Double oops," said Kip.

CHAPTER EIGHTEEN

What the Crow Knows

Caley and Kip were eating breakfast the next morning when Lucas slumped into his seat, a few stray feathers sticking out from his collar.

"Sorry I forgot to get you again," Kip told Lucas. "It was kind of an intense night. What did you find out?"

"Nothing. *Again.*" Lucas yawned, helping himself to some oatmeal. "The crow never changed into anything else. Crows are very light sleepers, by the way. Kept me up all night. I'd rather not do any more spying." He made a face, picked a nest twig from his teeth, and fell fast asleep, face-first in his oatmeal.

"Now what?" Caley turned to Kip.

Kip's eyes were fixed on the feathers in Lucas's collar.

The duchess cleared her throat. She had appeared right behind them. Kip nearly choked on his oats.

"Would you be so kind as to accompany me, Your Highness?" the duchess asked Caley.

There was a loud sploshing sound, and the duchess looked down to see a bowl of oatmeal had fallen on her tiny black shoes.

"Pardon *me*, Duchess!" Kip began swiping oatmeal around the duchess's shoes with his napkin.

"Leave it. You're making it worse," she said, snatching the napkin from Kip.

Caley saw Kip pocketing a feather from the duchess's dress as she float-fluttered off.

THE soft click of the duchess's shoes echoing in the hallways was the only sound as Caley followed her through the castle. She was sure—even if Lucas hadn't confirmed it—that the metal-winged crow who had seen them last night was the duchess, who was spying on her for Olpheist and probably taking her to him now. To her surprise, the duchess stopped at a door carved with the crest of the Sword. She knocked and led Caley into a dimly lit chamber, its walls lined with sinister-looking weapons. General Roon, dressed in his black military uniform and fur-tipped cape, was studying a large map carved into a wooden table and didn't look up as they entered.

"You were outside the castle after curfew." Roon's deep voice rumbled around the cavernous chamber.

"I went for a walk—"started Caley.

"At midnight," Roon cut her off, his eyes snapping up from the map at her. "With two others."

"They were keeping me company. I couldn't sleep. I have . . . bad dreams."

Roon began to walk slowly toward Caley.

"Do you? What haunts them, I wonder?"

Caley's gaze fell to her feet. Something about Roon made her feel like a child in trouble. Roon grabbed her chin in a gloved hand and jerked it up to meet his inky glare.

"Look at me when I talk to you!"

"General Roon, there is no need for unpleasantness." The duchess was glowering at him.

Roon's eyes slid to her with a silencing look; then he turned back to Caley, his glove tightening on her.

"That hurts," Caley protested.

"Dark forces are gathering." Roon conjured a concerned expression. "For your safety, I am implementing enhanced security measures."

He released Caley and turned back to his map.

"Leave."

Caley's eyes were fixed on the map. Positioned around it were models of the mechanical wolves she had seen in the Wandering Woods.

AS she left Roon's chamber, two mailbox-men clunked after Caley, peering suspiciously at her through the little slits in their helmets. They didn't let her out of their sight as she headed to class, down the long staircase leading to Doctor Lemenecky's lab.

Kip came hurrying up, frowning at the mailboxes.

"What's with them?"

"My security's been 'enhanced'," Caley told him.

They noticed a few students standing outside the lab door, looking puzzled. There was a note posted on the door:

CLASS CANCELED FOR REMAINDER OF TERM

Caley moved closer to Kip so the mailboxes couldn't hear. "I need to tell you something. In private."

Kip gave her a sly wink and began speaking in a loud, theatrical tone, glancing back to make sure her guards were listening. "Princess Caley! Since class is canceled, I wonder if you could help me with some homework Doctor Lemenecky left us. In your *rooms*."

He began to bolt up the stairs, and Caley raced after him with the mailboxes attempting to keep up in their awkward armor.

"Everything all right?" Neive was heading toward them, eyeing the mailbox-men.

"*Everything . . . is . . . all . . . right*," Kip replied slowly and loudly, so the mailboxes could hear, "but Doctor Lemenecky's class is canceled, so we are going to catch up on *homework*. So, Princess Caley won't be needing you because we will be doing *homework*."

"I think Neive should come anyway," said Caley.

"But . . . won't that be distracting . . . for the *homework*?" Kip was beginning to get that dense look he got whenever his brain was working too hard.

"Neive can help us . . . with the *homework*," prompted Caley.

Kip turned to Caley, his voice lowering. "But . . . we're not actually doing home—"

Neive grabbed Kip by his tie and yanked him through the door before he could say anything else. Caley hurried in after them, slamming the door on the guards, who were craning to get a look in.

"You're more dangerous than the Scabbard, you know that?" Kip squawked at Neive. "And if I ruin another tie, Mom's gonna kill me."

"Roon knows we were outside the castle last night," Caley informed them.

"The duchess!" Kip said right away. "She must have told him. She's trying to get Caley in trouble. Maybe even kicked out of the castle so Olpheist can get her."

Neive eyed Kip skeptically. "Even *if* the crow told Roon, it still doesn't prove she's the duchess."

"There's something else," Caley continued. "Roon had this map. And I saw models of the wolves from the Wandering Woods on it. I think *he's* building them."

"Everyone is blaming real wolves for the attacks," said Neive. "Roon's trying to start another war against baests."

"Roon's not our biggest problem," replied Kip. "Doctor Lemenecky's class is canceled. The Scabbard probably scared him off. It's up to us to save the castle. And *I* figured out how. Do you have the cat's-eye crystal?"

Neive regarded Kip, puzzled, and retrieved the crystal from the hidden shelf beneath Caley's bed.

"The cat's-eye only works if you have something from the place or the person you want to see." Kip held up a feather. "This feather is from the crow's nest. I got it from Lucas." He held up the feathery bit he'd snatched from the duchess's dress. "And this is from the duchess. If they're the same, the cat's-eye should be able to see, and we'll find out Olpheist's plan."

"It's not a bad idea," admitted Neive.

"It's genius!" Kip grinned.

"*If* it works." Neive handed Caley the crystal. "You should do it."

Kip gave Caley the feathers. "Don't forget, you have to take one of its lives. Let's hope it has a few left."

Caley threw the cat's-eye against the floor. It shattered to pieces. Nothing happened for a moment; then the pieces vibrated and reformed back together. She held the crystal tightly. A vague image began to form in it, as if through a frosted window. A desolate northern island, barren but for a lone hut, materialized under a veil of falling snow. A cloaked figure, bundled up against the storm, scratched for food in the frozen ground. The figure suddenly spun around, drawing a silver sword hilt as a crow landed on the hut. A bolt of lightning sizzled from the hilt, scorching the crow's wing. It spun to the ground, its tortured caw cracking the frigid air.

"What's happening?" Kip was squinting over Caley's shoulder. "I can't see. Try polishing the crystal."

Caley rubbed the crystal against her sleeve. The scene shifted to inside the hut. The figure leaned over a child in a basket beside a feeble fire. She lowered her cloak, removed an amulet from her neck, and placed it around the child's.

"It's you . . ." Neive stared into the cat's-eye with a look of astonishment. "And your mother."

A vicious wind shook the hut, and with it came a terrible wailing sound, like animals being hurt. Catherine Cross wrapped the infant in a green velvet cape with the Cross coat of arms, tightened her thick red hair into a knot, and walked out into a raging squall, whiting out everything. She drew her sword again and from it fired a frozen flame. Each snowflake hung motionless in the air around her. Nothing was moving: not the wind, not the clouds . . . it was as if the world had suddenly been petrified in place.

"Cool sword . . ." said Kip.

Catherine wheeled around, the sword clasped tightly in her hands, searching for something through the stillness. From the snow-shroud, a shadowy, animal-like mass exploded, slamming her to the ground.

"Athrucruth!" cried Kip.

Catherine's sword flew from her hands, and the world unfroze. From the mass, a hooded figure materialized. Catherine clawed for her weapon in the snow, but a streak of lightning hit her. She looked down at the burning wound in her chest, then up at the figure standing over her, holding a sword like her own, his face a boiling shadow.

Caley's blood froze. "It's him. Olpheist."

"Where have you hidden it?" A deathly voice came from the shadow.

Catherine shook her head defiantly. "You'll never get it."

Olpheist placed a spectral hand on Catherine's skull. She screamed in helpless agony as a vaporous light oozed from her ears, as if he were draining her mind. A child's cry made him turn to the hut and he released Catherine from his mortal hold. His sword spat out a vortex of wind, instantly slivering the hut, revealing the velvet bundle in the wreckage. Olpheist strode toward the child, his fingers clutching for the amulet around her neck.

There was a screech as a great hawk descended from the sky, grabbing the child in its powerful talons. Again, lightning streaked from Olpheist's sword, singeing the hawk, but it vanished into the storm. Olpheist let out a sick howl of rage and turned to the crow, bleeding in the snow.

"Find the child. Fail me again and you will know true pain."

The crow dragged itself to its feet and managed to take ragged flight on its shattered wing, aiming itself in the direction of the hawk's disappearance.

Olpheist walked into the blizzard, disappearing in the falling snow that had already begun to cover Catherine's body. Caley stared in raw disbelief as the image faded to white.

Neive began to gently take the cat's-eye crystal from Caley, which she was still clutching tightly in her hand.

"Look . . ." said Kip.

Another image was appearing in the crystal. On a blood-red dawn, the hawk set the bundle down on the doorstep of a run-down house in a run-down seaside town. A sign out front read:

GRUNCH HOME FOR WAYWARD WAIFS. CASH ONLY!

"Was that where you lived?" asked Kip.

Caley nodded—she couldn't seem to speak.

The hawk screeched until a light came on. The Gunch, in curlers and a hairnet, poked her face out the door and noticed the velvet robe at her feet. She unwrapped it and looked down at the baby staring back up at her.

"Caley Cross! Caley Cross!"

Albert the parrot was squawking excitedly in the hallway.

The Gunch eyed the robe appraisingly. It looked valuable, so she dumped the baby out and hurried back into her house with it.

Albert's insistent squawking was heard. A moment later, the door opened, and the Gunch reluctantly grabbed the baby. Her attention was drawn to a dark, feathery figure staring at her from across the street, her face revealed in the dim glow of first light.

It was Duchess Odeli.

The duchess transformed into a hawk and flew off. The Gunch quickly bolted the door behind her.

The crystal dimmed.

"The duchess isn't the metal-winged crow." Neive turned to Caley. "She's a *hawk*. And she saved you."

"I knew it all along!" said a nodding Kip.

Neive eyed Kip dubiously, then turned back to Caley. "Why didn't she ever say anything?"

Caley shook her head blankly. Her hand went to her chest. The amulet was vibrating slightly. At least one mystery was solved.

She finally knew where it came from.

"WHY didn't you tell me my mother was dead?" Caley was fighting back tears. "She's never coming back. You knew all along, and you never said anything."

The duchess sat in an armchair in her sparsely furnished room with Caley. She exhaled painfully as if feeling an old, deep wound.

"I tried to stop what happened. I am reminded of my failure every time I look at you—the very image of your mother. And I am so very sorry." The duchess put her hand on Caley's gently. "It seems like only yesterday Queen Catherine left here. Master Pim sent me to find her. It was not easy. For a year, I searched. She had hidden herself in a forgotten corner of your world, where she believed she was safe. She may have met your father there, but I know nothing of him. By the time I found you, he was gone. The night you were born, I heard two cries: one as you came into that world, the other . . . a sound I shall never forget. It was as if the sky had been stabbed. Your mother stole off with you into the night and sought the most desolate place she could find. But he found her."

"Olpheist."

The duchess nodded. "I have something to remind me of *him* too."

She raised the sleeve of her feathery dress to reveal her arm, scarred and withered from Olpheist's sword.

"The rest of it you know." The duchess covered her arm again. "I took you to that orphanage. I could not risk bringing you back here. I did my best to protect you. I left you with my cousin Albert, meaning to return for you as soon as it was safe. But it never was."

"But . . . if *you're* not the metal-winged crow, who is?"

"That I do not know. But if he is here, his master will not be far behind."

"And he wants whatever *this* is." Caley showed the duchess her amulet.

"There is only one person who might know the answer to that."

CHAPTER NINETEEN

Frogger

It was a dull gray morning, and Caley was on her way to the stable with Neive and Kip. She made sure they were out of earshot of the mailbox-men who were following her, as usual.

"I have to see Master Pim." Caley's hand went to her amulet.

"Good luck, with *them* watching." Neive scowled at the mailboxes.

Kip began gobbling bananas from his backpack. "Follow me."

Caley and Neive race-walked after Kip, with the mailboxes clanging after them. When they reached the tunnel leading down to the Equidium, Kip motioned for Caley and Neive to go on ahead. He tossed his banana peels on the floor, then emptied the rest of his backpack out and chased after them. The mailbox-men rattled into the tunnel entrance and proceeded to slip on the peels, mixed nuts, and baked goods Kip had dropped. The tunnel echoed with the sound of the mailboxes tumbling down the steep steps. It was like a kitchen had been turned upside-down. A few clangs and crashes could still be heard as Kip led Caley to Fearfew's stall.

"The best way out is up."

Caley hugged Kip and he instantly blushed. She fed Fearfew an animal cracker and began to lead him out of the stable.

Neive turned to Kip. "Your face is all red."

"From the running," replied Kip, turning even redder.

CALEY flew Fearfew up out of the Equidium arena, landing outside Pim's cottage. She frowned at the flower with the red button and gave the door a firm knock instead. Pim opened the door.

"Buzzer not working?"

He pressed the button, and Caley got a squirt of water in her face.

"You did that on purpose," said Caley.

"I do most things on purpose." Pim smiled, leading her inside. "But the results are often surprising."

"Never mind about the weird doorbells. Master Pim, I need to tell you something—"

"Frogger!"

Pim stood at the controls of an old-fashioned video arcade game hooked up to a bazkûl-breath gem-powered motor that sparked and sputtered. He gave the console a shake.

"Usually, if you jiggle it . . . ah . . . here we go . . ."

The word "FROGGER" lit up on the console, and the video screen came to life.

"Major Fogg brought this back from Earth, years ago. He made a few adjustments to get it working here."

Pim began to move a frog around the screen using the joystick.

"You have to get your frog home, past these obstacles . . ." He maneuvered his frog past a few cars. "Each push of this knob gets the frog to jump. See?" He turned to Caley, then back to the game. "Woah . . . almost got hit there! Better stay focused. Uh-oh, there's one of those . . . what do you call that?"

"Lawnmower."

"Mustn't get hit by *that*. Good jump, froggy! Thirty points already! Every safe step gets points. Here comes the river. Now it gets tricky . . ." Pim toggled the joystick, the fir tips on his fox ears quivering with concentration. "You have to land on the lily pads. You can jump on logs . . . and the backs of turtles . . . here's one . . . jump, froggy! You can jump on the alligators, too, but watch out for the jaws. Stay *completely* away from snakes. They're deadly! Sometimes you'll see another frog hanging onto a log, or in trouble. If you help it, you get bonus points. Jump . . . YES! My frog is safely home."

Pim turned to Caley with a smile that was almost as wide as the frog's.

"I got 310,000 points. Your turn."

Caley groaned, then reluctantly took the joystick and began to hop her frog toward the top of the screen.

"Don't be nervous." Pim hovered behind Caley. "Concentrate. Feel the frog . . ."

After a few minutes, Caley turned to Pim. "Is it finished?"

Pim read her score. "A total of 397,000. Impressive."

"I think I got bonus points for helping another frog."

"Just so. You might be a natural, like your mother."

"She played this?" Caley's fingers lingered on the joystick as if she might somehow feel her mother's hand on it too.

"Beat me every time," replied Pim. "Still holds the record. See? At the top of the leaderboard there."

Caley saw the initials "C.C." and the score: 860,630.

"But you have something to tell me," said Pim. "I mustn't distract you."

"You told me Olpheist was looking for something. I think I have it."

Caley took out her amulet and showed it to Pim.

"My mother gave me this before he killed her."

"The Hadeon Drop," Pim said. As usual, he didn't seem surprised by anything Caley said or did.

"What is it?"

"The Hadeon Drop is the seed of life, carried throughout the universe, waiting for a hospitable place to land."

"So, it's like . . . creation?"

"And destruction. For one does not exist without the other. Whoever commands the Hadeon Drop commands life and death."

Caley turned the amulet over in her fingers. "Is this why I can raise the dead?"

"And why you die a little each time you use it." Pim nodded. "A great and terrible price must be paid by the one who bears the Drop. It's why it has always been protected by the Watchers. They alone have the ability to use it wisely. But one of them was seduced by its power."

"Olpheist."

Pim's expression darkened. "He stole the Hadeon Drop and very nearly succeeding in destroying our world. After he was defeated, it eventually found its way to your mother, just as it has now found its way to you."

"I don't want it."

Caley removed the amulet from around her neck and held it out to Pim. He raised his hands defensively and backed away from her, his eyes suddenly wide with alarm.

"I cannot take it from you, even if I wanted to! Only the Watcher destined to bear it can wield its power . . . and resist it as well. To all others, it brings only madness and destruction."

"But I'm not a Watcher. I'm not even a good person. I have an *athrucruth* inside me. Like Olpheist!" Her hand holding the amulet was shaking now. "What if I destroy everything?"

Pim closed his eyes a moment and spoke quietly. "'Worlds turn or worlds burn.'" He regarded Caley thoughtfully. "Come to think of it, yes, you might destroy everything."

"Well . . . this . . . just . . . totally . . . sucks."

Caley slowly shook her head, tucking the amulet back inside her shirt.

"Not quite as bad as *always* losing to your mother in Frogger," said Pim. "She knew the secret."

"The secret?"

Pim began to lead Caley out of the cottage, pulling on a scarf against the chilly morning.

"I always get so caught up in getting my froggy home, not getting killed by—what did you call them?—*lawnmowers* and whatnot, that I forget the secret is to help other frogs along the way."

"Bonus points . . ." Caley said faintly. Her head was swimming, and the amulet around her neck was buzzing against her chest, almost painfully.

They had reached a gate at the end of the path leading from the cottage. Pim turned to her.

"Sometimes, when faced with an impossible task, helping friends allows us to find our strength. Choosing to walk alone in the darkness is one path. Choosing instead to walk with others, even when you're afraid—*especially* when you are afraid—can bring light even in the darkest of places."

"What if I'm not the light? What if I'm the darkness?"

"Ah, is this Fearfew?"

Pim gave Fearfew's muzzle a pat. The oroc gave an impatient snort, looking like he'd had enough of waiting in the cold.

"He's a handsome fellow."

"He behaves much better thanks to your magic crackers," Caley told him, holding out an animal cracker for Fearfew to gobble.

"Whatever you think, Caley Cross."

Pim bent to observe a withered blossom in an empty flower bed by the fence.

"Alas, the frosts are getting heavier, and the phantom flower has not bloomed. I'm afraid it never will before winter. A very long winter perhaps . . ."

He studied the reddening horizon a moment, then turned to Caley, a curious look on his face.

"The crow you mentioned last time we spoke. Do you recall how it found you?"

"I first saw it when I made some frogs come to life, back on Earth."

"Indeed." Pim frowned. "Raising the dead can raise a few eyebrows. Do you remember anything else?"

"Kids were teasing me. I guess I was angry. And then, you know . . . zombies. It happened before. A lot."

Pim's fox nose wrinkled in displeasure.

"Your anger draws Olpheist to you. He feasts upon it." He turned toward the castle in the distance. "Whatever you decide, I hope you'll at least stay for your investiture. I do love a ball. So long as they have decent music."

Pim patted Fearfew again and walked back to his cottage.

Caley swung up on Fearfew and flew above the forest, but it felt as if the weight of the whole world was hanging around her neck, about to drag her down forever.

CHAPTER TWENTY

Tiara Troubles

"So . . . this Hideous Drop—" Kip began.

"*Hadeon*," corrected Neive.

Caley had managed to slip back into the castle without being seen. She had dropped her armor off at the stable and sent a bee for Neive and Kip, who'd joined her on the way to the dining hall for lunch.

"It's like . . . powerful," Kip went on.

"It's what brings life or death to the universe." Neive side-eyed Kip. "So, yeah."

Kip shook his head, chuckling darkly.

"What's funny?" asked Neive.

"All *I* have to worry about is homework, too many brothers, and hand-me-downs. Caley's got, like, the evilest person ever after her, and she has to defeat him or the universe or wherever will be destroyed. Epic!"

"Not helpful," said Neive.

Caley shook her head hopelessly. "What am I going to do?"

"Don't get upset at anyone, that's for *sure*." Kip eyed Caley uneasily. "Because, you know, zombies and Olpheist being drawn to you. Oh, and we should have the ball. We still don't know who the metal-winged crow is, but it's a safe bet it doesn't know Caley has the Hideous Drop—"

"*Hadeon*," corrected Neive.

"Otherwise, the Scabbard or someone would have tried to get it. Plus, the castle's the only safe place. Maybe whatever Doctor Lemenecky was doing helped it. I vote we go along with things and try not to raise any suspicions—at least until we find out Olpheist's plan."

"Actually, that kind of makes sense," said Neive.

All Caley could do was shrug. So many people had said so many things to her that day, her brain felt like a newspaper left out in the rain: all the words ran together in a big black blob, and nothing made any sense. Not one thing she had ever done in her life had ever mattered one bit to anyone, and now everything she did—or didn't do—seemed like the most important thing in the universe, or wherever.

CALEY was picking at her lunch in the dining hall, still thinking about Olpheist and drops that started (or ended) all life, and what would happen if she ever lost her temper again, and she finally put her fork down because her appetite definitely *was* lost (maybe forever).

"You eating that?" Kip slid Caley's plate in front of himself without waiting for an answer.

"Princess Caley!"

They turned to see Ithica Blight making her way toward them with the Pingintees plodding behind.

"What does *she* want?" said Kip.

To Caley's complete amazement, Ithica curtsied to her.

"May I have a word with you after lunch in my rooms?" asked Ithica.

"What . . . ? Why . . . ? What . . . ?" Caley stammered.

"I thought it might be good for us to chat as you prepare for your ball. Perhaps I can give you some helpful advice, princess-to-princess."

"Princess-to-princess," echoed Pansy and Petunia so woodenly you could practically see sawdust coming out of their mouths.

Caley's head was spinning.

"Splendid," Ithica said flatly.

Everyone watched, speechless, as Ithica strode out of the dining hall with the Pingintees.

"Scariest thing I ever saw." Kip shook his head. "Ithica Blight acting nice. *And* her two mindless Pingintee parrots."

"Parrots are not mindless," said Lidia Vowell. "They have an outer layer of their brain that allows them to mimic speech for unknown reasons, although likely connected with socialization."

Kip turned to Caley, lowering his voice. "If you're going to her place alone, I suggest you go as an athrucruth."

"SUGAR?"

Ithica held out a golden sugar bowl for Caley. Ithica's rooms were way fancier than hers. Everything was trimmed with gold and had her initials, "I.B.," plastered all over it. Caley remembered the Gunch had a chronic case of irritable bowel syndrome she called her "I.B.'s." She realized she had just discovered the perfect nickname for Ithica (I.B.), even better than "A Bit Glitchhi," and she smiled to herself. Ithica smiled back. It didn't even look completely fake for once.

"Don't let your tea get cold, Princess Caley."

Caley stared into her teacup. It was probably poisoned.

"I've been drinking too much tea lately," she said, setting the cup down. "It's making me jittery."

"I feel you and I may have gotten off on the wrong foot."

You mean the one you keep trying to kick me down the stairs with? (Caley *wanted* to say that, but she just sat there staring suspiciously at her tea.)

"I'm afraid I've been a frightful *bore.*"

"That's . . . *one* word for it."

"It's a great responsibility, being in my position. One I try to bear with grace and humility."

"That's *two* words."

"And I realized I haven't had a moment's thought about you since you arrived."

Other than when you tried to kill me in the Equidium? (said the voice inside Caley's head).

"Despite our differences—I'm from Erinath, you're from some barbaric backward world—we have something in common—the most important thing of all: we're princesses. Of course, an investiture is terribly tedious. They put a tiara on one's head, and then one is supposed to be even more important than before."

"How's that even possible?"

Ithica shrugged in solidarity. "But a ball *can* be amusing. Do you have a date, by the way?"

"No."

"You must go with someone suitable. Our subjects expect it. We are the blank canvases upon which they project their tiny hopes and dreams."

Caley held a napkin up to her face. She'd never thrown up in her mouth until now (the downside, she supposed, of finally eating regular meals).

"I know!" It almost sounded like Ithica had a pulse (or at least a beating heart). "Let's find you someone to go to the ball with. Bee-Me . . ."

A bee appeared and displayed an image of a pasty, puke-faced prince with an upturned nose and braces. He looked like a boy version of Ithica.

"Prince Blens Blandon," said Ithica. "His father owns huge tracts of land. And he certainly has it in the looks department, don't you agree?"

"You said it . . ."

"Of course, it's expected the two highest-ranking royals will attend the ball together, so there is really only one person who could possibly go with you: Ferren Quik."

An image of Ferren appeared.

"Prince Ferren's been *begging* me to go to the ball with him, but it wouldn't be appropriate. *You* must go with him. I'm sure he will agree. I'll have him contact you."

"I must . . . ? He will . . . ? You *will* . . . ?"

"SHE'S up to something."

Neive met Caley in her rooms after she returned from Ithica's.

"Ithica Blight would never do something nice for anyone besides *herself*," Neive continued. "Plus, she always claims *she's* seeing Ferren Quik."

"So . . . he's *not* going to ask me?" said Caley.

There was a knock on the door and Neive answered it, returning with a tall package wrapped in gold paper.

"What's this?" asked Caley as Neive handed it to her.

She opened the package. Inside was a bouquet of blue buds.

"Bet they'll be pretty when they blossom," said Neive.

"Who sent them?"

"There's a card . . ."

Neive gave Caley the glowing leaf-note that was dangling from the bouquet. Caley read it. Then she read it again . . . and again . . . her eyes growing wider each time.

"Who's it from?" asked Neive.

Caley read it out loud.

Princess Caley Cross,

Please allow me the honor of escorting you to the Royal Ball.

Sincerely,
Prince Ferren Quik

The girls regarded each other . . . then hugged and screamed and jumped up and down. Caley's guards burst into the room to see if someone was being murdered or something, and Neive ushered them out.

"So, what do I do now?" said Caley. "Do I write him back? Or send a bee? Or do I have to say something to him in person? I don't think I could do that—say something to him in person. I mean, I guess I'd *have* to say something to him at some point . . . like . . . at the ball. *Would* I?"

"The first thing we have to figure out is clothes." Neive began looking through the box of Caley's clothes-roses and closed the lid with a frown. "You're not going to the ball in any of *these*. Your gown has to be amazing."

"Maybe Kip's mom can make me one!" Caley smiled.

·

THE first class of the afternoon was waltz lessons. The girls discussed who was going with whom to the ball. It seemed most of Caley's classmates now had dates. Taran O'Toole was going with Monty Ottley and her sister Tessa with Hudson Shotwell, a fourth-year boy. That created a mild scandal and a permanent grin on Tessa's face.

"At least we can tell them apart now," pointed out Amalia Tweedy.

Lidia Vowell (half-elk) was going with Ben Bruin (half-bear), which gave everyone a thrill because it was practically a mixed-species couple.

"Good morning, students."

Duchess Odeli appeared (suddenly and surprisingly, as usual) in the middle of the gym and nodded to the wooden cherubs on the walls, who began to play their instruments.

"Everyone choose a partner, and we shall begin."

The boys and girls moved slowly toward each other in the middle of the gym with mildly mortified looks, like they were being forced to duel instead of dance.

There was a tap on Caley's shoulder. She turned. It was Kip. "Dance?"

Before Caley could answer, Kip grabbed her hand and began casting her around the room like she was a fishing lure.

"I was going to ask you . . . about the ball—" Kip started to say.

"I was going to ask *you*—" blurted out Caley.

"If no one's asked you yet—" Kip talked over Caley.

"If your mom can grow me a dress—" Caley talked over Kip.

"OK, sure. We may as well go together." Kip nodded.

"Remember, gentlemen, your partner is a flower, not a

fire-sword," the duchess announced. "Do not hold her in a death grip."

"Wait . . . what?" Caley and Kip said together.

WHEN Caley woke up the next morning, she lazed in bed recalling a dream from the night before. She was a perfect princess with perfectly unproblematic hair who was dating the hottest boy in the kingdom and totally didn't have a monster living inside her. She gazed at her flowers. The blue buds had opened in the night and, as Neive predicted, were very pretty. Their fuzzy black centers gave off the most interesting aroma: sweet and sour at the same time. It reminded Caley of Chinese soup. And something else, too. She thought she'd seen flowers like that somewhere before but couldn't remember where.

Neive arrived and began helping her get ready for breakfast. It was Saturday, and they were going to the Gorsebrookes' so Kip's mom could get started on a ball gown for Caley.

"You'll probably want the heavy jumper," said Neive, fetching the box of clothes-roses. "It's cold."

Caley climbed out of bed—then held her head.

"What's wrong?"

"Nothing," Caley replied. "My head hurts. Maybe I'm coming down with encephalitis. Oh, and Kip asked me to the ball."

"Kip? Kipley *Gorsebrooke*?" Neive set the box of roses down. "But what about Ferren?"

"I hate to say no to people."

"You have to tell Kip, as soon as possible, or his feelings will be hurt. He's kind of sensitive."

Caley regarded Neive. "'Kind of sensitive.' That's the nicest thing you've ever said about him."

Caley was about to choose plain brown slacks and a sweater, but then she picked a flashy silver skirt and top because if she was going to be an actual princess, she decided she may as well start looking the part.

"That's pretty fancy for the Gorsebrookes," said Neive. "Remember, they shed."

"I'm hungry," Caley said absently. "Do they have Chinese food in Erinath?"

IN the dining hall, Caley was headed to her usual table with Kip and Lucas when Ithica Blight swooped over and led her off by the elbow.

"Princess Caley, can we chat about the Princess Pen?"

"Princess Pen?"

"It's what we call our VIP section at the ball. It's frightfully stuffy, but it *does* keep out the riffraff. I thought we might discuss who you'd like to invite."

Ithica steered Caley toward the tiara twits table at the front of the hall before she could say anything. To her surprise, there was a little throne at the head of the table with the Cross coat of arms. More surprising, everyone smiled at her through their braces. The effect of all that exposed metal—and their twinkly tiaras—was nearly blinding and made her dizzy, so she plopped herself in the throne.

"I hope you don't mind, but I had a proper seat put here for you," said Ithica. "With your investiture, people will be expecting more formality. It isn't appropriate for the aristocracy to dine with the lower classes."

Ithica limp-fish waved over in the direction of Kip and Lucas, who were staring back at Caley. Kip was so surprised to see Caley at Ithica's table, he stopped eating (which was even *more* surprising).

"*Love* your dress by the way," said Ithica. "Posh."

"That's a kind of chicken pox," said Pansy Pingintee.

"No, it's a small potty," said Petunia Pingintee.

Caley was eyeing some cantaloupe wedges on the table. They seemed to be smiling at her too. Ithica thrust a leaf-card in front of her. It was a seating chart for the Princess Pen.

"I have you here, front and center," Ithica told Caley, "beside me."

"Where's *my* seat?" asked Pansy, squinting at the chart with her piggy little eyes.

"And *mine*?" asked Petunia.

"You're in the 'special' section . . . over here . . ." Ithica pointed to a spot that was about as far away as you could get from the Princess Pen.

The Pingintees beamed at each other like they'd just won the lottery.

"Our dates will join us in the Pen," said Ithica.

"That reminds me, I need to send Ferren a note," said Caley.

"*Prince* Ferren," corrected Ithica. "It's best to use proper titles."

"He asked me to the ball . . . but I already told Kip I'd go with *him*."

Ithica wiped a nearly invisible speck of food from her nearly invisible lips.

"You mean Kipley Gorsebrooke? Whose father lost his title because he was a traitor? So, you intend to go to the royal ball with a . . . commoner?"

Everyone gasped. Princess Addled Puffdaddy (or whatever) looked like she was about to pass out.

"It's entirely up to you, of course," Ithica sniffed, "but we can't have non-royals running around the Princess Pen. Perhaps you would prefer not to sit with us." She began to cross Caley's name off the seating chart.

"But I want to be in the Princess Pen!" cried Caley (which had to be the weirdest thing she'd ever said).

"I'll inform Prince Ferren you will be attending the ball with him," said Ithica. "Everything is perfect."

"Perfect . . ." Caley repeated blearily; then she plonked a cantaloupe wedge on her head, like a tiara.

NEIVE and Kip were waiting for Caley outside the castle to go to the Gorsebrookes'. Caley appeared with the mailbox-men trailing after her (*very* closely this time).

Caley glanced around. It had been a while since she had been outside the castle, and it was not looking good. The tiled roof and turrets were shedding like an old snakeskin, and you could see right through some of the main roots. One of the gargoyles tumbled off a tower and did a swan dive into a fountain.

"We need a plan in case the castle doesn't make it to the ball," Kip said as they made their way to the worm station. "If Olpheist gets in, we have to get out of here. *Fast*." He turned to Caley. "Do you think we should ask Master Pim what to do?"

"I think . . ." Caley drawled, "we need to keep the riffraff out of the Princess Pen."

Kip and Neive regarded her as if she were about to tell them the punch line to some joke, but Caley wasn't smiling.

"Why is there cantaloupe on your head?" asked Neive.

•

CALEY and Neive watched Mrs. Gorsebrooke pick through a wicker basket in her rose-filled greenhouse while Kip helped himself to a second breakfast in the kitchen.

"I've gathered a few things, and if we can't find what you like, I will scour the kingdom until we do." Mrs. Gorsebrooke removed a tin of downy buds from her basket. "These are Robin's Wings, which should be the base for the gown. Soft as a feather but also very resilient, for dancing."

Neive nodded encouragingly at Caley. "She'll be doing *loads* of that, right?"

"Perfect . . ." Caley said absently, staring moonily at Mrs. Gorsebrooke's basket.

Mrs. Gorsebrooke rummaged through her basket and pulled out a green rose with multi-colored petal tips. "And for the gown itself, I think Field-of-Dreams. It's like a green meadow full of wildflowers."

"Green is your favorite color, isn't it?" Neive prompted Caley.

"Posh . . ." Caley nodded robotically without taking her eyes off the basket. Her head felt like a field of dreams, each one knocking against the next in the breeze.

"It's settled then," said Mrs. Gorsebrooke. "I'll start working on it right away, and it will be ready in time for the ball. Now, Miss Olander, what about you?"

"Me?"

"What would you like to wear to the ball?"

"I can't go." Neive shook her head. "It's only for nobles."

"You are Princess Caley's lady-in-waiting, which means you have every right to attend a royal ball."

Neive's face lit up; then she noticed Caley putting the

wicker basket upside down on her head like a crown, its contents emptying out all over her.

"Princess Caley has to *go* now," Neive said urgently, snatching the basket off Caley's head and pulling her out the door. "She has a lot of things on her head—I mean, *mind*—with the ball coming up!"

"Chicken pox . . ." Caley limp-fish waved back at Mrs. Gorsebrooke, who was staring after her with a perplexed expression.

"Caley, are you OK? You're acting funny," Neive said as she hustled Caley from the Gorsebrookes' with Kip.

"Potty," mumbled Caley.

AFTER the best sleep ever, Caley woke up feeling great. No dreams . . . or even any thoughts, come to think of it—or *not* to think of it. In fact, her head felt like a chalkboard wiped clean. She took a deep breath of Ferren Quik's flowers, which were still blooming and filling the bedroom with their intoxicating Chinese soup smell.

Weekends were normally a time when Caley rode Fearfew, but even the Equidium was falling apart, making the orocs too jittery to ride. Caley and Neive settled into one of the big overstuffed couches in the common room. Bazkûl-breath gems in the fireplace were attempting unsuccessfully to fend off the deep late-autumn chill that had settled into the castle, thanks to all the holes now riddling it.

Lidia Vowell nodded toward the doorway. Everyone turned to see Ithica Blight standing there.

"What does *she* want?" Kip scowled. "She never comes in here. The common room is too common for her."

"Oh, I almost forgot," Caley said casually, "I told Princess Ithica I'd help with the guest list for the after-after-after party for the ball. It's so exclusive, it's just her and me. Still, we have to keep out the riffraff."

"*Princess* Ithica?" repeated Kip. "You mean . . . 'A Bit Glitchhi?'"

"It's best to use proper titles, Mr. Gorsebrooke."

Kip looked at her and burst out laughing. Then he saw Caley wasn't laughing, and his face went flat.

"Who even *are* you?"

"A blank canvas," Caley replied crisply. "Now if you'll excuse me, I have an after-after-after party to organize."

Caley headed toward Ithica, who sneered at Kip with a smile so thin it could cut glass.

"Something fishy's going on around here," said Kip, staring at Ithica.

"That's speciest," replied Lidia. "Many fish are often quite adept at camouflage, giving them an undeserved reputation for being deceitful or dishonest."

"Something adeptly camouflaged is going on here," said Kip.

Neive stared steadily at Caley as Ithica led her off.

"WELCOME to the Royal Roost."

Ithica gestured around her private common room. Everything was blindingly gold, of course. The tiara twits and the Pingintees were sprawled on gilded armchairs gazing glassy-eyed out the windows while ancient servants shuffled around like tuxedoed turtles, bearing tea trays. Everyone looked bored and angry at the same time, like they were in prison, but with better clothes.

"We should put little bazkûl-breath gems in our tiaras for the ball," said a tiara twit.

"Are we wearing tiaras or coronets?" said another twit.

"Parures, perhaps?" said another.

"Diadems, definitely," said another.

"Whatever's poshest, obviously," declared Ithica. "Princesses are always on the cutting edge of fashion. By the way, Princess Caley, have you got an outfit picked out?"

"Kip's mom is growing me a gown."

Ithica put down her golden teacup so loudly it cracked in half. Her perma-puke-faced smile looked a bit cracked too.

"And will Mrs. Gorsebrooke be creating some sort of . . . peasant costume for you? Combined with that hairdo of yours, you will look quite bohemian."

"Boloney," said Pansy.

"Beluga," said Petunia.

Caley glanced around at the tiara twits and their perfectly straight, blond, sideswept bangs and picked at her curls self-consciously.

"Perhaps you don't understand, but it *is* a *royal* ball," Ithica went on frostily. "The people will be expecting something befitting your station. If you're not us, you're them. Are you *them*, Princess Caley?"

The Pingintees slowly stood, staring intensely back and forth between Caley and Ithica like pit bulls waiting for the "attack" signal.

"No . . . I'm you. I mean . . . *us*," stammered Caley.

"It's settled then," said Ithica. "I'll have my tailors grow you a gown. It's important you have the most perfect posh princess gown for the ball. Everyone must be entirely focused on you."

"Entirely focused . . ." Caley repeated, feeling entirely unfocused.

". . . AND following the arrival of the guests, you will dance
the first dance."

Duchess Odeli was going over the details of the ball with
Caley in her rooms while Caley picked at her hair in the mirror. She decided it had to be straight with sideswept bangs
for the big day, which was tomorrow. She had spent the better
part of the week ironing, boiling, and oiling it—which only
seemed to antagonize the hair into even curlier configura-
tions, like when you try to pick up a worm. Caley had also
attempted to dye it "Princess Pen Blond," but everything she
used on it only seemed to make it redder. It was like scratching a scab.

There was a knock on the door, and the duchess let in Major Fogg. He was carrying a contraption that resembled a cross
between a pasta maker and a miniature goat. Caley had ordered him to come up with something to fix her hair.

"This is designed to straighten and color it," said the major, patting his goat gizmo.

He began feeding clumps of Caley's hair into the mouth of
it while it made an ominous sputtering sound, like a lawnmower running over a rake.

"Princess Caley . . ." the duchess had to shout over the roar
of the gizmo, "Miss Olander informed me you have been acting strangely lately! Is everything all right?"

"Everything is perfect . . . except . . ."

"Yes?" said the duchess. "What is it? You can tell me."

"How big will my tiara be?"

"Your tiara? I imagine it will be a suitable dimension. May I inquire why?"

"So long as it's the biggest in the kingdom. And can it be lit up with bazkûl-breath gems?"

"Why in heaven's name would you want—Major Fogg, would you please turn off that thing!"

"Right-e-o." The major smiled, turning off the gizmo. "I must say, it's done a cracking job."

"Gracious, her head looks like it is encased in concrete!" sputtered the duchess.

Caley turned to the mirror. Her hair was straight, for the first time in her life, with sideswept bangs, and it was blond (in a cement-y sort of way).

"*Perfect . . .*" she smiled vaguely.

Major Fogg headed off as the duchess stared steadily at Caley as if attempting to read a street sign from far away.

"You are not yourself. Perhaps we should cancel the ball."

"NO!" Caley stood up and stomped her foot. Which was a mistake, because the weight of her cement-head sent her toppling across the room. She grabbed the curtains and hung on, attempting to steady herself.

"Very well," the duchess said stiffly. She curtsied and swiftly left.

Caley noticed a crow perched on a tree outside her window, staring intently at her.

"Pretty bird." Caley limp-fish waved at it and opened the window wide. The crow hopped along the branch, closer to the window, without taking its eyes off her. Caley noticed it had a shiny wing. It reminded her of something. But what? It was hard to think when you had no thoughts.

There was another knock on the door, and Neive entered

with Kip, who was holding a wooden box tied with a green ribbon. He did a double take when he saw Caley.

"Why is your head covered in cat litter? And what's that *smell?*"

"It's those." Neive pointed at the flowers Ferren had given Caley. They were rotting to bits, and a stinking black cloud was hanging over them. Neive started to pick them up. "I'll throw them out."

"NO!" Caley shouted. "They're from my perfect prince!"

"Perfect . . . prince?" repeated Kip.

"Show Caley what you brought!" Neive said before Caley could say anything else.

Kip thrust the wooden box at Caley awkwardly. "Mom finished your gown."

Caley wobbled past Kip with barely a glance at the box and stood at the mirror admiring herself some more.

Neive took the box from Kip and opened it in front of Caley to reveal a shimmering clothes-rose floating in water.

"Mom was up all night making sure it was growing properly," Kip said. "She told me to say she mixed in sea-beam that ripples like waves. She wants you to try it on right away, and if it needs any adjustment she'll still have time to fix it before tomorrow."

Caley turned from the mirror and started to shake her head, but her leaden locks made her knees buckle. Neive and Kip grabbed her and managed to sit her down, but she kept swaying, like Humpty Dumpty.

"I can't wear a peasant dress to my ball," said Caley.

"*Peasant?*" repeated Kip.

"Is there an echo in here?" Caley tapped her head and heard "echo in here" echoing around in it. "Princess Ithica is having a more suitable gown grown for me. I have to look posh for my perfect prince."

Kip stared at Caley uncomprehendingly, then at Neive, who stared at Caley with a look of mild horror.

"Who's this 'perfect prince'?" demanded Kip.

"Oh, I forgot to tell you. I'm going to the ball with Prince Ferren."

Kip's face had that dense look it got when he was thinking too hard.

"I can't go to my ball with a mixed-breed mutt," Caley went on.

"That's . . . a bit . . . harsh," Kip said slowly.

"Caley," said Neive, "something's wrong with you."

"Everything's *perfect*!" shouted Caley. "I'm going to a ball with a perfect prince, and my life is perfect for once, and you're both just trying to ruin it!"

"We're not trying to ruin anything." Kip glared at Caley. "And by the way, your life *isn't* perfect. Or did you forget about Olpheist and that Hideous Drop around your neck?"

"*Hadeon*," corrected Neive.

"Plus, I don't care who you go to your stupid ball with," Kip concluded.

"Perfect," said Caley lazily.

"*Perfect!*" snapped Kip. He stomped out, only stopping to grab a few animal crackers on a table.

"That was cruel," said Neive. "Kip's your friend."

"You don't even like Kip," replied Caley.

"We're *all* friends," Neive continued. "Your *real* friends. Unlike Ithica Blight. She's been filling your head with nonsense. I just can't figure out how it's managed to stay stuck in there. Maybe it's all that cement."

"You're not my friend. You're a *servant*. And servants need to know their proper place."

"I'll always be your friend," Neive replied evenly, "but you can find yourself another servant."

As she turned to leave, Neive caught sight of the crow. It saw her looking and flew off unsteadily, its metal wing glinting in the sun. Neive's eyes narrowed on it; then she hurried off without another word.

"You may go," Caley said, waving to the empty room.

CHAPTER TWENTY-ONE

The Ball

The morning of the ball, Caley woke from the poshest dream. She and Prince Ferren were married with a whole bunch of perfectly posh blond children with sideswept bangs. They were born with tiaras and braces, so there was almost no work involved in raising them. Everything was perfect, except for the athrucruth chained up in Doctor Lemenecky's Animals and Botanicals lab, who occasionally got loose and ate one of the children. Aside from that, her head was completely quiet—but for the faint sound of a solitary goldfish bumping into its bowl.

Caley lounged in bed and waited for Neive to come help her get ready. There was a knock on the door, but instead of Neive, it was Kip, holding a bouquet of lilies.

"Just thought I'd pop by to say no hard feelings." Kip held out the flowers. "And I brought these. For your big day."

"Just set them down with the others, Mr. Gorsebrooke." Caley limp-fish waved in the direction of Ferren's flowers.

"Whatever you say." Kip set the lilies down. "Good luck. Oh, and make sure you water him. *It!*"

Kip began to head out.

"Mr. Gorsebrooke."

Kip turned back to Caley.

"Do you know where Miss Olander is?"

"Who? Oh . . . *Neive*? No idea. She told me she quit."

"That's too bad."

"No kidding," Kip said sourly.

"Who's going to help me get my hair ready for my ball?"

Caley padded over to the mirror. Some cement had flaked off her hairdo overnight, and a few curly red bits were starting to poke out like weeds in a sidewalk.

"Actually, I don't need Neive," Caley said dreamily. "Everything is perfect."

"Whatever you say."

Kip opened the door, almost bumping into Ithica Blight, flanked by the Pingintees.

"Getting more perfect around here by the minute," Kip sniped, shoving his way past them.

"Princess Caley," began Ithica, "I brought your special ball gown. Give it to her, Lumpy."

Pansy Pingintee held out a gold box to Caley.

"Try it on; try it on." Ithica clapped lifelessly.

Caley stared vacantly in the mirror, picking at her hair.

Pansy turned to Ithica. "I don't think she can hear us."

Ithica limp-fish waved between Caley's face and the mirror. Caley didn't blink.

Ithica turned to the Pingintees with a vile smile. "The flowers worked just like I said they would. She's a vegetable." She pointed to the rotting blue flowers. "Dumpy, toss those in a trash-toad. Get rid of the evidence."

Petunia lumbered off with the flowers.

"I still don't get what's going on," said Pansy, scratching her fat forehead.

"I *told* you, dimwit," replied Ithica. "The flowers you stole from that bogger Pim's garden were Forget-Me-Lots. They make you forget who you are."

"Ohhhh! Like . . . what do you call it . . . amnesty?"

"*Amnesia*. And once she forgot who she was—a horrid little Earth worm—I made her think she was a perfect posh princess. Only she's *not* a perfect posh princess, is she, because there is only *one* perfect posh princess. And at the ball, everyone's going to see who the number one royal really is: *me*. The effects of the Forget-Me-Lots will have worn off by then. Just in time for my surprise."

"So . . . then . . . if Princess Caley's not posh . . . does that mean there's room for us in the Princess Pen?" asked Pansy hopefully.

"Wait . . . I'm confused." Petunia clomped back into the room. "Who's posh and who's not?"

There *was* one thing in Caley's head. A phrase came to her from out of nowhere: *Watch out for the Forget-Me-Lots . . .*

Who had said that, and what did it mean? Being blond was harder than it looked.

Ithica grabbed the gold box from Petunia and opened it in front of Caley. Inside was a blindingly gold clothes-rose.

"Time to get dressed for your big day."

"My big perfect posh princess day," Caley said dully.

She picked up the clothes-rose and blew on it. It sparkled dazzlingly, and the sparkles spread all over her, forming a gown constructed, head-to-toe, of little gold mirrors. It was so tight at the waist she could barely breathe, and then it ballooned into an enormous skirt the size of a prize pumpkin. It was like wearing a colossal disco ball made of bullion. The shoes were mirrored gold, too, with foot-long stiletto heels. She stood there, wobbling and winded.

The Pingintees started to snigger-snort, but Ithica silenced them with a "*Shush!*"

"These heels . . . are a bit . . . high," said Caley, attempting to keep her balance.

"They're perfect princess pumps," insisted Ithica. "You have to be the tallest princess because you're the poshest."

That certainly made sense, thought Caley (if anything did).

"Lumpy! Where's the special corsage?" prompted Ithica.

Pansy handed over some flowers, and Ithica attached them to Caley's gown.

"It needs one more thing," said Ithica. She placed a tinfoil tiara the size of a teacup on Caley's head. "Now you look like a proper posh princess!"

Ithica and the Pingintees headed out, cackling gleefully.

"Is that flower snoring?" asked Petunia, glancing back at the bouquet of lilies.

CALEY stood there for a long time, admiring herself in the mirror. Her gown was so gold and so bright she began to get a tan —or possibly a first-degree burn—from her own reflection.

"What on Erinath are you wearing, child?"

Caley looked around. Duchess Odeli was staring at her, aghast.

"I have been knocking and knocking. I thought something had happened to you, and now I see that it *has*. Someone has imprisoned you in some sort of torture device!"

"It's my perfect posh princess gown."

"Well, I certainly don't understand today's fashion. You're quite red. Do you have a rash?"

"Everything is *perfect* . . ." said Caley, scratching at her face, which was seriously stinging now. "I might need some sunscreen . . ."

"The ball is about to begin. Please, Your Highness, quickly . . ."

Caley took one step on her stilt-shoes and went skittering sideways past the duchess like a crazed crab.

"Not *that* quickly!" the duchess called, whooshing after her. "Royalty never runs!"

BY the time she reached the ballroom, the goldfish bumping back and forth inside Caley's brain had turned into a shark, shredding her head into little chunks of free-floating thoughts. It was nearly impossible to make sense of any of them: *Perfect posh potty princess in a Princess Pen . . . Forget-Me-Lots . . . Pretty bird . . .*

Caley gazed around blurredly. She was seated on a throne at the head of the ballroom. The once-magnificent room was crumbling, like the rest of the castle. The roots, holding up the floor-to-ceiling mirrors, were rotting off the walls. There were gaping holes where the ceiling was supposed to be, and you could see the cold autumn sky and menacing storm clouds closing in. Below the cornices, the carved cherubs holding musical instruments looked like pieces of parched driftwood. Everyone was in tuxedos and gowns, or military uniforms, milling around punch bowls and an enormous coronation cake. A liveried man announced couples as they entered.

"Princess Fenistera Fardsarrage and Prince Wilhelm Poting-Sackson."

Caley felt uncomfortable and tried to move, but she seemed to be wedged in tight to the throne. She caught her reflection in a mirror and was mortified to see she was packed into some sort of hideous golden getup, like the world's biggest bonbon. And what was up with her hair? As ridiculous as it usually looked, this was a whole other level. People were gawking at her with appalled expressions, and the tiara twits and their dates—who were all in some sort of velvet-roped-off pen—snickered and pointed.

"Why am I wearing this?" Caley turned to the duchess, who was seated beside her throne. "Am I going to outer space?"

"That is the gown you chose," replied the duchess.

"Kip's mom made me a gown. Where *is* Kip? And Neive . . . ?" Caley scanned around the ballroom.

The duchess regarded her with growing alarm. "Your rash is getting worse."

Caley felt her face. Something hot and nasty seemed to be bubbling beneath her skin.

"Princess Ithica Blight and Prince Ferren Quik," said the announcer.

Caley rubbed her eyes. No, she wasn't seeing things. Ithica Blight was walking into the ballroom with Ferren Quik. Despite her shark-shredded head, she remembered *she* was supposed to go to the ball with Ferren. Wasn't she?

"Princess Caley Cross will dance the first dance," said the announcer.

The cherubs on the ceiling began to play a creaky waltz, and everyone stopped talking and turned their attention to Caley.

"Where's your date?" a tiara twit taunted.

"Who would dance with *her*?" another twit teased.

Caley felt her face grow hotter, and now her hands were heating up too.

"I am putting a stop to this right now," the duchess told Caley firmly, taking her hand to lead her out.

Caley managed to wrench herself to her feet, alarmed to find she was at least a foot taller than usual. She had on hideously high heels, which made her look like a buffalo balancing on pogo sticks. One of the stilettos snapped, and the weight of her gown sent her toppling onto the dance floor. She landed with a thud that shook the chandeliers and shattered her gown. Her cement head cracked completely apart, and her curls sprang out like a bunch of springs from a busted cuckoo clock. The tiara twits, led by Ithica Blight, began laughing at her with a sound like jackals. Caley rolled around on the floor under the weight of her smashed gown, her legs kicking helplessly, like a turned-over tortoise. Just when she thought things couldn't get any worse, the hot nastiness on her face began to break the surface of her skin . . . like little volcanoes . . . and burst. She glanced at herself in the mirrors and saw her face was covered in enormous pimples, which were erupting like mini Mount Vesuviuses: great gushing geysers. A tiara twit took a picture with her bee. No doubt the post on Bee-Me would break the record for the most honeycomb emojis anyone ever got. The tiara twits' cruel laughter grew louder and louder while Caley continued tortoising and face-volcanoing, reflected infinite times in the ballroom mirrors—infinite infinitely humiliated Caley Crosses.

A hand held out a handkerchief. Caley looked up, surprised to see Ferren Quik. She wiped off her volcano-face as he helped her to her feet.

"Don't listen to them." Ferren nodded in the tiara twits' direction. "They're mean, and they do whatever Ithica tells them to do."

"Then why did you come to the ball with her?" asked Caley.

"My mother insisted." Ferren frowned. "I wanted to ask *you*, but I figured you'd go with Kip."

"Kip?" repeated Caley. "*Kipley Gorsebrooke?*"

"You're always hanging out. I thought you were going out with him."

"*Me?*" said Kip.

Caley turned, surprised, to see Kip and Lucas hurrying toward her in tuxedos.

"Sorry, we would have come sooner," started Lucas, "but Kip forgot to get me again. I think he stopped to eat coronation cake."

"'Never save the day on an empty stomach,'" said Kip, licking icing off his lips. "The Gorsebrooke motto. Those flowers your 'perfect prince' supposedly sent—" Kip gestured at Ferren, "were Forget-Me-Lots."

"They shrink your brain and swell your head," added Lucas.

Watch out for the Forget-Me-Lots. Caley picked out one memory from the swirling shark-sludge of her brain. She remembered who'd said that: Master Pim.

Now if she could just remember who Master Pim *was*.

"Those are pimple posies, by the way." Lucas pointed at Caley's corsage.

Caley tore them off, and her face instantly stopped volcanoing.

"Why would you send me Forget-Me-Lots?" She turned to Ferren.

"I didn't." Ferren shook his head blankly.

"Remember we saw the Pingintees outside Master Pim's garden?" said Kip. "I bet *they* were getting those flowers. Not hard to guess who for . . ."

Kip eyed Ithica Blight, who had gathered the tiara twits together: they were all attempting to out jackal-laugh each other at Caley.

"But then, if *you* didn't invite me to the ball . . ." Caley regarded Ferren, then pulled out his leaf-note invitation that she'd been carrying ever since she got it. She saw that each *i* was dotted with a lame little tiara. "I'm so stupid," she said, shaking her head. "I was so excited when I got this I never even noticed . . ."

Caley turned to Ithica. She felt her chest start to buzz. Her amulet was vibrating loudly.

"Your hand . . ." said Kip.

Caley looked down. Her hand holding the leaf-note was on fire. The note curled up in flames.

The cherubs suddenly stopped playing with a sound like a needle pulled from a record. Everyone was staring in horror at Caley's flaming fingers. There was a deafening silence, like a shoreline before a great wave hits; then the dead roots hanging from the walls began to writhe . . . and wriggle . . . and from out of the decay new shoots and stems exploded in every direction, fusing together to form giant zombie tree-hands. The zombie hands began clutching and clawing at everyone, and everyone began screaming and scrambling, terrified, from the ballroom. The tiara twits tumbled out of the Princess Pen, but a zombie hand scooped them up and shook them until their tiaras toppled off. Another zombie hand grabbed at Ithica Blight, who began to run around in circles, holding on to her tiara for dear life.

"Lumpy! Dumpy! HELP ME!" Ithica shrieked hysterically at the Pingintees.

The cousins shoved Ithica aside as they stampeded out of

the ballroom, squealing at the top of their lungs like pigs in a pit. The zombie tree-hands snatched Ithica up. There was a flurry of wooden fingers in front of her terrified face, and then she was dumped on the floor. The tiaras had been twisted into a set of braces the size of a restaurant sign and attached to Ithica's regular ones. They spelled out something:

A BIT GLITCHHI.

Ithica bolted from the ballroom, gibbering hysterically through her behemoth braces.

Caley managed a faint smile.

Then she died.

CALEY'S eyes flickered open. Kip's and Lucas's faces slowly came into focus, staring down at her, relieved. She managed to sit up, feeling lifeless and like she'd been stung by a million mosquitoes, like she always did after a zombie attack. She couldn't move a muscle, but her mind was suddenly working triple time. She remembered everything that had happened to her leading up to the ball and who Master Pim was. She also remembered him saying something about not getting angry (*see *Olpheist*). She had definitely gotten a bit steamed (or a bit bigger than a bit), she had to admit, as she glanced around the barren ballroom and the still-flailing zombie tree-hands.

While she was thinking about all this, the ceiling started to splinter apart.

"We have to get of here!" cried Kip.

Caley tried to stand, but her body was useless. Kip slung her arm over his shoulder and tried to haul her from the ballroom.

"You weigh a ton in this gown," he grunted.

Lucas grabbed Caley's other arm, but before they could take a single step, the floor disintegrated beneath them. Caley went hurtling through space. The ground reappeared and she lay there, the wind knocked out of her. A moment later, Lucas landed heavily beside her.

"Where are we?" Lucas slowly got to his feet and stared around.

"Under the castle," said Caley.

They were in the cavern where she and Kip had battled the queen venowasp. The castle's colossal taproots, glowing blue, squirmed around alarmingly.

"I think I'd rather be back in the *ballroom*." Lucas shivered.

"Where's Kip?" asked Caley, peering around the gloom.

They heard a sick cough and turned toward the sound, surprised by what they saw. It was Doctor Lemenecky. He was drinking from a vial of glowing blue liquid, and his beard was attaching itself to one of the castle's roots.

"Doctor Lemenecky," Lucas called out, "can you save the castle?"

Lemenecky coughed again loudly, lowering the vial.

"*Save* it? No, foolish boy, I am *killing* it. Conceivably . . ."

"But . . . why would you do that?" asked Caley.

"Because it is a murderer," replied Lemenecky calmly. "For a nen to become a great castle, a genocide must occur. As it grows . . . stealing the light . . . drinking the water . . . eating the soil . . . it destroys every other nen in its path. I alone escaped to avenge this evil." Lemenecky had a violent coughing fit, then continued in a rasping voice. "A nen like this has many defenses against its enemies. But it would never suspect its own kind. Each night I attach myself to its roots and poison it .

. . carefully, slowly, over time. This . . ." he held up the vial, "is the final blow of the woodsman's ax."

A vine streaked out and snatched the vial from Lemenecky and transformed back into Lucas.

"Give that to me."

A familiar voice rumbled across the cavern. Caley and Lucas turned to see General Roon emerge from a tunnel.

Lucas handed Roon the vial and pointed to Lemenecky. "He's poisoning the castle."

"And we must let him finish his work," said Roon, returning the vial to Lemenecky.

"You're *helping* him?" asked Caley.

"He required only a little encouragement from me." Roon stared down at Lemenecky. "My men found him like this in the forest when they were building my wall—a pathetic little stump clinging to life. I merely set him free to go about his revenge."

A bark rang out, and a bloodhound bounded into the cavern, his jaws snapping for the vial. Roon seized the dog by his studded collar and threw him with surprising strength clear across the cavern. The dog rolled several times with a sharp whimper and transformed into Kip, groaning in a heap.

Caley looked on helplessly as Lemenecky downed the remainder of the vial. He began to crumble like a rotten log, and the blue glow from his beard spread into the castle's roots, which also began to crumble. There was a deep, terrible moaning from high above the cavern, and the roots began to disintegrate, raining down on everyone's heads.

Caley noticed one of Roon's leather gloves had been torn off during Kip's attack. The color drained from her face as she saw what it concealed.

A mechanical arm.

"*You're* the metal-winged crow." Caley gasped.

"And you have something my master seeks."

Roon grabbed Caley and began to drag her from the collapsing cavern.

CHAPTER TWENTY-TWO

A Perfect Monster

Roon shoved Caley roughly to the ground as they emerged from the tunnels beneath the castle. A stinging sleet pounded down like nails. There was a sound like the bones of some gigantic beast breaking. Above them, the ancient castle collapsed, smashing apart like a thousand ships on a rocky shore. The inhabitants fled for their lives from the wooden wave crashing around them. The mechanical wolves Caley had seen in the Wandering Woods surrounded her and roared—a feral, frightening sound.

"Aren't they beautiful?" said Roon.

Caley stared in horror at the machine-beasts, bristling with metal claws and jaws, their empty yellow eyes fixed on her.

"Baestwraiths," said Roon. "A new army for a new age: a man age . . . a machine age . . . a *shadow* age."

There was another sound, faint at first, like cats circling for a fight, then rising as if all the hate in the world were a sound and the sound was seeking Caley. Roon knelt, and the baestwraiths parted for a hooded figure, materializing from the storm.

Olpheist.

Caley was on her feet, stumbling on leaden legs through the churning rubble of the castle. She fell heavily and lay facedown, unable to will herself to move, rigid with fear. The hateful wailing faded. The only sound was her ragged, panicked breath. She forced herself to stand. She was outside a windswept cottage on the edge of the ocean. The screen door swung open, and her mother was standing there, her green eyes smiling, red hair caught in the wind.

"I've been waiting for you," said her mother. "Isn't this what you always dreamed of?"

The sight of her mother brought hot tears to Caley's eyes. More than anything, it *was* what she had always dreamed of, so deeply and so desperately and so hopelessly.

Her mother held her hands out to her.

"Give me the Hadeon Drop, and I will give you this dream. Forever."

Caley reached for her mother's perfect embrace.

"Caley . . ."

Someone was calling her.

"CALEY!"

It was Kip's voice.

A single black tear rolled down her mother's cheek. Caley slowly shook her head.

"I can't go home."

As she spoke the words, the sky split apart and black rain began to fall, vaporizing everything: the cottage, her mother . . . that beautiful world melting away from her. She was back outside the castle again. Olpheist stood before her.

Kip ran toward Caley, swiping rain and dirt from his eyes.

"Whatever he's doing, don't listen to him! It's a trick!"

Without a glance at Kip, Olpheist drew a silver sword hilt

and flicked it in the air like swatting a fly. It spat a rope of wind, lassoing Kip into the air by his neck. Olpheist took a step toward Caley. He was so close now, she could feel the tomblike chill coming from him.

"You can escape your dreams, but there is no escaping your destiny. The Hadeon Drop was meant to come to you. And you were meant to come to *me*. Together, we will be immortal."

Caley was frozen before Olpheist, his words tightening around her like a noose. She could feel her amulet thrumming against her chest.

"Do not fear me. I am your only companion in the darkness. And I alone know who you truly are: A monster. A perfect monster."

Caley wrenched her eyes over to Kip, still held in the grip of Olpheist's sword, fighting for his last breath.

"You have . . . no idea," Caley managed to gasp.

The instant she said this, her body atomized as the annihilating bomb inside her sent out a shock wave. Its force slammed into Olpheist, incinerating him where he stood. In his place, another shock wave spread, answering the call of the first. Two athrucruths met like galaxies colliding. There was no pain, no thought, only immeasurable, unstoppable fury—all the pain and darkness from Caley's life, ripping into her enemy. Red . . . everything was blood red and burning as the athrucruths attacked each other again and again, locked in a death spiral until Caley's rage was finally spent.

Caley knelt in the cold mud, human again. Olpheist lay there beside her, his face writhing with half-formed shadow creatures, like maggots on some dead thing. She reached for his fallen sword with shaking hands. But she felt the sword's weight, and it slipped from her fingers. Caley had hurled all her anger at Olpheist, and with it, the last of her strength. Her head slumped. Then she felt a red-hot stab of pain. She stared down at the burning sword stuck in her chest—then up at Olpheist, who held it, rising to his knees to face her.

"You could have joined me. Now you will be alone forever."

Caley could only find enough breath to make the sound of a gasp as Olpheist reached for the amulet around her neck.

Then everything was still and black as eternity.

Until . . . a light . . . the faintest light, like a lone star in an empty heaven. It grew brighter. The face of Caley's mother came into focus, bending over her. She placed her hand on Caley's heart. A great warmth surrounded her. For an instant, another figure appeared in the distance behind her mother. Then blackness again.

Caley's eyes blinked open. Her wound was gone. She felt for the amulet.

Gone too.

Kip came stumbling across the burnt crater the athrucruths had left, wiping metallic ash off himself with a dazed look.

"What happened?"

"I think . . . I died," said Caley.

"Oh . . ." Kip nodded. "Anything else?"

A vine wriggled out of the rubble and transformed into Lucas.

There was a terrible cry, like an animal tearing itself from a trap. Great roots wrenched from the hill where the castle had stood, fusing with its ruined rooms and halls to form a colossal wooden creature, its head scraping the storming sky.

"The nen . . ." said Lucas, awestruck.

A fire-sword suddenly sunk into the nen's foot. Flames leapt up its leg with frightening speed. The nen thrashed blindly at Roon, holding a fire-sword, ant-sized beneath him.

A sharp caw cracked the air, and a hawk swooped from the storm, its powerful talons scratching at Roon's eyes. Roon transformed into a crow, his metal wing slashing murderously at the hawk before flying off in a blind retreat. The hawk landed and transformed into Duchess Odeli, smoothing her feathery dress and watching the crow disappear.

"There is no need for unpleasantness."

The sky was lit by a tremendous glow, and the nen—all in flames—staggered off into the forest, quaking the earth with its steps.

Hungry snarls made everyone turn. The baestwraiths came swarming toward Caley.

"Despite the etiquette I have been attempting to instill in you," the duchess said, "I suggest it might be wise, at this point, to *run!*"

It was all Caley could do to stand. Kip and Lucas each took one of her arms and began to pull her away from the things, but Caley knew they wouldn't outrun them with her.

"Let me go!"

But Kip and Lucas only tightened their grip on her arms.

There was a chest-thumping blast as a rocket burst above them, creating a colossal blazing bazkûl. It dove, melting the baestwraiths with a single burning breath.

Everyone turned to see Major Fogg, his hand on a plunger, give a cheery thumbs-up.

"I promised fireworks for the ball. Sorry it took so long. Had a bit of bother getting the bazkûl sorted out . . ."

The bazkûl did a loop, dove again, and spat out a volley of

baby bazkûls. One of them latched onto Major Fogg and carried him off into the exploding sky.

"Or a bit bigger than a bit . . . !"

The beating of wings made everyone look up to see Neive landing Fearfew, with Arrow and Dream behind her. Neive grabbed Caley's hand and hauled her up on Fearfew as Kip and Lucas swung up onto their orocs. In a heartbeat, they were soaring above the shattered earth where the nen castle had stood.

CHAPTER TWENTY-THREE

Home

The orocs set down outside the little toadstool cottage in the woods. The storm had stopped, and a few stars began to poke through the clouds. The evening was suddenly calm and quiet. It felt to Caley as if she had been in one of Lucas's epic tapestry adventures and he had fallen asleep and the world had nodded off along with him.

The nearby trees parted, and everyone turned to a huge figure lumbering toward them. When they saw who it was, they froze.

The Scabbard.

Part of his head looked like a melted candle from the slugdevil attack, and his one good eye resembled a fried egg.

Lucas hid behind Kip, who tried to hide behind Lucas, who began to turn into an ivy again.

"Good evening!"

Master Pim was hurrying toward them.

"No need to be alarmed." Pim pointed his staff toward the Scabbard. "He is a friend. Shall we go inside?"

Everyone quickly followed Pim into his cottage, craning nervously back at the Scabbard.

"I'll put on some tea," said Pim. "There are blankets by the fire. Warm yourselves."

Everyone huddled by the fire as Pim began to set out tea and biscuits, which Kip began to gobble almost before he could put down the plate.

"I'm sorry I was unable to attend your ball," Pim told Caley, "but after Miss Olander informed me Olpheist had discovered the whereabouts of the Hadeon Drop, I went straight away for help." He glanced out the window at the Scabbard, who was standing watch. "I found him, half-alive, in Doctor Lemenecky's laboratory."

"Slugdevil." Kip coughed guiltily.

"He will heal. That is his curse. The Scabbard was General Roon's first experiment. He bears no love for his creator. And now you have seen the general's latest ghastly invention—nature twisted into the machinery of domination and destruction." Pim turned back to the others. "But tell me, how was the ball?"

"Olpheist returned," Caley began.

"Caley died," said Kip.

"Not sure if the nen will survive," added Lucas. "Doctor Lemenecky was poisoning it."

"Like I said all along." Kip nodded.

Neive gave him a look.

Pim settled into his rocking chair next to the others. "I sent the Scabbard to determine the cause of the nen's distress, and he confirmed what you told me: Doctor Lemenecky was indeed attempting to kill it."

"*That's* why Lucas's termites went after him in Animals and Botanicals class!" Kip smacked his forehead with exasperation. "I should have figured it out. They were meant to attack the most rotten parts of the castle first. Which I guess was . . . Doctor Lemenecky."

"Poor fellow." Pim shook his head. "And most unlike his

kind. Nens are the noblest of beings. Once a nen castle has taken root, the other nens willingly sacrifice themselves to become part of it, for only one castle can grow at a time. Squirrels plant them, by the way . . . did you know that? Though how they decide when and where is beyond my understanding."

Caley and Neive exchanged quick, amazed looks.

"I'm certain General Roon led Lemenecky into believing the castle was somehow his enemy. Perhaps it helped salve the guilt he must have felt for surviving when the other nens did not. At any rate, I do not believe h e would have carried out his mad scheme if not for the general's insidious influence. These are dark times, and everyone is at the mercy of their worst instincts." Pim gazed around at the solemn faces staring back at him. "And the music?"

"Music?" repeated Caley.

"At the ball. Fanfares and waltzes and such, I presume?"

"We never got around to dancing."

"No, no, no, no, nooooo! That won't do. We shall have our *own* ball." Pim sprang up and put on a record. The cottage filled with music. "Have you heard of the Beatles?"

"Does he want us to . . . dance?" Lucas glanced nervously at the others.

"I can't dance in *this*." Caley stared down at her dented disco ball atrocity.

"I've got something you could wear . . ."

Kip reached into the pocket of his tuxedo and handed Caley a small wooden box.

She opened it. Inside was the clothes-rose Kip's mother had grown for her.

"You saved it," said Caley, delighted.

"In case you changed your mind," replied Kip.

Caley stood up and blew on the rose. It sparkled, and the sparkles spread over her disco ball, which mercifully vanished. In its place was a gown made of delicate green strands, soft as a cloud, with Field-of-Dreams flowers blossoming throughout it. Caley did a twirl and the gown spun with her, filling the little cottage with the heavenly scent of a summer garden.

"Well, go on." Neive nodded to Kip. "Princess Caley has to have the first dance."

Kip walked woodenly up to Caley.

Pim's fox nose furrowed. "We need a little atmosphere . . ." He tapped his staff on the floor, and the walls and ceiling vanished. In their place, stars appeared, blazing with constellations.

Caley and Kip put their arms around each other and danced in awkward silence a moment.

"You're definitely not 'Scarcely So' anymore," Kip finally said.

"You mean . . . my anagram?"

"I'll have to come up with a new one because, you know, you defeated Olpheist and saved the universe or wherever. You're not *scarcely* anything."

Caley grinned and tightened her grip on Kip.

"C'mon, Lucas . . ."

Neive was holding out her hand for Lucas to dance. Lucas looked like he wanted to turn into a vine again, but Neive pulled him onto the floor.

"Hold on!" Kip called.

He pulled another box from his pocket and handed it to Neive. She regarded it, puzzled, and opened it. It was another clothes-rose.

"I couldn't find you before the ball to give it to you," said Kip.

Neive regarded Kip with her usual look (disbelief), but this time, she was smiling. She blew on the clothes-rose, and a warmly glowing pearl-gray ball gown materialized around her.

"It's beautiful," said Neive. "And it matches my hair."

"Moon Meadow," noted Kip. "And mom used some Butterfly's Breath so it'd be nice and soft."

Neive and Lucas began to dance.

"Looks like Lucas was paying attention in dance class," said Kip as he grabbed Caley again and began to spin around. "I think *I'm* doing pretty good too—"

As soon as he said this, he tripped over one of his own big feet and almost banged into the Frogger game.

"Oops!" Kip grinned sheepishly, then noticed the game. "The old guy has some strange stuff in here."

"It's a game from my world," said Caley. "There's a secret. You can't go home. Not until you help another frog. Bonus points. Good thing I remembered that with Olpheist. Thanks to you."

"Scary Close!"

"My new anagram? Why that?"

"Because the closer you get to you, the scarier things are. It's dangerous around you!"

Caley had to admit, Kip had a point.

"*All you need is love!*" Pim sang along to the music and bopped around the cottage. "Everyone change partners!"

Lucas turned from Neive and bowed solemnly to Caley. She curtsied back, and they started to dance.

"You're very brave," said Caley.

"To dance?"

"At the castle. You and Kip. You saved my life."

A smile slowly spread across Lucas's face.

"'Brave.' No one's ever called me that before."

Neive and Kip regarded each other warily. Kip's hair bristled, and Neive's nose twitched. Finally, Kip screwed up his courage and held his hand out to Neive. She took it, and they began to twirl around the cottage.

'Good thinking getting Lucas to spy on Caley," said Neive. 'That was pretty clever."

"How did you know," Kip said, "that Olpheist found out where the Hadeon Drop was and that Caley was in trouble?"

"Squirrel sense."

Kip stared at Neive, mystified.

"My baest. Sort of. Try not to blab it to everyone."

"You're a *squirrel*." Kip flashed a triumphant smile. "I knew it all along!"

Neive was about to give Kip some serious side-eye . . . but she burst out laughing instead.

"Dogs might be loyal, and brave, but they've got *terrible* noses for mysteries."

Pim turned the music up, and everyone danced until the floorboards shook. The constellations came alive and formed the starlit shapes of animals dancing along with them: bears, rabbits, dogs, frogs, crickets, even a squirrel or two. Eventually, Caley saw Pim put on his hat and scarf and slip out the door. She bundled herself in a blanket and quietly followed.

They walked in silence to a small garden tucked in hay for the winter. Pim stopped to admire a small brown flower.

"Oh! Still one left, so late in the season. A special breed of hope lily. Although it is quite plain looking, it has the most wonderful smell in all the world. Give it a sniff."

Caley regarded the lily suspiciously.

"Nothing unpleasant will happen; gardener's honor."

Caley bent down to smell the flower, but it jumped over her shoulder and bounded off into the night.

"Well . . . it *is* a *hopping* hope lily." Pim shrugged. "Never *have* been able to smell one."

"Why would you grow a flower with the world's most wonderful smell if no one can actually *smell* it?"

"Once you've smelled the most wonderful smell in the world, everything after that is bound to be a disappointment. There'd be no hope for any other smells, and I have found that hope is often the only thing that keeps one going."

Caley grinned. It made sense (in a Pim sort of way).

"I shall miss our walks." Pim began to head back to the cottage with Caley. "Winter is almost upon us. The world is going to sleep. Perhaps for a very long time."

"Master Pim, what's going to happen to Erinath?"

"War is coming. Some will fight; others will hide behind walls. But in the end, I fear we all will be swept up in a terrible struggle."

"You were wrong," said Caley. "You thought I could protect the Hadeon Drop, but it's gone. Olpheist has it. He's still alive."

"But *you* are also alive, if my old eyes do not deceive me. How is that, without the Hadeon Drop? For, as your friend said, you died."

"Something . . . brought me back."

"The One." Pim nodded. "Oh, I know the One does not play favorites, but I like to think it leans toward love in the end. Olpheist—full of hatred, seeking immortality and power above all—could not prevail against such a force."

Caley touched her heart where her mother's hand had been, her face suddenly full of anguish.

"I saw my mother. And there was someone else. He was like a ghost. Was it my father? I could have stayed with them. Did I lose my chance for all time?"

"It is not about the family you have lost," said Pim. "It is about the one you find."

Caley heard the sound of her friends' voices drifting from the cottage twinkling through the trees. She thought about Neive, and Kip, and Lucas. For the first time in her life, there were people who were important to her. The thought of it made her heart warm. But what if she were to lose them too?

What if one day, the darkness won?

They had arrived at the cottage gate. Pim turned to Caley, his orange eyes shining as if he had heard her thoughts.

"Growing up, you never knew the simple joys of love and friendship, and so you came to believe the world was filled with evil. Now you find a light in the most unexpected place, perhaps most surprisingly in *yourself*. And your choice remains—will you hold a candle to the darkness . . . or blow it out?"

The night suddenly brightened. A full moon appeared above the trees, and its silver rays hit a lone, shriveled blossom poking up from the cold ground. It burst open. In its center, the galaxy was slowly spinning—a billion points of light in a great cosmic dance.

Pim's face lit up like the blossom.

"The phantom flower. It seems there is still a little magic left in the world after all."

CALEY woke to the sound of a whistling kettle. Everyone had slept, curled up in their blankets near the fire. Pim was stirring a pot of porridge over glowing bazkûl-breath gems as the first light of day crept across the cottage. Neive began to set the table for breakfast. Kip was still asleep, growling a bit, his hair bristling. Caley figured he must be chasing a squirrel in a dream. Outside, the sky was clear and deep blue, the sun hinting on the horizon. Snow had fallen overnight, blanketing the world in a crisp white coat.

Winter had come. Pim carried the porridge pot to the table. Kip's nostrils twitched, and he sprang to his feet, wide-awake.

"I'm famished!" Kip pounced on the table, plunking the entire pot of porridge in front of himself. He looked around at the others staring at him. "Oh . . . anyone else hungry?"

They ate in silence as Pim bustled about the cottage gathering supplies in a large burlap sack that he began to drag to the door. Caley went to help.

"Better put this on . . ." Pim handed Caley a clothes-rose.

She blew on it, sad to see her beautiful ball gown replaced by a thick rough cloak held in place by a sturdy woven belt.

"Not quite as fashionable, I'm afraid," said Pim, "but you'll be warm at least on the journey."

They headed out the door with the sack. The Scabbard took it from them and slung it over his shoulder. It looked about the size of a school bag on him.

"Where should I go?" Caley turned to Pim.

"Somewhere far from here. The nen has fallen. You are not safe. Olpheist once again possesses the Hadeon Drop. He will eventually regain his powers. But he fears you now."

"What can *I* do against him? If he gets stronger . . ."

"I have something for you."

Pim reached into one of the pockets of his overalls and drew out a silver sword hilt.

"I have been waiting to give this to you. But I needed to be sure you were ready to accept it. This was your mother's. To wield a Watcher's sword, you must find the One within yourself. This sword is called 'The Light.'"

Pim held the sword out to Caley. She hesitated, then took it. The gleaming metal gave off a surprising warmth in her hand. The rising sun hit it, and it sent out dazzling rainbows, as far as the eye could see. Pim nodded, a faint smile crossing his face.

"Find the Watchers—if there are any left. Begin your training. The road ahead will be long, and the destination far from certain." Pim turned to the Scabbard. "He knows the way."

Caley tucked the sword into her belt and headed back to the cottage. "I have to say goodbye."

"Goodbye to who?" Neive stepped through the door. "I'm coming with you. You never officially fired me."

Caley stared at Neive, remembering now the cruel words she had said to her when they'd last seen each other in the castle.

"Only if you come as my friend. Not as my servant."

"I'll always be your friend," said Neive. "Even when you forget."

"You're going to need a tracker." Kip bounded out of the cottage with Lucas. "I'm ninety-eight percent bloodhound. *And* Equidium champion."

Caley regarded Kip, surprised.

"It's a noble cause, isn't it?" Kip shrugged. "Save the world from tyranny. Dad would approve." His face fell. "Mom's gonna kill me . . ."

"I'm coming too," said Lucas. "I've always wanted to go on an adventure. A *real* one, not one just made up in some tapestry."

"Lucas, I don't think *either* of your parents would like that," said Caley.

A huge grin broke out on Lucas's face. "No, they won't. Especially my father."

Pim cleared his throat. "It is very gallant of you young people, but I'm afraid it is quite out of the question. Such a large party would attract unnecessary attention. Not to mention it is most dangerous. I cannot allow you to be put in further peril. You have already risked too much."

"They're coming, if that's what they want," Caley said in a firm voice, standing beside her friends. "We wouldn't be here without them."

"And as for danger," added Kip, "it's my middle name."

"I thought it was Gustus," said Lucas.

Caley and Neive swallowed smiles as Kip shot Lucas a look.

"Very well." Pim regarded the young people grimly. "In which case, Miss Olander, it is better *you* keep this . . ."

He handed Neive a leaf. She unwrapped it. Inside was the nut the squirrels had given her.

"You will know what to do with it when the time comes." Pim fixed Neive with the full intensity of his brilliant orange eyes. "I feel that you, child of the wild woods, will have a part to play in the great drama that lies ahead." He turned to the others. "And now you must be off, and quickly."

Everyone hurried toward the orocs. Caley turned and walked back to Pim, giving him a big kiss on his cheek. Pim looked surprised and even blushed.

"You said I should do one silly thing before teatime every day." Caley winked.

Pim tipped his straw hat to Caley with a little bow and began to head back to his cottage, clearing the snow from the path with a magical wave of his staff.

Everyone climbed up on their orocs. The Scabbard gave a sharp whistle. From out of the trees thundered a mammoth gray oroc, and he swung up on the snorting beast.

Kip stared at the Scabbard nervously. "So . . . should we call you . . . 'Scabbard'? Or . . . 'Mr. Scabbard'? Or . . ."

"Sliigo Killiman," he grunted.

"Pardon me?"

"My name. Sliigo Killiman."

Kip swallowed hard. "I'll stick with 'Scabbard.'"

Caley shifted forward on Fearfew to make room for Neive, but Kip trotted over on Arrow and offered his hand to her.

"Arrow is the fastest," Kip explained with a serious face. "Especially with two people. I'm just being practical."

Neive nodded and swung up behind Kip with a trace of a smile.

The orocs took to the sky. Caley glanced back at the little toadstool-like cottage in the woods. She wondered if she would ever see it or Master Pim again and considered what strange sights would lay ahead.

"So, where are we going?" Kip called to her.

Caley looked around at her friends and thought of Pim's words, *It's about the family you find,* and realized this must be what home felt like.

"I don't know," she said. "But we're going together."

Caley tightened her fingers on Fearfew's glowing mane, urging him toward the dawn.

ABOUT THE AUTHOR

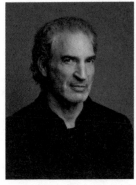

Photo credit: Benny Fong

When he's not writing Caley Cross, Jeff Rosen creates award-winning children's television series like *Bo on the Go, Poko, Animal Mechanicals, The Mighty Jungle, Pirates!, Monster Math Squad,* and *Space Ranger Roger.* He was the principal writer of the beloved *Theodore Tugboat.* Jeff's programs have been viewed around the world and translated into numerous languages.

Jeff was a founding creative partner of WildBrain (formerly DHX Media), a global children's content company, home to *Peanuts, Teletubbies, Strawberry Shortcake, Caillou, Inspector Gadget,* and *Degrassi.*

Jeff got the idea for Caley Cross when some horses escaped from his daughter's riding academy and roamed the city, popping into various shops along the way, mixing it up with the locals. The books have nothing to do with that, but you never know where ideas will lead.

An accomplished painter, Jeff's work can be found in galleries, at http://jeffrosenart.com/, and on Instagram @jeff.rosen

Jeff lives in Halifax, Nova Scotia, with his wife and vampire poodle, Vlad.

Gobbledy: A Novel, Lis Anna-Langston, $16.95, 978-1-68463-067-7. Get ready to meet everyone's favorite alien in the attic. Ever since Dexter and Dougal's mom passed away, life has been different—but things take a whole new turn when a shooting star turns out to be a creature from outer space!

Eye of Zeus: Legends of Olympus Book 1, Alane Adams. $12.95, 978-1-68463-028-8. Finding out she's the daughter of Zeus is not what a foster kid like Phoebe Katz expected to hear from a talking statue of Athena. But when her beloved social worker is kidnapped, Phoebe and her two friends must travel back to ancient Greece and rescue him before she accidentally destroys Olympus.

Above the Star: The 8th Island Trilogy, Book 1, Alexis Chute. $16.95, 978-1-943006-56-4. *Above the Star* is an epic fantasy adventure experienced through the eyes of three unlikely heroes transported to a new world: senior citizen Archie; his daughter-in-law, Tessa; and his fourteen-year-old granddaughter, Ella. In this otherworldly realm, all interests are at war, all love is unrequited, and everyone is left to unravel the truth of who they really are.

The Leaving Year:A Novel, Pam McGaffin. $16.95, 978-1-943006-81-6. As the Summer of Love comes to an end, 15-year-old Ida Petrovich waits for a father who never comes home. While commercial fishing in Alaska, he is lost at sea, but with no body and no wreckage, Ida and her mother are forced to accept a "presumed" death that tests their already strained relationship. While still in shock over the loss of her father, Ida overhears an adult conversation that shatters everything she thought she knew about him. This prompts her to set out on a search for the truth that takes her from her Washington State hometown to Southeast Alaska.